BOOKS BY ANTHONY BURGESS
IN NORTON PAPERBACK

Re Joyce

Nothing Like the Sun

Honey for the Bears

The Wanting Seed

A Clockwork Orange

The Doctor Is Sick

The Long Day Wanes: A Malayan Trilogy

TREMOR OF INTENT

ANTHONY BURGESS

W. W. NORTON & COMPANY

NEW YORK   LONDON

For information about permission to reproduce selections from this book, write to
Permissions, W. W. Norton & Company, Inc., 500 Fifth Avenue, New York, NY 10110

Manufacturing by Courier Westford
Book design by Barbara M. Bachman
Production manager: Anna Oler
Library of Congress Cataloging-in-Publication Data

Burgess, Anthony, 1917-1993.
Tremor of intent / Anthony Burgess.
pages ; cm.
ISBN 978-0-393-34639-8 (pbk.)
1. Scientists—Russia (Federation)—Fiction. 2. Espionage, British—Fiction. I.
Title.
PR6052.U638T74 2013
823'.914—dc23
2013016304

W. W. Norton & Company, Inc., 500 Fifth Avenue, New York, N.Y. 10110
www.wwnorton.com

W. W. Norton & Company Ltd., Castle House, 75/76 Wells Street, London W1T 3QT

1 2 3 4 5 6 7 8 9 0

To

J. McMichael

M.B., Ch.B.

gratefully

But between the day and night
The choice is free to all, and light
Falls equally on black and white.

—W. H. AUDEN

The worst that can be said of most
of our malefactors, from statesmen to
thieves, is that they are not men
enough to be damned.

—T. S. ELIOT

TREMOR OF INTENT

ONE

THE POSITION AT THE MOMENT IS AS FOLLOWS. I JOINED THE gastronomic cruise at Venice, as planned, and the *Polyolbion* is now throbbing south-east in glorious summer Adriatic weather. Everything at Pulj is in order. D.R. arrived there three days ago to take over, and it was good to have a large vinous night and talk about old adventures. I am well, fit, except for my two chronic diseases of gluttony and satyriasis which, anyway, continue to cancel each other out. There will be little opportunity for either to be indulged on this outward voyage (we shall be in the Black Sea the day after tomorrow), but I dribble at the glutinous thought of the mission-accomplished, unbuttoned-with-relief week that will come after the turn-around. Istanbul, Corfu, Villefranche, Ibiza, Southampton. And then free, finished. Me, anyway. But what about poor Roper?

D.R. handed over, as arranged, the ampoules of PSTX; I have, of course, my own syringe. I know the procedure. A sort of proleptic wraith of poor Roper is already lying on the other bunk

of this Bibby cabin. I explained to the purser that my friend Mr
Innes had been called by unforeseen business to Murflater but
that he would be making his way by road or rail or ferry or something to Yarylyuk and would be joining us there. That was all
right, he said, so long as it was clearly understood that there
could be no rebate in respect of his missed fifteen hundred miles
of cruising (meaning gorging and fornication). Very well, then.
For Roper all things are ready, including a new identity. John
Innes, except in fertilisers. The bearded face of that rubbery man
from Metfiz looks sadly back at me from the Innes passport. He
has been many things in his time, has he not, that all-purposes
lay-figure. He has been a pimp from Mdina, a syphilitic
computer-brain skulking in Palaiokastritsa, a kind of small Greek
Orthodox deacon, R. J. Geist who had the formula, even a distin-
guished Ukrainian man of letters set upon for his allegations of
pederasty in the Praesidium. And now he is John Innes, who is a
sort of egg-cosy for soft-boiled Roper.

I well understand, sir, Her Majesty's Government's palpitating need to have Roper back. Questions in the House, especially
after Tass passed through the jubilant news of the breakthrough
in rocket-fuel research and Eurovision showed the Beast gliding
through May-day Moscow. What I cannot so well understand is
the choice of myself as the agent of Roper's repatriation, unless,
of course, it is the pure, the ultimate trust which, if I were not
modest, I would say I have earned in my fifteen years of work for
the Department. But you must surely be aware of a residue of
sympathy for a schoolfellow, the fact that until his defection we
maintained a sort of exterior friendship, though with many lacu-
nae (war, peace, his marriage, my posting to Pulj); his last communication with the West was a picture post-card to myself, the

message cryptic and, so I gather, still being pored over by the cipher-boys: *Two minutes to four—up all their pipes—martyrs' blood flows through them.* Let us get certain things straight about Roper. Approach Number One will never work. I don't think for one moment that Roper can be persuaded to go *back* to anything. He has this scientist's thoroughness about disposing of the past. He never rummaged among old discarded answers. If he's a heretic at all it's your heresy he subscribes to—the belief that life can be better and man nobler. It's not up to me, of course, to say what a load of bloody nonsense that is. It's not up to me to have a philosophy at all, since I'm nothing more than a superior technician.

I understand the reason, sir, for two approaches to Roper, persuasion first and force after. There's the propaganda value of freedom of choice, even though the horse's-mouth official letters in my jacket-lining neigh fantastic offers. And then, after a month or so, the judgement. Anyway, I confront Roper. I prepare to confront him by being not myself but Mr Sebastian Jagger (the rubber man wasn't needed, of course, for my fake passport). Jagger, typewriter expert; why didn't you christen me Qwert Yuiop? Jagger goes ashore and, in some restaurant lavatory, is swiftly transformed into something plausible and quacking, totally Slavonic. And then, if things go as they ought to go, a swift taxi journey to wherever Roper is at that hour of night, to be peeled off from the rest of the delegates of the scientific *sbyeẓd*. And then it will be I, very much the past, very much the old ways, not merely smelling of a West that has given him no answers but smelling of himself, an old formula discarded.

You think he can be persuaded? Or rather, do you think I can find it in my heart to be all that persuasive? How far am I (I am able to speak boldly now, this being my last assignment) convinced enough to want to convince? It's all been a bloody big game—the genocidal formulae, the rocketry, the foolproof early warning devices mere counters in it. But nobody, sir, is going to kill anybody. This concept of a megadeath is as remotely unreal as specular stone or any other mediaeval nonsense. Some day anthropologists will comment in gently concealed wonder on the ludic element in our serious flirting with collective suicide. For my part, I've always played the game of being a good technician, superb at languages, agile, light-fingered, cool. But otherwise I'm a void, a dark sack crammed with skills. I have a dream of life, but no one ideology will realise it for me better than any other. I mean a warm flat, a sufficiency of spirits, a record-player, the whole of *The Ring* on disc. I would be glad to be rid of my other appetites, since they represent disease, and disease, besides being expensive, robs one of self-sufficiency. A doctor I met in Mohammedia on that hashish-ring assignment persuaded me that a simple operation would take care of both, since they are some-how cognate. Ultimately I have a desire for a spacious loghouse on a vast Northern lake, conifers all about, all oxygen and chloro-phyll, paddle-steamers honking through the mist. The bar on board the *Männikkö* is stocked with drinks of intriguing nomen-clature—*Juhannus, Huhtikuu, Edustaja, Kreikka, Silmäpari*—and the captain, who has a large private income, is round-buyingly drunk but never offensive. They serve mouth-watering food—fish soused and salted, garnished with gherkins; slivers of hot spiced meat on toasted rye—and there are blonde pouting girls who twitch for savage anonymous love. Some day I will have that operation.

Look in my glands and not in the psychologist's report. I am mentally and morally sound. I tut-tut at St Augustine, with his 'O

God make me pure but not yet'. Irresponsible, no appointment duly noted in the diary, the abrogation of free will. If you, sir, were really reading this, you would frown an instant, sniffing a connection between St Augustine (though of Canterbury, not Hippo, not less worthy but duller), Roper and myself. He was the patron saint of the Catholic college in Bradcaster where Roper and I were fellow-pupils. You have the name of the school in the files but you have not its smell, nor the smell of the city surrounding it. Bradcaster smelt of tanneries, breweries, drayhorses, canals, dirt in old crevices, brick-dust, the wood of tram-benches, hash, hot pies with gravy, cowheel stew, beer. It did not, sir, smell of Rupert Brooke's or your England. The school smelt of Catholicism, meaning the thick black cloth of clerical habits, stale incense, holy water, fasting breaths, stockfish, the tensions of celibacy. It was a day-school, but it had room for forty or so boarders. Roper and I were boarders, our homes being so far away, exiles from the South—Kent I, Dorset he— who had sat for scholarships and got them. The best Catholic schools are in the North, since the English Reformation, like blood from the feet when the arteries harden, could not push up so far so easily. And, of course, you have Catholic Liverpool, a kind of debased Dublin. There we were then, two Southern exiles among Old Catholics, transplanted Irish, the odd foreigner with a father in the consular service. We were Catholics, but we sounded Protestants with our long-aaaaa'd English; our tones were not those of pure-vowelled orthodoxy. And so Roper and I had to be friends. We had adjoining desks and beds. There was nothing homosexual about our relationship. I think we even found each other's flesh antipathetic, never wrestling as friends often do. I know I would cringe a little at Roper's whiteness, exposed for bed or the showers, fancying that a smell of decay came off it. As for heterosexuality, well, that was fornication, you see. The heterosexual act was a mortal sin outside the married state, that was made very clear. Except, we accepted, for such foreigners as had had Catholicism before we got it and hence had sort of founder members' special concessions.

Meaning swarthy foreigners like little Cristo Gomez, Alf Pereira, Pete Queval, Donkey Camus of the Lower Fifth. They had money, and they would buy women (the ones that hung round the corner of Merle Street and London Road) whom they would take to the derelict art-room, the cricket pavilion (a hairy boy called Jorge de Tormes was secretary to the First Eleven at that time), even the new chapel. That was discovered *in flagrante* and ended in a thrilling ceremony of expulsion. What must the Blessed Sacrament have thought, looking down on those moving buttocks in the aisle? It was surprising that so much was able to be got away with, considering how the Rector, Father Byrne, was so strong against sex. He would come round the dormitories some nights, smelling of neat J.J., feeling under the bedclothes for impure thoughts. On various occasions, having felt under the bedclothes with special lavishness, he would stand at the end of our dormitory to deliver a sermon on the evils of sex. He had a fine Irish instinct for the dramatic and, instead of turning on the lights, he would illuminate his ranting face with a pocket-torch, a decollated saint's head brave above a kind of hell-glow. One night he began with:

'This damnable sex, boys—ah, you do well to writhe in your beds at very mention of the word. All the evil of our modern times springs from unholy lust, the act of the dog and the bitch on the bouncing bed, limbs going like traction engines, the divine gift of articulate speech diminished to squeals and groans and pantings. It is terrible, terrible, an abomination before God and His Holy Mother. Lust is the fount of all other of the deadly sins, leading to pride of the flesh, covetousness of the flesh, anger in the thwarting of desire, gluttony to feed the spent body to be at it again, envy of the sexual prowess and sexual success of others, sloth to admit enervating day-dreams of lust. Only in the married state, by God's holy grace, is it sanctified, for then it becomes the means of begetting fresh souls for the peopling of the Kingdom of Heaven.'

He took a breath, and a voice from the dark took advantage of the breath to say: 'Mulligan begot a fresh soul and he wasn't married.' This was Roper, and what Roper said was true. Mulligan, long since expelled, had put a local girl in the family way; it was still well remembered.

'Who said that then?' called Father Byrne. 'What boy is talking after lights out?' And he machine-gunned the dark with his torch.

'Me,' said Roper stoutly. 'Sir,' he added. 'I only wanted to know,' he said, now illuminated. 'I don't see how an evil can be turned into a good by a ceremony. That would be like saying that the Devil can be turned into an angel again by just being blessed by a priest. I don't see it, sir.'

'Out, boy,' cried Father Byrne. 'Out of bed this instant.' His torch beckoned. 'You there at the end, turn on the lights.' Feet pattered and horrible raw yellow suddenly struck at our eyes. 'Now then,' cried Father Byrne to Roper, 'down on your knees, boy, and say a prayer for forgiveness. Who are you, worm, to doubt the omnipotence of Almighty God?'

'I wasn't doubting anything, sir,' said Roper, not yet out of bed. 'I was just interested in what you were saying, sir, even though it is a bit late.' And he thrust out a leg from the bed, as from a boat to test the temperature of the water.

'Out, boy,' shouted Father Byrne. 'Down on that floor and pray.'

'Pray for what, sir?' asked Roper, now standing, in faded blue shrunken pyjamas, between his bed and mine. 'For forgiveness because God's given me, in his infinite omnipotence, an enquiring mind?' He, like myself, was something over fifteen.

'No, boy,' said Father Byrne, with a swift Irish change to mellifluous quietness. 'Because you cast doubts on the miraculous, because you blasphemously suggest that God cannot'—crescendo—'if He so wishes turn evil into good. Kneel, boy. Pray, boy.' (fff.)

'Why doesn't He then, sir?' asked Roper boldly, now down, though as if for an accolade, on his knees. 'Why can't we have what we all want—a universe that's really a unity?'

Ah, God help us, Roper and his unified universe. Father Byrne was now attacked by hiccups. He looked down sternly at Roper as though Roper, and not J.J., had brought them on. And then he looked up and round at us all. 'On your knees, all of you, hic,' he called. 'All of you, hic, pray. A spirit of evil stalks, hic, pardon, this dormitory.' So everybody got out of bed, all except one small boy who was asleep. 'Wake him, hic,' cried Father Byrne. 'Who is that boy there with no, hic, pyjama trousers? I can guess what you've been doing, boy. Hic.'

'If somebody were to thump you on the back,' said Roper kindly. 'Or nine sips of water, sir.'

'Almighty God,' began Father Byrne, 'Who knowest the secret thoughts of, hic, these boys' hearts—' And then he became aware of a certain element of unwilled irreverence, the hiccups breaking in like that. 'Pray on your own,' he cried. 'Get on with it.' And he hiccuped his way out. This was looked on as a sort of victory over authority for Roper.

He was having too many victories over authority, solely because of the exceptional gift of scientific enquiry he'd been demonstrating. I remember one fifth-form chemistry lesson in which Father Beauchamp, an English convert, had been dully revising the combining of elements into compounds. Roper suddenly asked:

'But why should sodium and chlorine *want* to combine to produce salt?'

The class laughed with pleasure at hope of a diversion. Father Beauchamp grinned sourly, saying, 'There can't be any question of *wanting*, Roper. Only animate things *want*.'

'I don't see that,' said Roper. 'Inanimate things must have wanted to become animate, otherwise life wouldn't have started on the earth. There must be a kind of free will in atoms.'

'*Must* there, Roper?' said Father Beauchamp. 'Aren't you rather tending to leave God out of the picture?'

'Oh, sir,' cried Roper impatiently, 'we ought not to bring God into a chemistry lesson.' Father Beauchamp chewed that for two seconds, then swallowed it. Tamely he said:

'You asked the question. See if you can answer it.'

I don't know when all this business of electrovalent methods of combination started, but Roper must, in those late nineteen-thirties, have known more than most school-boys knew, and chemistry teachers for that matter. Not that Father Beauchamp knew much; he'd been learning the subject as he went along. What Roper said, I remember, was that the sodium atom had only one electron on its outer shell (nobody had ever taught us about outer shells) but that the chlorine atom had seven. A good stable number, he said, was eight and very popular with the constituents of matter. The two atoms, he said, deliberately came together to form a new substance with eight electrons on the outer shell. Then he said:

'They talk about holy numbers and whatnot—three and seven and nine and so on—but it looks as though eight is the really big number. What I mean is this: if you're going to bring God into chemistry, as you want to do, then eight must mean a lot to God. Take water, for instance, the substance that God made first, at least the Bible says about the spirit of God moving on the face of the waters. Well, you've got six outer electrons in the oxygen atom and only one in the hydrogen atom, and so you need two of those to one of oxygen to get water. God must have known all this, and yet you don't find eight being blown up as a big important number in the teachings of the Church. It's always the Holy Trinity and the Seven Deadly Sins and the Ten Commandments. Eight comes nowhere.'

'There are,' said Father Beauchamp, 'the Eight Beatitudes.' Then he had a brief session of lip-biting, not sure whether he ought to send Roper to the Rector for blasphemous talk. Anyway, he let Roper alone, and the rest of us for that matter, bidding us read up the stuff in our books. A twitch started in his right eye and he couldn't stop it. It was Father Byrne in the dormitory all over again. The sending of Roper to the Rector over God and Science was deferred till a year later, when Roper and I were in the Sixth Form, he inevitably doing science, myself languages. He told me all about it in the refectory afterwards. We were eating a very thin Irish stew. Roper kept his voice down—it was a

rather harsh voice—and one lock of his lank straw hair lan-
guished in the steam from his plate.

'He tried to get me to pray again, kneeling on the floor and all
that nonsense. But I asked him what I was supposed to have done
wrong.'

'What was it?'

'Oh, Beauchamp told him. We had a bit of tussle about physical and chemical change and then somehow we got on to the
Host. Does Christ reside in the molecules themselves or only in
the molecules organised into bread? And then I decided I'd had
enough of pretending you can ask questions about some things
and not about others. I'm not going to Mass any more.'

'You told Byrne that?'

'Yes. And that's when he shouted at me to get down on my
knees. But you should have seen the sweat start out on him.'

'Ah.'

'I said what was the point of praying if I didn't believe there
was anyone to pray to. And he said if I prayed I'd be vouchsafed
an answer. A lot of bloody nonsense.'

'Don't be too sure. There are some very big brains in the
Church, scientific brains too.'

'That's just what he said. But I told him again that there has to
be one universe, not two. That science has to be allowed to knock
at all doors.'

'What's he going to do with you?'

'There's not much he can do. He can't expel me, because
that's no answer. Besides, he knows that I'll probably get a state
scholarship, and there's not been one here for a hell of a long
time. A bit of a dilemma.' Roper getting the better of authority
again. 'And the exam isn't far off now, and he can't very well

send me somewhere for special theological instruction. So there it is.'

There it was. I was still in the Church myself at that time. My own studies were technical and aesthetic, not posing any fundamental questions. I was studying Roman poets who glorified Roman conquerors or, in the long debilitating pax after conquest, pederasty and adultery and fornication. I was also reading, fretting at their masochistic chains, the correct tragedians of the Sun King. But there was one member of the staff who was Polish, a lay brother called—after the inventor of the Russian alphabet—Brother Cyril. He'd only come to the school three years before and there was nobody for him to teach, since he knew only Slavonic languages and a little English and very little German. But one day I found him reading what he told me was Pushkin. I took a liking to those solid black perversions of Greek letters and at once my future (though naturally, sir, I did not know this yet) was fixed. I romped through Russian and was allowed to take it as a main subject for the Higher School Certificate, dropping Modern History. Modern History, sir, has had its revenge since then.

TWO

I DID NOT KNOW at that time—the time of hearing Roper on the molecular structure of the Eucharist—how soon both our futures were about to begin. The year was 1939. Roper and I were both coming up to eighteen. Father Byrne had intimated, in various morning assemblies, that the Nazi persecution of the Jews was nothing more than God's own castigation of a race that had rejected the Light, a castigation in brown shirts with a crooked cross. 'They crucified our loving Saviour, boys.' (Roper, sitting next to me in the prefects' front row, said quietly, 'I thought it was the Romans who did that.') 'They are,' cried Father Byrne, 'a race on whom Original Sin sits heavy, much given to sexuality and money-making. Their law forbids neither incest nor usury.' And so on. Father Byrne had a long and rubbery body and more than he needed of neck. He now, with great skill, made himself both neckless and tubby and gave us a sort of Shylock performance, full of lisping dribbling and hand-rubbing. 'Dirty Chrithtianth,' he spat. 'You vill not cut off your forethkinth.' He loved to act. His best performance was of James I, and he would willingly spice any teacher's history lesson, whatever the period being taught, with a session of blubbering and slavering and doubtful Lallans. But his Jew was not bad. 'Oh yeth, ve vill do you all down, dirty Chrithtianth. You vill have none of my thpondulickth. Oy oy oy.'

Roper and I were too liberal to laugh at this. We understood that the Nazis were persecuting Catholics as well as Jews. We learned a bit about evil now from the newspapers, not from the religious tracts that stood in a special rack in the school library. Concentration camps fascinated us. Mashed bloody flesh. Bayonets stuck in the goolies. Sir, say what you will, we half-become what we hate. Would we, any of us, have had it otherwise, the film run back to the time when there were no gas-chambers and castrations without anaesthetic, then a new, sinless, reel put in the projector? We will these horrors to happen and then we want to feel good about not wreaking vengeance in kind. Roper and I, instead of Father-Byrne-Shylock dribbling over the reports from black Germany, would have done better to sweat it all out in a decent bout of sex in the chapel. I said to Roper:

'What about good and evil?'

'It seems reasonable to suppose,' said Roper, chewing on a fibre of stewed mutton, 'that good is the general name we give to what we all aspire to, whatever thing it happens to be. I think it's all a matter of ignorance and the overcoming of ignorance. Evil comes out of ignorance.'

'The Germans are said to be the least ignorant people in the world.'

He had no real answer to that. But he said: 'There are particular fields of ignorance. They're politically ignorant, that's their trouble. Perhaps it's not their fault. The German states were very late in being unified, or something.' He was very vague about it all. 'And then there are all those forests, full of tree-gods.'

'You mean they have atavistic tendencies?'

He didn't know what the hell he meant. He knew nothing now except the trilogy of sciences he was studying for the Higher School Certificate. He was becoming both full and empty at the same time. He was turning into a *thing*, growing out of boyhood into thinghood, not manhood—a highly efficient artefact crammed with non-human knowledge.

'And,' I asked, 'what will you do when war breaks out? Just say that it's all a matter of ignorance and the poor sods can't help it? Because they'll be coming for us, you know. Poison gas and all.'

He suddenly seemed to realise that the war was going to touch him as well as other people. 'Oh,' he said, 'I hadn't thought about that. That's going to be a bit of a nuisance, isn't it? There's this question of my state scholarship, you see.' There was no doubt that he was going to get one of those; his examination results were going to be brilliant.

'Well,' I said, 'think about it. Think about the Jews. Einstein and Freud and so on. The Nazis regard science as a kind of international Jewish conspiracy.'

'They have some of the finest scientists in the world,' said Roper.

'Had,' I said. 'They're getting rid of most of them now, That's why they can't win. But it'll take a long time to persuade them they can't win.'

That was a lovely summer. Roper and I, with ten pounds each in our wallets, hitch-hiked through Belgium, Luxembourg, Holland and France. We had a month of bread and cheese and cheap wine, of the *'J'aime Berlin'* pun about Chamberlain the umbrella man, of war talk under brilliant sun. We spent one night in our sleeping-bags near the teeth of the Maginot Line, feeling well protected. We were back in England three days before war broke out. Our examination results had come through in our absence in soon-to-be-locked-up Europe. I'd done well; Roper had done magnificently. There was some talk of my going to the School of Slavonic Studies in London; Roper had to wait for news of his scholarship. We were both drawn, during the interim time, to the only community we knew; we went back to school.

Father Byrne was now very good as Suffering Ireland. He came from Cork and hinted that his sister had been raped by the Black and Tans during the Troubles. 'Warmongering England,' he cried in morning assembly. Antichrist Germany never came into it. 'She has done it again, declaring war, backed by the Jews with their wads of greasy notes.' A brief impersonation of International Finance. 'This war, boys, is going to be a terrible thing. Europe will soon be swarming, if not swarming already, with ravaging and pillaging soldiery. It will be Ireland all over again, the leering and tramping louts, not a thought in their heads but this damnable sex, an abomination before Almighty God and His Blessed Mother.' Soon Roger Casement was brought in. And then he gave us the news that all scholarships were temporarily suspended. I said to Roper, after a morning of yawning lounging in the school library, 'Let's go out and get drunk.'

'Drunk? Can we?'

'*I* certainly can. As for *may*, who's to stop us?'

Bitter beer was fivepence a pint in the public bars. We drank in the Clarendon, the George, the Cuddy, the King's Head, the Admiral Vernon. Bradcaster smelt of khaki and diesel-fuel. There was also a sort of headiness of promise of the night—this damnable sex. Did not the girls in the streets seem to flaunt more, more luscious-lipped, bigger-breasted? It was always unwise ever to think Father Byrne *totally* wrong about anything. Over my sixth pint I saw myself in uniform of a subaltern of the 1914–18 War, girls panting as they smelt the enemy blood coming off me as I passed the ticket-barrier at Victoria Station, London, home for a spot of leave. Hell in those trenches, girls. Tell us more. I said now to Roper:

'Going to volunteer. This dear country we all love so much.'

'Why?' swayed Roper. 'Why so much? What has it done for you or for me?'

'Freedom,' I said. 'It can't be so bad a bloody country if it lets buggers like Father Byrne attack it in morning assembly. You think about that. What are you going to choose—England or bloody Father Byrne?'

'And,' said Roper, 'I thought I'd be going to Oxford.'

'Well, you're not. Not yet you're not. They're going to have us both sooner or later. Best make it sooner. We're going to volunteer.'

But before we could go and do that, Roper was sick. He had no true hearty English beer-stomach. He was sick in a back-alley near the Admiral Vernon, and this rationalist moaned and groaned prayers like 'Oh Jesus Mary and Joseph' as he tried to get it all up. The scientific approach to life is not really appropriate to states of visceral anguish. I told Roper this while he was suffering, but he did not listen. He prayed however: 'Oh God God God. Oh suffering heart of Christ.' But the next day, very pale, he was prepared to go with me to a dirty little shop that had been turned into a recruiting centre. The cold deflation of crapula perhaps made him see himself as temporarily empty of a future; the only thing he could be filled with in these times was his generalised young man's destiny. And, of course, that went for me too.

'What will our parents say?' wondered Roper. 'We should really write and tell them what we're doing.'

'Reconcile yourself to the jettisoning of another responsibility,' I said, or words to that effect. 'We'll send them telegrams.' And off we went to see a sergeant with a dreadful cold. I put in for the Royal Corps of Signals. Roper couldn't make up his mind. He said:

'I don't want to kill.'

'You dod't have to,' said the sergeant. 'There's always the Bedics.' He meant the Medics. The Royal Army Medical Corps. RAMC. Rob all my comrades. Run Albert matron's coming. Roper bravely joined that mob.

It seems strange, looking back, that the British armed forces had as yet no room for genuine skills, except of the most elementary trigger-squeezing, button-pressing kind. All the time Roper was in the army, nobody ever once thought that here was a brain that could be utilised in the development of the most horrible offensive weapons. For that matter, my own ability to speak French and Russian quite well, and Polish moderately well, was seized on with no eagerness. I even had difficulty in transferring to the Intelligence Corps when it was formed in July, 1940. My officers spoke French with a public school accent; the British have always been suspicious of linguistic ability, associating it with spies, impresarios, waiters, and Jewish refugees: the polyglot can never be a gentleman. It was not until the Soviet Union became one of our allies that I was allowed to bring my Russian into the open, and then there was long delay before it was used. It was used when there was some sort of programme of Anglo-American aid to Russia; I was brought in as a junior assistant interpreter. This sounds big enough stuff for one still so young, but it was only to do with the provision of sports equipment for the ratings of Soviet naval vessels. There was a bigger job that at one time I thought I might get, something to do with the putting of a bay leaf in every tin of American-aid chopped pork, the Russians finding pig-meat so ungarnished unpalatable, myself to explain that this would slow up deliveries, each bay leaf having to be dropped in separately by hand, but I never got the job. And now back to Roper.

He wrote to me first of all from Aldershot, saying that a bomb had dropped near Boyce Barracks and he'd been thinking more than usual about death. Or rather what Catholics call the Four Last Things Ever To Be Remembered: Death, Judgement, Hell and Heaven. He'd succeeded, he said, in blotting those doctrines out pretty well when he'd been in the Science Sixth, but what he wanted to know was this: did these things perhaps exist—the after-death things, that was—for somebody who believed in them? He'd been put in rather a false position, he thought, from the point of view of religion. When he'd arrived at the Depot as a recruit, they'd called out: 'RCs this side, Protestants that, fancy buggers in the middle.' His intention had been to declare himself an agnostic, but that would have put him right away among the United Board. So he said he was an RC—'on the surface, the army being all surface'. When he became a sergeant he found himself possessed not merely of authority but of Catholic authority. There was this business of helping to march the men to Mass on Sunday mornings. And the priest in the town church was decent, friendly, English not Irish, and he asked Roper to use his influence to make more of the men go to communion. But, after this bomb had dropped near Boyce Barracks, which was very early in his army career, he'd been made aware of the talismanic power of having 'RC' in his paybook. 'You're an RC,' some of his barrack-room-mates had said. 'Going to stick close to you we are next time one of those bastards drops.' What Roper said in his letter was: 'There seems to be a certain superstitious conviction among the men that the Catholics have more chance of "being all right" when death threatens. It's as though there's a hangover of guilt from the Reformation among the common people—"We didn't want to get away from the Old Religion really, see. We was quite happy as we was. It was them upper-class bastards, Henry VIII and whatnot, that made us break away, see."'

And poor Roper, cut off from his science—though he learned the tricks of his corps so well that he was very quickly promoted—and living more with his emotional and instinctive needs, began to be aware of emptiness. 'If only I could be reconverted or else converted to something else. What's the point of fighting this war if we don't believe that one way of life is bet-

ter than another? And that's not the same as saying that our way
is bad but the Nazi way is worse. That won't do. You can't fight
negatively. A war should be a sort of crusade. But what for?'

And then, God help us, Roper started to read poetry. 'But'
he wrote, 'I can't get much out of this very difficult poetry. I've
got a scientific brain, I suppose, and I like a word to mean one
thing and one thing only. That's why I've been going back to
people like Wordsworth, who really does say what he means,
even though you can't always agree with what he says. But at
least there's a man who made a religion for himself, and, when
you come to think of it, it's a scientific religion in a way.
Nature—trees and rivers and mountains and so on—is something that's really there, it encloses us. I think of those Nazi
bastards coming over and blasting England, and I get a sort of
picture of England suffering—I don't mean just the people and
the cities they've built, but the trees and the countryside and the
grass, and I feel more bitter than if it was Christ on His cross. Is
this some sort of new religious sense I've got? Would you say it
was irrational?'

A delightful and inevitable progression from bare reason to
sentimentality to sex. He wrote to me from Chesham in 1943,
saying that he was doing some sort of course on Army Hygiene
and, in his spare time, going out with a girl called Ethel. 'She's
tall and fair and has blunt fingers and is very wholesome, and she
works in a snack-bar on the High Street. Would you say I was late
in losing my virginity? We go out into the fields and it's all very
pleasant and not very exciting, and I don't feel any guilt at all.
Would it be better if I did feel guilt? I seem to have come very
close to England since I stopped believing in Catholicism, close
to the heart or essential nature of England I mean. What I find

there is a sublime kind of innocence. England would take neither Catholicism nor Puritanism for very long—those faiths built on sin just rolled off like water from a duck's back. And then, when I think of Nazi Germany, what do I find but another kind of innocence, a sort of malevolent innocence which enables them to perpetrate the most incredible atrocities and still see nothing wrong there. Is there anybody anywhere who is feeling guilt for this war? I lie in the cornfield with Ethel and, to spice it up with guilt, I imagine this is adultery—she isn't married—or incest, but it won't work. Of course, in a way it *is* incest, for we're all supposed to be bound together in a big happy family, brothers and sisters, directing our sexual hate, all hate being really sexual, against the enemy.'

The really significant letter from Roper came from defeated Germany. 'I shall never eat meat again,' he said, 'never as long as I live. The camp was full of meat, layers and layers of it, some of it still alive. Human meat, sweet surely because it was so near the bone, with the flies buzzing over it and grubs moving. The smell was of a massive cheese factory. We were the first in, and we wasted no time in squirting our patent Mark IV antiseptic sprays, retching while we did it. I had met this word *necropolis* before and thought it to be a sort of poetic term for describing a city at dead of night, a city of locked houses from which all the living seemed to have fled. Now I saw what a necropolis really was. How many dead or dying citizens did this contain? I had not thought it possible that so many dead could be brought together in one place, and all arranged and stacked so neatly, sometimes dead with still alive. I passed along the neat made-in-Germany streets that had house-high hedges of piled corpses on either side, spraying away, but the spray, for all its powerful smell of clean kitchen-sinks and lavatory-bowls, couldn't at all erase the stink of the dead.'

That, sir, was Roper—QMS Roper—in the spearhead of the invasions of cleaners-up after the German surrender. The letter, and the three letters that followed (he was just talking the anguish out on the paper), spoke of vomiting and a mad fear that the near-corpses would suddenly topple their fully dead brothers from the pile and come to lap up half-digested protein. They also told of nightmares of a sort we all had, all those of us who'd entered the death-camps and stood paralysed, our mouths in *rictu* but whether for retching or out of sheer incredulity the mouths themselves could not at first tell. We had to gape; it was the only possible oral response to what we saw and smelt. We didn't want to believe, since belief that a civilised nation had been capable of all this must overturn everything we'd ever taken for granted about civilisation, progress, the elevating power of artistic, scientific, philosophical achievement (who could deny that the Germans were a great race?). For my part, I went in as sole sergeant-interpreter with a small Russo-American group (I have deliberately forgotten where the death-camp was) and found, what I should have known, that words, whether Russian or Anglo-American, were otiose.

Strangely, my own nightmares featured Roper more than myself, perhaps because Roper had written those letters. I could see him very clearly as I read them—pale, fattish, bespectacled (with those steel-rimmed respirator-spectacles that made the wearer look like an idiot child), a shaggy straw nape under the eaves of the steel helmet. In my dreams he did my moaning for me, vomiting up such dream-objects as the flywheels of clocks, black-letter books, wriggling snakes, and he sobbed very idiomatic German, full of words like *Staunen* (astonishment) and *Sittlichkeit* (morality) and *Schicksal* (destiny). His own night-mares were of the forced evening walk (a lovely sunset, the birds' last song) through groves of corpses, along with burrowing into hedges of blue flesh and (this was fairly common with all of us) actual necrophagy or corpse-eating. And then dreaming Roper allowed himself to appear as a sort of British Christ, John Bull Jesus crucified on his own Union Jack. The crucifixion was either punishment or expiation or identification—he couldn't tell which. He'd done very little reading outside of physics and chemistry and very simple poetry.

But guilt was in his letters. These crimes had been committed by members of the human race, no different from himself. 'We should never have let this happen,' he wrote. 'We're all responsi-ble.' I wrote back:

'Don't be so bloody stupid. The Germans are responsible and only the Germans. Admittedly, a lot of them won't have that because a lot of them won't believe what's been done in their name. They'll have to be shown, all of them. You can start off with the German women.' That's what I'd been doing. In a way, with their deep belly-consciousness or whatever the hell it is, the German women were already lining up to be punished. They didn't think it was that, of course; they thought they were just on the chocolate-buying game like the women of any conquered country. But the deep processes of genetics were calling out for exogamy, fertilisation by foreign bodies, and the deeper moral processes were shrieking for punishment. Wait, though: aren't those aspects of the same thing? Isn't the angry punitive seed more potent than the good gentle stuff that dribbles out in the pink-sheeted marriage-bed? Isn't miscegenation a means of

destroying ethnic identity and thus getting rid of national guilt?
For my part, I didn't then ask such questions of the stocky
women of Bremen. I got stuck into them, not sparing the rod. At
the same time, showing my teeth and manhood, I was dimly
aware that their menfolk, dead or merely absent, had got the better of me by making me one of themselves—brutal, lustful,
something from a Gothic bestiary. Ah, what a bloody Manichean
mess life is.

THREE

POOR ROPER FOUND a woman in Elmshorn. Or rather she found
him. She married him. She needed the leisure of marriage to
enforce a lesson diametrically opposite to the one I'd been trying
to teach. Though Roper and I were both in the British Zone of
Germany we never met, and it wasn't till the marriage was a couple of years old and the lessons well under way—back in
England, in fact, with both of us civilians—that I was able to
indulge my not very-strong masochistic propensities (vicarious,
anyway) and see the *Ehepaar* (these lovely German words!) in
cosy domestic bliss.

I remember the occasion well, sir. Roper said shyly, 'This is
Brigitte,' having got the introductions arse-backwards. He
realised it and then said, in confusion, *'Darf ich vorstellen—*
What I mean is, this is my oldest friend. Denis Hillier, that is.'

Roper had been released from the army no earlier than anyone else, despite the scholarship that was awaiting him at
Manchester University (not Oxford, after all) and his obvious
potential usefulness in the great age of technological reconstruc-

tion that was, we were told, coming up. He was now in his third year. He and this Brigitte had had a twelve-month engagement, she waiting in Elmshorn with the ring on her finger, he getting his allowances and a flat sorted out in that grey city which, when you come to think of it, has always had some of the quality of a pre-Hitler *Stadt*—rich musical Jews, chophouses, beeriness, bourgeois solidity. I understand that that picture has now, since the immigration of former subject peoples longing to be back with their colonial oppressors, been much modified. It is now, so I gather, much more like a temperate Singapore. Perhaps the German image only came out fully for me when I saw Brigitte, almost indecently blonde, opulently busted, as full of sex as an egg of meat, and a good deal younger than Roper (we were both now twenty-eight; she couldn't have been more than twenty). She'd contrived to stuff the Didsbury flat with cosy Teutonic rubbish—fretwork clocks, an elaborate weatherhouse, a set of beer-mugs embossed with leather-breeched huntsmen and their simpering dirndl-clad girl-friends. Lying on the sideboard was a viola, which Roper, perhaps never having met one in England, insisted on calling a *Bratsche*, her dead father's, and she could play it well, said proud Roper—nothing classical, just old German songs. There seemed to be only one thing of Roper's in the stuffy Brigitte-smelling living-room, and that was something hanging on the wall, framed in passe-partout. It was the Roper family-tree. 'Well,' I said, going to look at it. 'I never realised you were so—is *Rassenstolz* the word?'

'Not race,' said Brigitte, whose eye on me had been, since my entry, a somewhat cold one. 'Family-proud.' For that matter, I hadn't taken to her at all.

'Brigitte's family goes back a long way,' said Roper. 'The

Nazis did some people a sort of service in a manner of speaking, digging out their genealogical tables. Looking for Jewish blood, you know.' I said, still looking at past Ropers:

'No Jewish blood here, anyway. A bit of French and Irish, some evident Lancashire.' (Marchand, O'Shaughnessy, Bamber.) 'A long-lived family.' (1785–1862; 1830–1912; 1920– This last was our Roper, Edwin.)

'Good healthy blood,' smirked Roper.

'And in my family no Jewish,' said Brigitte aggressively.

'Of course not,' I said, grinning. And then, 'This Roper died pretty young, didn't he?' There was a Tudor Roper called Edward—1530–1558. 'Still, the expectation wasn't all that long in those days.'

'He was executed,' said this Roper. 'He died for his beliefs. It was my grandfather who dug up all this, you know. A hobby for his retirement. See, there he is—John Edwin Roper. Died at eighty-three.'

'One of the first Elizabethan martyrs,' I said. 'So you have a martyr in the family.'

'He was a fool,' pronounced Roper, sneering. 'He could have shut up about it.'

'Like the Germans who saw it through,' I suggested.

'My father died,' said Brigitte. Then she marched out to the kitchen.

While she was clattering the supper things I had to congratulate Roper and say what a handsome, intelligent, pleasant girl she seemed to me to be. Roper said eagerly:

'Oh, there's no doubt about the intelligence' (as though there might be some doubt about the other qualities). 'She speaks remarkably good English, doesn't she? She's had a rough time, you know, what with the war. And her father was a very early casualty. In Poland it was, '39. But she's not a bit reproachful. Towards me, I mean, or towards the British generally.'

'The British were never in Poland.'

'Oh, well, you know what I mean, the Allies. It was all one war, wasn't it? All the Allies were responsible, really.'

'Look,' I said, giving him the hard eye, 'I don't get all this. You mean that your wife, as a representative of the German nation, very kindly forgives us for Hitler and the Nazis and the bloody awful things they did? Including the war they started?'

'He didn't start it, did he?' said Roper brightly. 'It was we who declared war on him.'

'Yes, to stop him taking the whole bloody world over. Damn it, man, you seem to have forgotten what you did six years' fighting for.'

'Oh, I didn't actually fight, did I?' said literalist Roper. 'I was there to help save lives.'

'Allied lives,' I said. 'That was a kind of fighting.'

'It was worth it, whatever it was,' said Roper. 'It led me to her. It led me straight to Brigitte.' And he looked for a moment as though he were listening to Beethoven.

I didn't like this one little bit, but I didn't dare say anything for the moment because Brigitte herself came in with the supper, or with the first instalments of it. It looked as though it was going to be a big cold help-yourself spread. She brought serially to the table smoked salmon (the salty canned kind), cold chicken, a big jellied ham (coffin-shaped from its tin), dishes of gherkins, pumpernickel, butter—a whole slab, not a rationed wisp—and four kinds of cheese. Roper opened bottled beer and made as to pour some for me into a stein. 'A glass, please,' I said. 'I much prefer a glass.'

'From a stein,' said Brigitte, 'it smacks better.'

'I prefer a glass,' I smiled. So Roper got me a glass with the name and coat-of-arms of a lager firm gilded on it. 'Well,' I said, doing the conventional yum-yum hand-rubbing before falling to, 'this looks a bit of all right. You're doing very nicely for yourselves, *nicht wahr?*' At that time British rations were smaller than they'd been even at the worst point of the war. We now had all the irksome appurtenances of war without any of its glamour. Roper said:

'It's from Brigitte's Uncle Otto. In America. He sends a food parcel every month.'

'God bless Uncle Otto,' I said, and, after this grace, I piled smoked salmon on to thickly buttered black bread.

'And you,' said Brigitte, with a governess directness, 'what is it that you do?' The tones of one who sees a slack lounging youth who has evaded call-up.

'I'm on a course,' I said. 'Slavonic languages and other things. I say no more.'

'It's for a department of the Foreign Office,' smiled Roper, looking, with his red round face and short-cropped hair and severely functional spectacles, as German as his wife. It was suddenly like being inside a German primer: Lesson III— Abendessen. After food Roper would probably light up a meerschaum.

'Is it for the Secret Police?' asked Brigitte, tucking in and already lightly dewed with fierce eater's sweat. 'My husband is soon to be a Doktor.' I didn't see the connection.

Roper explained that only in Germany was a doctorate the first degree. And then: 'We don't have secret police in England, at least I don't think so.'

'We don't,' I said. 'Take it from me.'

'My husband,' said Brigitte, 'studies the sciences.'

'Your husband,' I said, 'will be a very important man.' Roper was eating too hard to blush with pleasure. 'Science is going to be very important. The new and terrible weapons that science is capable of making are a great priority in the peaceful work of reconstruction. Rockets, not butter.'

'There is much butter on the table,' said Brigitte, stonefacedly chewing. And then: 'What you say I do not understand.'

'There's an Iron Curtain,' I told her. 'We're not too sure of Russia's intentions. To keep the peace we must watch out for war. We've learned a great deal since 1938.'

'Before you should have learned,' said Brigitte, now on the cheese course. 'Before England should this have known.' Roper kindly unscrambled that for her. 'It was Russia,' said Brigitte, 'that was the fiend.'

'Enemy?'

'*Ja, ja, Feind*. Enemy.' She tore at a piece of pumpernickel as though it were a transubstantiation of Stalin. 'This Germany did know. This England did know not.'

'And that's why Germany persecuted the Jews?'

'International *Bolschevismus*,' said Brigitte with satisfaction. Then Roper started, eloquently, going on at length. Brigitte, his teacher, listened, nodded approval, cued him sometimes, rarely corrected. Roper said:

'We, that is to say the British, must admit we have nearly everything to blame ourselves for. We were blind to it all. Germany was trying to save Europe, no more. Mussolini had tried once, but with no help from those who should have helped. We had no conception of the power and ambition of the Soviet

Union. We're learning now, but very late. Three men knew it well, but they were all reviled. Now only one of them is living. I refer,' he said, to enlighten my ignorance, 'to General Franco in Spain.'

'I know all about General bloody Franco,' I said coarsely. 'I did a year in Gibraltar, remember. Given the chance, he would have whipped through and taken the Rock. You're talking a lot of balls,' I added.

'It is you who talk the balls,' said Brigitte. She picked up words quickly, that girl. 'To my husband please listen.'

Roper talked on, growing more shiny as he talked. There was one thing, I thought in my innocence: here was a man who, when he got down to research, as he would very shortly, would be quite above suspicion—a man who would be susceptible to no bland-ishments of the one true fiend. What I didn't like was this busi-ness of England's guilt and need to expiate great wrong done to bloody Deutschland. I took as much as I could stand and then broke in with:

'Ah God, man, how can you justify all the atrocities, all the suppression of free thought and speech, the great men sent into exile when not clubbed to death—Thomas Mann, Freud—'

'Only the smutty writers,' said Brigitte, meaning *schmutzig*.

'If you're going to wage war,' said Roper, 'it's got to be total war. War means fighting an enemy, and the enemy isn't necessar-ily somewhere out there. He can be at home, you know, and he's at his most insidious then. But,' he conceded, 'do you think that anybody really enjoyed having to send great brains into exile? They wouldn't be argued with, many of them. Impossible, a lot of them, to convince. And time was very short.'

I was going to say something about ends not justifying means, but I remembered that it was right for prisoners-of-war to drop razor-blades into the enemy's pigswill and that, if they'd bombed Coventry, we'd bombed Dresden. That if they'd been wrong we'd been wrong too. That killing babies was no way to kill Hitler, who'd had to kill himself anyway at the end. That history was a mess. That Fascism had been the inevitable answer to Communism. That the Jews could sometimes be as Father Byrne had portrayed them. I shuddered. Was somebody brainwashing me? I looked at Brigitte, but she, replete, glowed only with sex. I clenched my teeth, wanting her on the floor then and there, Roper looking on. But I merely said:

'You've joined Father Byrne in condemning the warmonger-ing English. And, of course, the money-grubbing Jews. You two would get on well together now.'

'That horrible Church,' said Roper passionately. 'Jewish meekness, turning the other cheek, draining the blood from the race. Nietzsche was right.' Brigitte nodded.

'What the hell do either of you know about Nietzsche?' I asked. 'I bet neither of you's ever read a word of Nietzsche.'

Brigitte began: 'My father——' Roper said, mumbling a bit: 'There was a very good summary of his philosophy in the *Reader's Digest*.' He was always honest. '——at school,' ended Brigitte. I said:

'Oh, my God. What do you want—blood and iron and black magic?'

'No,' he said. 'I want to get on with my work. The first thing is to get my degree. And then research. No,' he repeated, some-what dispirited now (perhaps that was overeating, though: he'd tucked away half a chicken and a slab of ham and a bit each of the four kinds of cheese, all with bread in proportion). 'I don't

want anything that causes war or could be used to make war
more terrible than it's been already. All the dead, all the innocent
children.'

'My father,' said Brigitte.

'Your father,' agreed Roper. It was as though they were toasting him. And for a moment it was as if the Second World War
had been conjured expressly to kill off Herr Whoever-he-was.

'Yes,' I said. 'And my Uncle Jim, and the two children evacu-
ated to my Aunt Florrie's house who found a bomb in a field, and
all the poor bloody Jews and dissident intellectuals.'

'You say right,' said Brigitte. 'Bloody Jews.'

'We must never be allowed to start another war like that one,'
said Roper. 'A great nation in ruins.'

'Not starving, though,' I said. 'Plenty of Danish butter and
fat ham. The best-nourished bastards in Europe.'

'Please,' said Roper, 'do not call my wife's people bastards.'

'What is that word?' asked Brigitte. 'Many strange words he
knows, your fiend.'

'Friend,' I amended.

'A great nation's bones picked over by Yanks and Bolshevists,'
said Roper, 'and the French, a rag of a nation, and the British.'
Strangely, two cathedral choirs sang in my head, antiphonally;
Babylon the Great is fallen—If I forget thee, O Jerusalem. I said:

'You always wanted a unified universe. Tautology and all.
Remember that no science now can be wholly for peace. Rockets
are for outer space but also for knocking hell out of enemies.
Rocket fuel can speed man into the earth or off it.'

'How did you know about rocket fuel?' asked Roper, wide-
eyed. 'I never mentioned—'

'Just a guess. Look,' I said, 'I think I'd better be going.'

'Yes,' said Brigitte very promptly, 'be going.' I looked at her, wondering whether to be nasty back, but her body got in the way. Perhaps I'd said enough already. Perhaps I'd been discourteous. I still had fragments of Uncle Otto's ham in my back teeth. Perhaps I was ungrateful. I said to Roper:

'It's a messy sort of journey back where I'm going.'

'I thought you were in Preston.'

'No, a country house some way outside. A matter of a last bus.'

'Well,' he said unhappily, 'it's been nice having you. You must come again some time.' I looked at Brigitte to see if she would corroborate that in smile, nod, word, but she sat stony. So I said:

'*Danke schön, gnädige Frau. Ich habe sehr gut gegessen.*' And then, like a fool, I added: '*Alles, alles über Deutschland.*' Her eyes began to fill with angry tears. I got out without waiting to be shown out. Jolting on the bus into town, I kept seeing Brigitte's great *Urmutter* breasts wagging and jumping inside their white cotton blouse. Roper would undo a button, and then the catechism would start: 'Whose fault was it all?'—'England's, England's' (most breathily). It would continue, intensifying, to the point where she would lose interest in catechising. I turned myself into Roper. Oh yes, cupping a fine firm huge Teutonic breast I too would breathily revile England, would blame my own mother for the war, would say, preparing for the plunge, that not enough Jews had been plunged into gas-chambers. And afterwards I would take it all back, though not in any chill disgust of *post coitum:* rather I would call her an evil bitch, very hot, and strafe her. And then it would start again.

That was a significant event in Roper's life, sir. I mean his going into the death-camp and seeing evil for the first real time—

not the pruriently reported evil of the Sunday rags, but stinking palpable evil. For the sake of scientific rationalism he'd jettisoned a whole system of thought capable of explaining it—I mean Catholic Christianity; face to face with an irrational emptiness he'd made himself a sucker (ah, how literally) for the first coherent system of blame that had been presented to him. There's another letter I haven't mentioned, a letter in reply to that letter of mine advising him to get stuck into the German women:

'I've tried to do what you said. It's reminded me in a queer way of the old days of going to confession. Blasphemous, those still in the fold would think. I met this girl in a small beer-place, she was with a German man. I was a bit drunk and a bit more forward than I'd have normally been. The man sort of slunk off when I came to their table. I think it was her brother. Anyway, I bought her several beers and gave her three packets of Player's. To cut a long story short, before I properly knew what was happening I found we were lying on the grass in this sort of park place. It was a lovely evening—*Mondschein,* she kept saying. That was right for what they call LOVE. Then, when I saw part of her bared body under the moon, it all came over me—that camp and all that bare wasted flesh there, not at all like hers. I sort of grabbed hold of her in a kind of hate you could call it, and I even screamed at her while I was doing it. But she seemed to like it, *"Wieder wieder wieder,"* she seemed to keep on crying. And then it seemed to me that I'd done wrong to her, raped her even, but, worse than that, I was sort of corrupting her by all this, she took such pleasure in what was meant to be hate but became a great joy I was sharing with her. I loathe myself, I could kill myself, the guilt I feel is shocking.'

The day before I got this letter I received a telegram from

Roper. It said: 'DESTROY LETTER WITHOUT READING PLEASE PLEASE WILL WRITE EXPLAINING.' He never did write explaining. What he did instead was to expiate his fancied wrong to the woman shrieking for more in the moonlight. Girl rather than woman. Brigitte must have been very young at that time.

FOUR

IT WAS A LONG TIME, time enough to forget Uncle Otto's smoked salmon and coffined ham and his niece's unpleasantness, before Roper and I met again. When we did meet again, he was, over-fulfilling his wife's prophecy, a *real* doctor, not just, like horrible dead Goebbels, a man with a first degree. He rang me up at home, very breathy and very close to the telephone, as though it were an erogenous zone of Brigitte's. Urgent, he said. He needed advice, help. I could guess what it was going to be. *Wieder wieder wieder. Ach*, the lovely bloody *Mondschein*. I suggested a Soho restaurant the following evening. A German restaurant, since he liked German things so much. There Doctor Roper, white hope of research in cheap rocket fuel, got very drunk on sparkling hock and moaned and whined. His wife was playing away. And he loved her so much still, he said, and he'd given her everything any decent woman could—

'What exactly has happened?' There was a vinous touch of satisfaction in my voice; I could hear it and it was hard to suppress.

'He was in the house one night when I got back late, a great red German lout, and he had his coat off and his shirt open, a big fair hairy chest, and he was drinking beer out of a can and he had his feet on the settee, and when I walked in he wasn't one bit abashed but just grinned at me. And she grinned too.'

Abashed. 'Why didn't you bash him and kick him out?'

'He's a professional wrestler.'

'Oh.' I had a swift vision of Roper on the ropes, neatly cat-cradled in them, a parcelled crucifixion. 'How did all this start?'

'We took this house, you see, and it's in a fairly slummy part of London, because houses are the very devil to get in London but—'

'You've been in London long?'

'Oh yes.' He stared at me as though his coming to London had been headlined in the more reputable newspapers. 'Hard to get, as I say, but the Department helped and we didn't want a flat any more, and Brigitte said that she was to be an *Englische Dame* with stairs to go up and down—'

'Come to this wrestler.'

'We went into a pub for a drink, you see, in Islington it was, and then there was this big blond man talking bad English with a very strong German accent. She spoke to him, talking about *Heimweh*—that's homesickness, she was homesick, you see, for somebody to speak German to, and she found that he came from about thirty miles from Elmshorn. So that was it pretty well. He's under contract to wrestle in England or something and he said he was lonely. A very big man and very strong.'

'Wrestlers usually are.'

'And very ugly. But we had him back for supper.' Roper spoke as though ugliness would not normally get you an invitation. 'And very—you know, absolutely no intelligence, with this big grin and his face all shiny.'

'That was after eating, I take it?'

'Oh no, all the time.' Roper was growing as obtuse as his wife to the tones of irony or sarcasm. 'But he did eat like a pig. Brigitte cut him more and more bread.'

'And she's rather taken to him, has she?'

Roper began to tremble. 'Taken to him! That's good, that is. I came home one night, late again, very tired, and you know what I found?'

'You tell me.'

'On the job.' Roper's voice rose. His hands clenched and unclenched. They seized the sparkling hock and poured a size-able tremulous measure. Then, panting, he said, loudly so that people looked at him, 'On the bloody job. I saw them. His big bloody muscles all working away at it, enjoying it, and she was there underneath him crying out *Schnell schnell schnell*.' The solitary waiter, a German, took this for a summons and started to come too. I waved him away. To Roper I said:

'Oh no.'

'Oh bloody yes. And even he had the bloody grace to see this was all filthy and wrong and he didn't grin this time, oh no. He slunk out, carrying half his clothes. You know, it was as though he expected me to hit him.'

'You should have knocked the daylights out of him,' I said. An improbable idea. 'And so that's the end of that. I never thought that marriage would work, somehow.'

He looked at me wet-lipped. Part of his dithering now seemed out of shame. 'But it did, you know,' he mumbled. 'It took me a long time to forgive her. But, you see, seeing them like that—I don't quite know how to put this. Well, it gave us a new lease of life, in a way.'

I understood. Horrible, but life remains life. A new lease of.

'You mean, even though you *were* tired coming back home at night, you were able to—'

'And she was sort of penitent.'

'So she should be. If I ever caught any wife of mine—'

'You wouldn't understand.' A flash of drunken sweetness peered, then went. 'You're not married.'

'All right. So now what's your trouble?'

'It didn't last all that long,' he mumbled. 'It was working late and not eating enough, I suppose. I've been having this bit of tummy trouble, canteen food.'

'This was all right, though, was it?'

'Oh yes.' We'd had *Kalbsbraten* followed by *Obsttorte*. Roper, in a distracted kind of passion, as though waging a secondary war at threshold level, had cleaned my plates as well as his own. 'She's been going on at me as an effete Englander, no ink in my pen, no pen at all, only a little *Bleistift*. Now I've become one of those who encouraged the Jews to engineer Germany's downfall.'

'Well, you always were, weren't you? As an Englishman, I mean?'

'I'd seen the light,' said Roper in dark gloom. 'That's what she used to say. Now she's brought this bloody big blond beast back again.'

'So there was a sort of interim, was there?'

'He was on the Continent, doing a kind of tour. Now he's in London, wrestling in the suburbs.'

'Has he been back in the house?'

'For a late supper. Not for anything else. But I can't vouch for what happens in the afternoons.'

'You condoned it, you bloody fool. They've both got you now.'

'He's not abashed any more. He grins and goes to the fridge to get more beer. She calls him Willi. But the name he wrestles under is Wurzel. On the posters it says *Wurzel der Westdeutsche Teufel*.'

'Wurzel the mangle.'

'The West German Devil is what it means.'

'I know, I know. What do you want me to do about it? I can't see that there's anything I *can* do.' But then—and they should have done this before—my professional ears pricked. 'Tell me,' I said, 'do you discuss your work with her at all? Does she know the sort of thing you're doing?'

'Never.'

'Does she ever ask?'

He thought for a moment. 'Only in the most general terms. She doesn't really understand what sort of work a scientist does. She didn't get much schooling, what with the war.'

'Do you bring papers home?'

'Well—' I'd made him just a little uneasy. 'She wouldn't understand them even if she could get at them. I keep them locked up, you see.'

'Oh, you innocent. Tell me, has she any relatives or friends in East Germany?'

'None that I know of. Look, if you think she's on the spying game you're greatly mistaken. Whatever's going on is sexual, you take my word for it. Sex.' This damnable. His mouth began to collapse. The whine came gargoyling out. 'It's not my fault if I get so tired in the evenings.'

'And on Sunday mornings too?'

'I don't wake early. She's up hours before I am.' Now the tears were ready to flood, and I was ready to get him out of here before the fierce fat manageress came. I grinned to myself, remembering Father Byrne sermonising in the dormitory. I paid the bill, leaving all the change, and said, as we left, me supporting his left elbow:

'I can make a professional job of this, you know. Watching them, I mean. And if you want evidence for a divorce—'

'I don't want a divorce. I want things to be as they used to be. I love her.'

We walked down Dean Street towards Shaftesbury Avenue. 'There was a time,' I said, 'when you were always having a jab at authority. Very independent you were, Renaissance man, knocking at all doors. You seem to need to lean on something now. Somebody, I mean.'

'We all need to lean. I was very young and inexperienced then.'

'Why don't you go back into the Church?'

'Are you mad? One goes forward, not back. The Church is a lot of irrational nonsense. And you're a right sod to talk, aren't you?' The Bradcaster way of speech had burrowed deep into us, despite our Southern background. 'Been out of the Church yourself since God knows when.'

'Since taking up this kind of work, to be precise. A question of loyalties. In my dossier my religion is down as C of E. It's safe. It means nothing. It offends nobody. The Department has an annual church parade, believe it or not. When all's said and done, the Pope remains a foreigner.'

'Beat him up,' said Roper, not meaning the Pope. 'Teach him a lesson. You've done unarmed combat and judo and so forth. Knock his teeth in, the big blond swine.'

'In Brigitte's presence? That won't exactly endear you to her, will it? She called me your fiend, remember.'

'Get him alone, then. Outside at night. Back at wherever he lives.'

'I don't see how that's going to teach Brigitte a lesson. The true object of the exercise. Good God, this is really the war all over again, isn't it?'

We were approaching Piccadilly Underground. Roper stopped in the middle of the pavement and began to cry. Some young louts stared at him, but more in commiseration than in the traditional guffawing contempt. The sex-patterns were merging with this new generation. But not for Roper, not for me. Sex was, for us, still damnable. I persuaded him to wipe his eyes and give me his address. Then he tottered off underground to reach it, as though it were somewhere in hell.

I was going to do things my way, not Roper's. At that time my position in the Department, as you remember, sir, was still more or less probationary. It was not yourself but Major Goodridge who gave me permission—treating it rather like an exercise—to spy on Brigitte Roper, *geboren* Weidegrund, and this Wurzel man. I think I was even praised for initiative. Each afternoon after that Soho meeting I waited outside the Roper residence just off Islington High Street. It was a dingy bleak little terraced house, the windows unwashed perhaps because window-cleaners were too proud to call in this district. The dust-bins stood, all along that street, like dismal battered front-door sentinels. At one end of the street was a dairy, cloudy milk-bottles stacked outside; at the other was a dirty-magazine shop. As this was a working-class district, it was deserted in the day—except for curlered wives in slippers, shopping. Watching was difficult. But I only had to do three days of it. At last the Wurzel man came—muscular, ugly, complacent, dressed in a deplorable blue suit. He knocked, then looked up at the sky, whistling, sure of his welcome. The door was opened, though Brigitte did not show herself. Wurzel went in. I took a walk long enough to smoke a *Handelsgold* Brazilian cigar. Then, spitting out my butt, I too knocked. And again. And again. Bare feet coming downstairs. A voice speaking through the letter-slit, Brigitte, unswitched to English: *'Ja? Was ist's?'* I said, in gruff demotic:

'Registered parcel, missis.' She opened up minimally. Ready for that, I pushed in, feeling the ineffectual counterpush of those large Teutonic breasts (though not seeing, not looking) as she cried after me marching up the stairs. A shout of bemused and part-fearful enquiry answered her. It was like two people playing at Alps. His sound, as well as a rank cigarette-smell, told me where the bedroom was. Poor Roper. The landing was full of books spilling from shelves. Brigitte was panting up after me. I entered the bedroom, crossing to its furthermost corner before turning to face them both. She, now in, clad only in a gaudy bathrobe, recognised me, the fiend. And now I took in the beast on the bed—gross, stupid, totally—like Noah—uncovered. There was no spying going on here, that was certain. But could one ever be sure? I said very loudly:

'Go on, pig. Out. Out before I you into the street all naked kick, swine.'

He saw I was not the husband. He stood up on the bed, seeking balance as on a trampoline, totally and obscenely bare, his little bags swinging. He gorilla-spread his fat arms, grunting at me. He had some idea of leaping at me from the bed-foot, but I was too far away. And then, as in the ring, the bloody fool, he beckoned me in with his fingers. We were to engage to the crowd's roars and boos. I could see at once that he was fit only for rigged bouts, a throw-seller, spectacular enough with the Irish whip and the flying mare, the flying head scissors, the monkey climb, but no good at all in genuine shoot moves. A script-boy. *Cats and big thing after with Tiger Pereira.* 'Cats' meaning 'catspaw' meaning 'draw'. The 'big thing' an act of anger or marching off in a huff to the crowd's delight. I knew a little about wrestling.

He jumped from the bed. Brigitte's pots and jars shook on their dressing-table. Good God, I now noticed on the wall a group photograph of the Sixth Form at St. Augustine's, Roper and I arm-folded side by side, Father Byrne smiling, damnable sex off his mind that day. And now Wurzel advanced, bad teeth snarling, theatrically terrible. We needed more space really. Relying too much on initial intimidation, Wurzel did not expect my sudden rush with a head-butt to the midriff. His arms were wide open, heaven help him. Surprised, he was taken aback by my rapid hug, from a kneeling position, of his left leg. He was about to chop at my nape, but I was ready for this. I leaned my whole weight and had him on his back, breathless. He was a horrible big soft fleshy feather-bed. I lay on him, his posture Mars Observed. He tried to get up, but I bore down hard. Then I dealt my speciality, a hand-edge on the larynx, *einmal, zweimal, dreimal.* By rights Brigitte should have been hammering me with a shoe or something, but I saw her bare feet by the door, quite immobile. *'Genug?'* I asked. He gurgled what might have been *'Genug'* but I gave him no benefit of the doubt. His thick arms lay quite flaccid, more ornament than use. I bit his left ear very viciously. He tried to howl, but coughs got in the way. I rose from the bed of him in a single nimble push, then he was after me, flailing and coughing, trying to howl expressions with *Scheiss* in them. On Brigitte's dressing-table was a pair of nail-scissors, so I picked these up and danced round him, lunging and puncturing. '*Genug?*' I asked again.

This time he just stood, panting when not coughing, squinting at me warily. 'I go,' he said. 'I wish mine gelt.' So she took money, did she? 'Give it him,' I said. From the pocket of the bathrobe she drew out a few notes. He snatched them, spitting. I found an even better weapon on the dressing-table—a very long nail-file with a dagger-end. 'One minute to dress,' I said, 'and then out.' I began to count the seconds. He was pretty quick. He didn't bother to lace his shoes. 'And if you give the *Herr Doktor* any more trouble—' Brigitte's eyes were on me, not on him, I now had time to notice. She bade him no good-bye as I back-punched him, grumbling, out on to the landing. On the landing he saw Roper's books and, very vindictive, he swept his fist along a top shelf and sent some of them bumping and swishing to the floor, I said: 'Smutty swine, you. Uncultured shitheap,' and I kicked his arse, a large target. 'Make a fire, shall we? Burn them all?' He rounded and snarled at me in the landing-dark, so I thrust him downstairs. Bumping against the stairwell wall he dislodged a little picture that had been unhandily nailed not firmly rawlplugged. It was an old-fashioned woolly monochrome of Seigfried, his gob open for a hero's shout, his hand grasping Nothung. This angered me. Who were they in this house to think that Wagner was theirs? Wagner was mine. I banged Wurzel down the last few steps and then let him find his own way to the front door. Opening it, he turned to execrate a mouthful as elemental and nasty as a bowel movement. I raised my hand at him, and then he slammed out.

All this time I had had my raincoat on. Going back upstairs I took it off, as well as my jacket. Entering the bedroom for a new, but still cognate, purpose, I was already loosening my tie. As I'd expected, Brigitte was lying naked on the bed. In a very few seconds I was with her. It was altogether satisfactory, very gross and thorough. I rode into Germany again, a hell become all flowers and honey for the victor. She didn't want tenderness, victim self-elected, also the mother I and the enemy had been tussling to possess. I re-enacted the victory ride three times. Afterwards (it was now dark) she spoke only German to me, language of darkness. Should she make tea, would I like some schnapps?

'Did you always take money from him?' I asked. 'Do you want money from me now?'

'Not this time. But if you come again.'

We shared a black aromatic *Handelsgold*. 'You'll have to leave him, you know,' I said. 'This sort of thing won't do at all. Go back to Germany. They're building fine new *Dirnenwohnheime* there. Düsseldorf. Stuttgart. That's your line. A lot of money to be made. But leave poor Edwin alone.'

'I too have thought of that. But here in London is better. A little flat, no *Dirnenwohnheim*.' She did a theatrical shudder; I felt it in the dark. In the dark, above the bed, Roper and I looked out at our coming world, arms folded; Father Byrne had smiled through the act of light, the act of dusk, the act of darkness. Well, I too, were I Brigitte, would much prefer a flat and a poodle in warm sinful London to one of those cold regimented German whorehouses. I said:

'Have you any money?'

'I have saved some. But if I am divorced I am deported.'

'It's up to you. But for God's sake get out of his life. He's got work to do, important work.' Lying here, right hand splayed on her right breast, its nipple rousing itself from flaccidity, I felt both loyal and patriotic. 'Each of us must do,' I added sententiously, 'the thing that is given us to do.' My cigar had gone out; there was no point in feeling for the matches to relight it. Roper and British science were to be saved. I felt a gush of generosity. 'This,' I said, turning to her, 'can count as another visit.'

FIVE

DID I DO RIGHT to tell her to do what, and very soon after, she did? I did not see her again, though, had I had time and inclination to wander Soho or Notting Hill, I might well have spied her, smart with her little dog. I rang up Roper and told him of the discomfiture of Wurzel the West German Devil. He was elated. He thought a marriage could be saved through the elimination of what Brigitte would call the *Hausfreund*. He said nothing to Brigitte nor she to him of Wurzel's being kicked downstairs and out of doors. Let bygones be. Brigitte had been more tolerant, more loving (this seemed to me the best signal of the decision I had articulated for her); again (and this she might have done, had she not been going to leave) she told no lying story to Roper about attempted rape by his best friend or fiend (see: here is his cigar-butt, hurriedly crushed out). But, after a week, Roper came to my flat. This I had expected. I had waited in every evening, expecting it, listening to *Die Meistersinger*. When Roper rang, Hans Sachs was opening Act III with his monologue about the whole world being mad: *'Wahn, wahn—'*

'I can guess what she's done,' I said. 'She's gone back on the job. The job she'd already been doing in Germany.'

'There was no real proof of that,' he snivelled, grasping his whisky-glass as though to crush it. 'Poor little girl.'

'Poor little girl?'

'An orphan of the storm.' Oh my God. 'A war victim. We did this to her.'

'Who did? Did what?'

'Insecurity. Instability. The crash of all that meant anything. Germany, I mean. She doesn't know where she is or what she wants.'

'Oh, doesn't she? She doesn't want you, that's certain. Nor did she really want that bloody Wurzel. She just wants to do a job she can do.'

'Independence,' said Roper. 'Unsure of herself. She always talked about working, but she'd not been trained for anything. No education. That damnable war.'

That damnable. 'Oh my God, Roper, you're the end. You're totally incredible. She's just a natural prostitute, that's all. Good luck to her, if that's what she wants. But now you've got to forget all about her and get on with your work. If you're lonely, call on me any time. We'll go out and get drunk together in low pubs.'

'Drunk,' said Roper thickly. 'We're drunken beasts, that's what we are. Warmongers and ravishers and drunken beasts. But,' he said, when he'd taken a swig as though toasting that, 'she may come back. Yes, I'll be waiting for her. She'll come back crying, glad to be home again.'

'Get a divorce,' I said. 'Get a private detective on the job. They'll find her sooner or later. Evidence. No trouble at all.'

He shook his head. 'No divorce,' he said. 'That would be the final betrayal. Women are not what we are. They need protecting from the great destructive forces.'

I nodded and nodded, very grim. He'd mixed Brigitte up with the Virgin Mary (whom we'd all at school got into the habit of calling, as though she were a spy-ring or automation company, the BVM) and Gretchen in Goethe's *Faust*. '*Das Ewig-Weibliche zieht uns hinan,*' I quoted. But he didn't recognise the quotation.

What I should have foreknown, sir, was that Roper would be thrown into a great empty pit where nothing was really to be trusted any more, where there was no belief in anything. *Anything?* There was the value of his work, wasn't there? Roper, gently but firmly led by Professor Duckworth, was professionally absorbed in that, but there must have been great areas of his brain suffering from inanition. Brain? Perhaps heart or soul or something. Blame England, yes, for Brigitte's defection, but—let it come slowly—blame also the whole of Western Europe, blame even Germany for not being a good father to her. But you can't fill the irrational past with blame. You need something positive. We all need our irrational part to be busy with something harmless (the housewife's hands knitting while her eyes take the television in), letting our rational part get on with what, perhaps stupidly, we suppose to be the important purpose of life. Here, in brief, is the peril of being a scientist brought up on a fierce and brain-filling religion. He starts, in his late teens, by thinking that his new sceptical rationalism (bliss was it in that dawn to be alive) makes nonsense of Adam and Eve and transubstantiation and the Day of Judgement. And then, too late, he discovers that the doctrines don't really count; what counts is the willingness and ability to take evil seriously and to explain it. Supernature abhors a supervacuum. When I returned from that Serbo-Croat refresher course you, sir, sent me on, I was pleased to find that Roper seemed to be living a nice, decent, normal, middle-class British life. I rang his home one evening to see how he was getting on, and I heard a voice somehow beer-flushed and, behind the voice, the noise of well-in-hand gaiety. A few people in, he said. Do come round, meet the boys and girls. News of Brigitte? News of who? Oh, her. No, no news. 'Come round,' he said, 'I've joined the Labour Party.'

'You've joined the—'

He rang off. He had joined the— Well, then, that was a relief. The NATO powers could breathe freely again. What could be safer than that he should be a member of the political party which provided either H.M. Government or Opposition? No more nasty guilt now, no more there - can - be - no - God - if - He - failed - to - strafe - England, breathed breathily as, each hand crammed with warm Brigitte, he dug his hot spoon into that delicious honey-pot. I went round. Lights and merriment in the bay-window. A dark-haired girl let me in. The hall-light was bright: she was slim and sallow, dressed for no nonsense in a tweed skirt and yellow jumper. 'Oh, you must be—' Roper came into the hall. 'Ah, there you are' His hair, like that of some pioneer labour leader, was shaggy and tousled. The living-room and dining-room had only recently, he told me, been knocked into one: forgive the smell of size. These were his friends, he said: Brenda Canning, a merry ginger girl in flashing glasses and jingling trinket-bracelet; Shaw, shy, who worked with Roper; Peter, no, sorry, Paul Younghusband—a round man who smiled from striking a chord on a guitar; Jeremy Cavour, long, with a pipe, his ample grey hair parted on the left. Others. 'Not really a party,' said Roper. 'More of a study-group meeting.' There were cheese, bread, a carboy of pickles, bottles of light ale on the dining-table.

'What are you studying?' I asked. 'Oh,' said Roper, 'there's been a bit of talk about some of us scientists getting together to hammer out a sort of pamphlet. Socialism and Science. We hadn't really got down to the title, had we, Lucy?'

Lucy was the girl who had opened the door, unintroduced to me perhaps because we'd already made functional contact, introductions perhaps being purely decorative or phatic. This Lucy was standing close to him and seemed to me, at that moment of being addressed, to touch him with a gentle thrust of the hip. Ah, I thought, they are friends. I looked at her with more attention, soon with something like favour—wide-mouthed (generous), gate-toothed (sensual), small-eyed (shrewd), high-browed. It was a neat figure; the voice was a decent kind of South London. An attractive girl on the whole, but breathing of no gross earth-mother like Brigitte. The house looked very tidy; Lucy had opened the front door; Lucy said to me now:

'Can I get you some beer? All we have, I'm afraid.' I noted the 'we', saying:

'In a stein, please.' Roper clouded over. 'Sorry, stupid of me,' I said. 'There aren't steins any more.' This was at once taken up by a small man in the corner, weak-and-intellectual-looking, rings under his eyes. He cried:

'The house of Stein is fallen. Ah, Gertrude, Gertrude.' The round man with the guitar, Peter or Paul or something, improvised a silly jingle to the tune of 'Chopsticks':

'Einstein and Weinstein and Kleinstein and Schweinstein and Meinstein and Deinstein and Seinstein and Rheinstein and—' Roper smirked at me: what witty and erudite friends he now had. They all seemed to be scientist's assistants, none of them under thirty, most of them adolescently content with an evening of singsong and light ale. Light ale was now given to me. 'Thank you,' I said. 'What will you have, Winny?' asked Lucy of Roper. A choice, was there? Beer was all they had, she'd said. 'Lemon barley water,' said Roper. 'A small glass.' Well, the loss of Brigitte hadn't sent him howling to the drink. Or perhaps it had; perhaps he was being looked after now.

'Winny she calls you,' I said, when Lucy had gone to the kitchen.

'That's short for Edwin,' said Roper, smiling.

'Oh, Roper, Roper, I've known your name is Edwin for the last twenty years.'

'As long as that? How time goes.'

'Have you done anything about a divorce yet?' I asked.

'Plenty of time,' he said. 'Three years for desertion. I see now it could never be the same again as it used to be. Have you ever read Heracleitus? Everything flows, he said. You can't step into the same river twice. A pity. A terrible, terrible pity. Poor little girl.' I got in quickly, forestalling the *Weltschmerz*, with:

'How about *this* little girl?'

'Lucy? Oh, Lucy's been a very great help. Just a good friend, you know, nothing more. She cooks me the odd meal. Sometimes we have a meal out. A *very* intelligent girl.' This seemed to have something to do with her skill with a menu, but then he said: 'She works our computer for us. Don't you, Lucy?' he smiled, water-ily, as he took lemon barley from her. 'Our computer.'

'That's right,' she said. I felt that perhaps she would have preferred Roper to designate their relationship *not* in professional terms. To me she said: 'Are you a member of the party?'

'Oh, I'm progressive. I believe in soaking the rich. But I also believe in Original Sin.'

'Poor old Hillier,' smirked Roper. 'Still not emancipated.'

'My belief,' I said, 'has nothing to do with Father Byrne. People tend to choose the worse way rather than the better. That's something experience has taught me. I use the theological term for want of a better one.'

'It's all environment,' said Roper. 'All conditioning.' He would have said more, but Lucy told him to save it. 'Everybody wants to sing,' she said. 'Don't you think we ought to have business first?'

'Business.' The word made Roper very serious and chin-jutting. 'We have a bit of discussion,' he told me. 'Brenda there takes the main conclusions down in shorthand. You'll stay, won't you? You may have some useful ideas to contribute. A fresh mind, you see. Perhaps we in the group are growing a little too familiar with each other's. Minds, I mean. But,' he chuckled, 'don't say anything about Original Sin.'

When the discussion started (and it was a very earnest sixth-form-type discussion, full of fundamentals), I found myself switching on the professional ear. But any hammering-out of the position of science and technology in a progressive society had to be above suspicion. Britain, whatever party happened to be in power, was now committed to socialism. This group was concerned with laying down a series of articles for a Socialist scientist's creed. The pipeman Cavour was presumably to do the actual writing of the proposed pamphlet, since he tried to fix all conclusions in a ponderous literary form, going er and ar in search of the *mot juste*, correcting people's grammar. 'Something like this,' he said. 'We er hold that the past is dead and the future is er upon us. Meaning the Scientific Revolution. We think in world terms, not er the antique terms of nationalism.

Ultimately we envisage a World State and World Science. Ar.'
Brenda, her token-bracelet jangling, was getting it all down.
Lucy sat in one of the two moquette-covered armchairs, Roper
on the arm. He seemed happy. He seemed to have got over sin.
He was safe, sir.

Of course he was safe, cuddled by a humanitarian and rational philosophy which occasionally gives Britain a government.
The whole Roper case, if I may call it that at that stage, was perhaps ready to bubble with a political extremism that, during a
long Tory summer, sought fulfilment in a country that wasn't
merely doctrinaire about a World State and World Science. Must
a man be blamed for being logical? I don't know how far Lucy,
who seemed to be a very serious girl, helped. I was out of
England long before Roper. What I'm trying to say, sir (or would
be trying to say if I were saying it), is that you can't condemn a
man because an ineluctable process carries him. If you wanted
Roper's logic—and you did and still do—you have to swallow it
all. That is why I can't attempt any serious moral persuasion
when, the day after tomorrow, late at night, I eventually reach
him. The bribes, of course, he'll, and very rightly, scorn. It will
have to be the ampoule, the forcible abduction of a Soviet citizen
temporarily disguised as a drunken British tourist. And I'm doing
this for the money.

I'm doing this for the money, for the terminal bonus (I am
most bribable now) which, in my retirement, I shall need. If it
were not for the retirement I should not be proposing to play a
mean trick on a friend. But, as I've already told you in a *real* letter—dispatched, received, ruminated, replied to—I am retiring
precisely because I'm sick and tired of having to play mean
tricks. You might as well, while my hand is in, have the lot.

Lot what? Lot the next to the last in this shame's auction to bidding oblivion of the shabby contents of my long-leased spy-house. You have my report of the successful betrayal of Martinuzzi, very brief, totally factual. The lying code-message about Martinuzzi's being on the double game was, as we knew it would be, intercepted. When Martinuzzi was taken over to Rumania he expected, I suppose, praise, bonuses, promotion. We know what he got. End of Martinuzzi. Of Signora Martinuzzi and the three bambini in Trieste also the end, but that, of course, irrelevant. The explosion of a paraffin stove in the little Casa Martinuzzi on the Via della Barriera Vecchia and the burning alive of mother and eldest child, as well as the cat and her kittens, was just an unfortunate accident. A spy should not give hostages to fortune: that's what whoever was responsible really meant. I was sick; I vomited a bellyload into the gutter. What made my shame worse was the visit of some British louts with guitars and emetic little songs; they filled the Opera House with infantile screamers. Their income, I read, amounted to something like two million lire a week; Martinuzzi was lucky to get half of that sum a year. All right, Martinuzzi was the enemy, but to whom do you think I felt closer? My very good fiend, Brigitte might have said. I spent some of my own few million lire on arranging for the adoption of the remaining two of the enemy's children; both need the most delicate plastic surgery. I don't mind games, but when they get too dirty I don't think I want to play any more.

You won't receive this letter, for this letter has not been written. But, if I get Roper back to you, and if you do to Roper what I fear you will, despite the promises in the letters in my coat-lining, I shall at least have rehearsed some of the content of his defence. The time is now two minutes to four. I shall forgo tea and a tabnab and not eat much dinner. To my satyriasis I say 'Down, sir, down.' I must be fit for the day after tomorrow, recognising my duty to my retirement. A little nap now, then. As ever, or rather *not* as ever, D.H. (729).

PART II

ONE

DRY WITHIN, WET WITHOUT, HILLIER AWOKE. IT WAS REALLY very hot. He had lain down on his bunk in his old grey holiday Daks and a green sleeveless Luvisca shirt; now the shirt was soaked and the slacks felt clammy. He was also aware of the smell of himself. Adam had awakened to the scents of a garden; fallen Adam in his early forties was greeted, as a kind of smell-track to painful light, by tobacco-smoke woven into his skin and a vague effluvium of sour meat-juice, also—like a space-traveller freely floating outside, but not too far outside, his capsule—an exter-nalisation of his own breath: burnt potato and tannery. Hillier got up, tasting his mouth and frowning. He should have switched on the electric fan. He did so now, stripping. The coolness exorcised that small bad dream he'd had—the buffeting with rose-branches, the yelling crowd, his breathless crawling up a road that grew steadily hillier. That, of course, was a dream of his own name; the huge coil of rope he'd been carrying was explained by the name of his quarry. He should by rights have dreamed of new names—a hunter and an island.

He surveyed himself naked in the dressing-table mirror. The body still looked as if it were for use, pretty lean. But he had the impression that it now wanted to sag under the stress of an adventurous past whose record was scored on the flesh—wound-scars, the pitting of an old disease. On his left flank was an indelible brand, a literal one. Soskice, who had eventually been smashed, dying cursing, had watched and grinned with all his blue and yellow teeth while the white-hot iron had been applied. 'S,' he had lisped. 'A signature on one of my lesser works, your body mangled, though not mangled to the pitch of unrecognisability.' Strapped to the chair, Hillier had tried to impose another meaning on the brand as, in its mirror-form, it slowly descended. His mother's name—Sybil. That would do. Welcome it, welcome it, he had told his body as Soskice's executioner voluptuously delayed the searing impact. And then. Yearn to it, desire it, he had counselled his skin. It's a poultice, it's good for you. He had not screamed, feeling the intolerable bite, the pain itself S-shaped. The S had hissed into his very bowels, the sphincter—weakest of all the muscles—bidding them open to expel the snake whose body was all teeth. Soskice had been disgusted, but no more so than Hillier. 'I didn't mean that,' Hillier had moaned. 'I apologise.' And they had left him for a time in his mess, delaying the consummation. And that delay had (oh, it was a long story bringing in a man called Kosciusko) saved his life. The S now stared back from the mirror, the reversed S of the brand itself. A spectacular thing to carry into retirement. Many a woman had commented on it, tracing the serpentine course, forward and back, in languid wonder after love. And in the languor of retirement Soskice and Brayne and Tarnhelm and Chirikov and Artsibashev would rest, the violent enemies, as fellow-heroes in a remote saga as flavoursome with nostalgia as a dog-eared school Virgil.

Hillier had not yet unpacked. All he did now was to click open the shabbier of his two suitcases and take out from under his boxes and tins of cheap cigars—Sumovana, Castaneda, Huifkar Imperiales—an old rainbow bathrobe. He did not think it likely that anyone would enter his cabin while he was out taking a shower. Nevertheless he thought he had better find a hiding-place for his Aiken and its silencer, as well as for the box of PSTX ampoules. These latter were a new thing and he had not yet seen them in action. A subcutaneous injection was, so he had been told, immediately followed by drunken euphoria and great amenability. Then sleep came and, after sleep, no hangover. He looked round the cabin and hit on the lifebelt locker above the dressing-table. That would do for the time being. You could never tell, you could never be sure. The fiend is slee. His embark-ation would have been noted; no disguise is totally deceptive. Before going for his shower, Hillier surveyed the new face he had given himself. Discreet padding had swollen the cheeks to an image of self-indulgence which his normal leanness hypocriti-cally belied. The greying moustache, the greying hair rendered thinner, the contact lenses which made hazel eyes dark brown, the nose flared, the mouth pulled to a sneer—these, he told him-self, belonged not to Hillier but to Jagger, a typewriter technician on holiday. This was the penultimate disguise. And Roper's dis-guise? This was a great age for beards; nobody pulled beards any more or shouted 'Beaver'. Hillier packed the beard with the ampoules and the Aiken. The plump Edwardian mannekin on the yellowing card of lifebelt instructions pulled his strings tight, looking indifferently out at Hillier-Jagger—as functional as a spy and as dehumanised.

Hillier went out on to the corridor. This was A-Deck. A scent which reminded first-class passengers that they were paying extra for luxury breathed here, stroking the closed cabin-doors. No smell of engine-oil or galley cabbage, rather something rose-petalled and landlocked. Soft lights hid behind voluted plastic. Hillier locked his door, clasping the key in his bathrobe-pocket as he made for the bathroom. Suddenly the quiet of the corridor erupted into the noise of squabbling. A cabin-door three down from Hillier's own burst open, a boy emerged backwards, shouting. Oh God, groaned Hillier. Children. He didn't like children. They were too vigorous but also too honest, the enemies of intrigue. Besides, they got bored on voyages, they got in the way. This boy was about thirteen, an awkward age. 'I only wanted to borrow it,' he was complaining. The accent was not patrician. 'I only wanted to see what it was about.'

'You're too young,' said a girl's voice. 'I'll tell dad. Go and have a nice game of quoits or something.'

'I bet I know more about it than you do,' said the boy. 'And I don't mean quoits.' He was small and compact and dressed like a miniature adult tourist—Hawaiian shirt, tapering brown slacks, sandals, though no camera on his chest. He was also, Hillier noticed, smoking what smelt like a Balkan Sobranie Black Russian. And then, coming closer (he must pass the door to get to the bathroom), he saw the girl. At once, with a kind of groan of habituation, his body made its stock responses—tightening of the larynx, minimal pain in the frenum, a shuddering re-stoking of the arteries, a sense of slight levitation. She was beautiful:

corn-hair piled up carelessly, a nose like an idealisation of a broken boxer's, a mouth whose scolding ought at once to be stopped
with kisses. She was in a straight gold dress, deep-cut; legs, arms,
neck were bare, honeyed, superb. She was about eighteen.
Hillier's groan came up like a dreaming dog's.

'And,' said the boy, 'dad wouldn't give a damn. Nor would
she. Flat out they are, both of them. They're only interested in
one thing.'

Me too, thought Hillier. He now saw what it was the boy
wanted from his sister. A book by a certain Ralph Quintin, its
title large: *Sex and Patterns of Cruelty*. Hillier was shocked. She
should not be reading that, one so young and— Her eyes were
large, blue pools after Eden's first rainfall. They looked on Hillier
widely, then narrowed nastily at her brother. 'Dirty young pig,'
she said.

'Pigs,' said the boy, 'are not dirty. A fallacy. Just like the one
about goats smelling.' She slammed the door. Hillier said to the
boy:

'Dirt is an inescapable part of the animal condition. That's
why we take baths. That's why I'm going to the bathroom now.
Unfortunately you're standing in my way.'

The boy stared up at Hillier and then, at the leisure appropriate to a holiday, moved, ending by flattening himself against the
wall. 'You're new,' he said, puffing up Russian smoke. 'You've
only just got on. We, on the other hand, are founder members.
We got on at Southampton. It's all eating,' he told Hillier confi-
dentially. 'They gorge themselves till they're sick. That's why
some of them get off at Venice and totter back home overland. I
hope you like it.'

'I'm sure I will.'

'I shouldn't try to make my sister, though. She's mad about sex, but it's all what D. H. Lawrence calls sex in the head. She just likes to read about it. Would you like one of these Black Russians?' From the breast pocket of his Hawaiian shirt he drew out a box, also a Cygnus butane lighter.

'I'm a cigar man,' said Hillier. 'Thanks all the same.'

'Try one of my Reservados after dinner,' said the boy. 'They've got some of this very special Remy Martin behind the bar. In a reproduction Louis XIV decanter. Nobody knows how old it is.'

'I look forward to that,' said Hillier. 'And now I must have my shower.'

'You do that,' said the boy. 'I dare say we'll be meeting again at the hour of the apéritif.'

Precocious young bastard, thought Hillier, as he went to the bathroom. Sex in the head, eh? Down, wantons, down. A passer-by hooted loudly from the blue Adriatic. Hillier turned the knob of the bathroom door. He gaped at what he saw inside.

This was all too totally absurd. He had seen that fair beauty legitimately, clothed at her cabin door. Here, to balance that vision, was another, very dark, unclothed. She stood drying herself, a dusky Indian, her hair loose, a midnight river flowing to her buttocks.

'I'm terribly sorry,' gulped Hillier. 'The door wasn't—'

She already had the bath-towel about her, the ship's name *Polyolbion* draping her as if she were its beauty-queen. She was less embarrassed than Hillier. Her face was that of a cool straight-nosed Aryan, though burnt to the richest coffee. 'No,' she said, 'the door wasn't. I'm often careless.' It was a kind of finishing-school English with a Welsh lilt. She coolly watched while Hillier let himself out. She seemed to do nothing about re-locking the door. Trembling, Hillier went for his shower. The voyage was beginning either well or badly, depending on which way you looked at things. He had come aboard stringently braced for action. He was already being seduced by flesh, the two extremes of the continuum as it were pegged out for him in a matter of minutes. He took his shower very cold, gasping, then strode back to his cabin looking straight before, inseducible.

The cabin door was open. Someone was singing inside, opening and closing dressing-table drawers. His suitcases were being rummaged. But a cheerful face, unabashed, turned to greet him. 'Mr Jagger would it be, sir? And how about the other gentleman?'

Hillier relaxed as he entered. Of course, the cabin steward. 'Could you,' he said, 'do something about getting me a drink? Whisky, I think—a whole bottle. And some ice.'

'And the other gentleman? Mr Innes?'

'Delayed. He's joining us at the next port.'

'Yarylyuk, that will be. A queer sort of a place.' He laid some of Hillier's shirts in a drawer, singing again.

'I suppose,' said Hillier, 'you'll want some money.' He had already hung his summer jacket in the wardrobe. He went to the wallet there.

'It's the usual thing, sir, as you'll know. A sweetener some people call it.' The tones were either of East London or of Sydney, really both, the sea really, two ends of the sea. Hillier paid out pound notes till the steward's hand ceased to be a table and became a clamp. 'Thank you, sir. Wriste, my name is. Wriste.'

'Wrist?'

'With an e at the end. A queer sort of a name you'd say. Most call me Rick or Ricky. That's short for Richard.' He was about thirty-five, dressed in blue denim trousers and a horizontal-striped singlet. His skin was well tanned and salted, the sumptu-ousness of line and shadow to be found on an inland Northern face thoroughly pickled out. This man had been long at sea. His eyes had a far-focused look. He was toothless but wore no den-tures and, as if to point the fishiness of his mouth, he pouted when speaking, holding the pout when he'd finished, then letting the pout settle very gently to a normal spread. His thin dark brown hair seemed glued to his scalp. He wore well-fitting house-shoes of very expensive leather. 'Any particular brand, sir? We have this very good one, exclusive to the Line. Old Mortality it's called. Oh, by the way, sir, a letter for you. Came aboard at Venice, quite a lot of mail there was, you'd be surprised. But it's all business-men, you know, tycoons. They have to be kept informed.'

It was an official envelope, OHMS, correctly addressed to Sebastian Jagger, Esq.

'You'll want to read it, I suppose, sir. I'll go and get your Old Mortality.' Wriste went out singing. Hillier was aware of a strong thump of apprehension under his ribs. What warning? What change of plan? He opened the letter. It was, as he'd expected, in code: ZZWM DDHGEM EH IJNZ OJNMU ODWI E XWI OVU ODVP—Long, quite a long message. Hillier frowned. He had no means of breaking the code. Nothing had been said to him about the sending of messages after embarkation. He had neither book nor machine in his luggage. He looked again at the enve-lope. Inside, previously unnoticed by him, was the thinnest slip of paper, hardly bigger than a cracker motto. On it a rhyme had been typed:

November goddess in your glory
Swell the march of England's story.

And underneath a cheery message: *Regards from all here*. Hillier's pulse slowed in relief. It was nothing, then, after all. A facetious farewell from the Department, then, in code like every other letter he had received. A sort of crossword puzzle with cryptic clue. Something for his leisure, when he should have leisure.

When Wriste returned, bearing whisky and an ice-bowl, Hillier was already in evening shirt and black lightweight trousers. He had stowed the code message in the back pocket. Later, perhaps, he would— 'We do dress tonight, do we?' he asked.

'Big ones for dressing, all of them,' said Wriste, 'even on the first night out. Want to convince themselves they're having a good time. And you should see the women.' His fish-lips pursed to a point to whistle one sad note. 'Plunging necklines? You've no idea. No half-measures with this sort of lot, I'll say that. That's what I appreciate about the rich. Not always all that generous, though.' He was pouring a healthy slug of Old Mortality for Hillier, gold winking through caves of ice. Hillier noticed that there were two glasses on the tray. He motioned to Wriste to have one himself. Wriste took it as his due, cockily saying 'Cheers'.

The whisky was of a smoothness Hillier had forgotten existed. He poured himself another. A mood of quiet excitement came over him as he knotted his black tie: the evening ahead, plunging necklines, the smell of the rich. Wriste got on with the

unpacking. 'Although,' he said, 'the couple in here was very generous. To me, that is. Got off at Venice, motoring down the East
Coast. Ravenna, Rimini, Ancona, Pescara, Bari, Brindisi. Then
into somebody's yacht there. A nice sort of a life. Every day
there was a dozen of Guinness paid for for me and my mate. He's
a winger in the First Class.'

'I should be honoured,' said Hillier, 'if you would—'

'I expected no less of you, sir,' said Wriste. 'Me and Harry
will be proud to drink your health every night. On holiday in
Venice, was you, sir?'

'Business,' said Hillier. He might as well try out his new persona before getting on-stage. 'I design typewriters.'

'Do you really, sir?' Wriste hushed his voice as if more
impressed than by any other revelation he'd ever heard in this
cabin. 'I suppose you've been doing a bit of work for the Olivetti
people.'

Careful, careful. 'Hardly in Venice,' said Hillier.

'Of course not, sir. But it's funny that that should be your
line. I have a sister who's a secretary, and she was called in on one
of these surveys. They'd brought out this typewriter with
different-sized letters like in ordinary printing. Which I know a
bit about, having worked on a ship's printing press, but not on *this*
ship. You know, an em twice as big as an en. You know, a fat o
and a thin i. Well, they thought a lot of her opinion. You, of
course, being in the game, would know what her objection was.'
Wriste waited, poising a wad of handkerchiefs above a drawer.

'Correction is very difficult,' said Hillier, 'if you don't have a
uniform-sized type. In fact, you just daren't make a typing error
at all. That sort of thing would drive a typist mad.'

'That's it,' nodded Wriste. 'You've got it.' He displayed to

Hillier pink toothless gums. 'And now, sir, what can I do for you?' It was as though Hillier had come through a test, which indeed he had. Wriste shut the handkerchief drawer and came closer. 'Anything about seating arrangements in the dining-saloon, for instance?'

Hillier weighed in his head the light and the dark. 'There's a girl along here,' he said. And then, 'No.'

'If it's who you're thinking of,' said Wriste, 'I understand your point. A forward little sod, that brother of hers is. Big money there, though. The old man's Walters, the big flour man. I get the idea that his missis, younger than he is she is, she wants to see him off. Forcing second helpings on him all the time. Those two kids are by his first marriage. The lad, Alan his name is, was on one of these TV quizzes in the States. Knows it all, they reckon. You keep away from there. Drive you cracked he will.'

'There's an Indian lady,' said Hillier.

'Not moving very far afield, are you, sir?' said Wriste. 'You could bust your G-string on this vessel. Crying out for it a lot are. Neglected wives. Still, keep it on the corridor by all means. Less far to go. You're thinking of Miss Devi. Sort of secretary she is to this big fat foreign tycoon. Mr Theodorescu. Speaks lovely English he does, though, Oxford-educated I should imagine. At least she's *called* his secretary. See how much *she* knows about typewriters.' Wriste thought a moment, eyes down. 'It means fixing things in the purser's office. I'll have to be quick. A few quid should do it.' Sighing, Hillier handed over a five-pound note. He would not be able to live like this in his retirement. 'But,' said Wriste with great sincerity, 'if there's anything at all I can do—*anything*—you've only got to ask.'

TWO

GOING TO THE First Class bar, Hillier expected the last word in cushioned silk walls, a delicious shadowless twilight, bar-stools with arms and backs, a carpet like a fall of snow. What he found was a reproduction of the Fitzroy Tavern in Soho, London W.1, the Fitzroy as it used to be before the modernisers ravaged it. The floor had cigarette-ends opening like flowers in spilt beer; a man with long hair and ear-rings was playing an upright piano that must have cost a few quid to untune; on the smoked ceiling there were tiny chalices made out of silver paper and thrown up to stick, mouth down, by their bases. The long wooden bar-counter was set with small opaque windows which swivelled on ornate Edwardian frames, obstacles to the ordering of drinks. A job-lot of horrid art-student daubs covered the walls. There even seemed to be a hidden tape-recording of Soho street sounds, the Adriatic brutally shut out. The Tourist bar, Hillier thought, must have a very luxurious décor, no fun to the decorators.

The passengers, though, were not dressed like touts, yobs, junkies and failed writers. They were dressed like First Class passengers, a dream of rich rippling textures, and some of the men had golden dinner-jackets, a new American fashion. The aroma of their smokes was heady, but some of them seemed to be drinking washy halves of mild beer. Hillier's professional nose at once divined that they were really disguised cocktails. He had not expected that he would have to fight his way to the bar, but this, to the rich, must be part of the holiday. There was, however, no paying with money and no handfuls of soaked change. That would be taking verisimilitude too far. Hillier signed for his large

Gordon's and tonic. And the barman, who had got himself up to look dirty, would undoubtedly have liked to look clean.

Hillier was at once accosted by the forward youth called, he remembered, Alan Walters. He was dressed in a well-cut miniature dinner-jacket and he even had a yellow Banksia in his buttonhole. Hillier hoped, for the lad's own sake, that his glass of tomato-juice did not contain vodka. Master Walters said: 'I've found out all about you.'

'Oh, you have, have you?' said Hillier, with a pang of fear that perhaps the boy really had.

'That man Wriste told me. For thirty bob. A very mercenary type of man.' His accent was not right, not rich enough. 'Your name's Jagger and you're connected with typewriters. Tell me all about typewriters.'

'Oh no,' said Hillier, 'this is meant to be a holiday.'

'It's all nonsense about people not wanting to talk shop on holiday,' said Alan. 'Shop is all most people have to talk about.'

'How old are you?'

'That's an irrelevant question, but I'll tell you. I'm thirteen.'

'Oh, God,' murmured Hillier. The nearest group of drinkers—fat men become, with subtle tailoring, merely plump; silk-swathed desirable women—looked at Hillier with malice and pity. They knew what he was going to suffer; why had he not been here before to suffer equally with them?

'Right,' said the boy. 'Who invented the typewriter?'

'Oh, it's so long ago,' said Hillier. 'I look to the future.'

'It was in 1870. There were three men—Scholes, Glidden and Soule. It was in America. They were financed by a man named Densmore.'

'You've just been reading this up,' said Hillier, uneasy now.

'Not recently,' said Alan. 'It was when I was interested in firearms. Technically, I mean. I'm still interested practically.' The neighbour drinkers would have liked to ignore Alan, but the boy was, after all, a kind of monster. They listened, drinks poised, mouths open. 'It was the Remington Company, you see, who first took it up. A typewriter is a kind of gun.'

'The Chicago typewriter,' said a voice. 'It ties up well enough.' Hillier saw that the Indian girl, Miss Devi, had just joined the nearest group. She was holding a martini. She was very beautiful. She was dressed in a scarlet sari embossed with gold images of prancing, tongued, many-armed gods. A silver trinket embellished her nose. Her hair was traditionally arranged—middle parting, plaits on each side of it. But the remark about the Chicago typewriter had come from the man standing by her. This must be her boss, Mr Theodorescu. He was of a noble fatness; the fat of his face was part of its essential structure, not a mean gross accretion, and the vast shapely nose needed those cheek-pads and firm jowls for a proper balance. The chin was very firm. The eyes were not currants in dough but huge and lustrous lamps whose whites seemed to have been polished. He was totally bald, but the smooth scalp—from which a discreet odour of violets breathed—seemed less an affliction than an achievement, as though hair were a mere callow down to be shed in maturity. He was, Hillier thought, about fifty. His hands were richly ringed, but this did not seem vulgar: they were so big, strong and groomed that the crusting of winking stones was rather like adornment by transitory flowers of acknowledged God-given instruments of skill and power and beauty. His body was so huge that the white dinner-jacket was like a moulded expanse of royal sailcloth. He was drinking what Hillier took to be neat vodka, a whole gill of it. Hillier feared him; he also feared Miss Devi, whom he had seen nearly naked. There had been a man who had inadvertently spied a goddess bathing. Actaeon, was it? Was he the one who had been punished by being turned into a stag and then devoured by fifty dogs? This boy here would know.

This boy said: 'It was Yost who was the real expert. He was an expert mechanic. But the Yost method of inking soon became obsolete. What,' he coldly asked Hillier, 'was the Yost method of inking?'

'I used to know,' said Hillier. 'I've been in this game a long time. One forgets. I look to the future.' He'd said that already.

'Yost used an inked pad instead of a ribbon,' said Alan sternly. Others looked sternly at Hillier too. 'It's my opinion,' said Alan, 'that you know nothing about typewriters. You're an impostor.'

'Look here,' bullied Hillier, 'I'm not having this, you know.' The god whom Hillier took to be Mr Theodorescu laughed in a gale that seemed to shake the bar. He said, in a voice like a sixteen-foot organ-stop:

'Apologise to the gentleman, boy. Because he does not wish to disclose his knowledge to you does not mean that he has no knowledge. Ask him questions of less purely academic interest. About the development of Chinese typewriters, for instance.'

'Five thousand four hundred ideographic typefaces,' said Hillier with relief. 'A three-grouped cylinder. Forty-three keys.'

'I say he knows nothing about typewriters,' said Alan staunchly. 'I says he's an impostor. I shouldn't be surprised if he was a spy.'

Hillier, like a violinist confidently down-bowing in with the rest of the section, started to laugh. But nobody else laughed. Hillier was playing from the wrong score.

'Where's your father?' cried Mr Theodorescu. 'If I were your father I would take you over my knee and spank you hard and then make you apologise to this gentleman. Abjectly.'

'He's over there,' said Alan. 'He wouldn't do anything.' At a table just by the Fitzroy Street entrance a dim swollen man was being adjured, by a frizz-haired woman much his junior, to down that and have another.

'Well, then,' said Mr Theodorescu, veering round massively as by silent hydraulic machinery, 'let me apologise on the boy's behalf.' He shone his great lamps on Hillier. 'We know him, you see. You, I think, have just joined us. In a sense, he is all our responsibility. I believe he is sincerely sorry, Mr—'

'Jagger.'

'Mr Jagger. Theodorescu myself, though I am not Rumanian. This is Miss Devi, my secretary.'

'I regret to say,' said Hillier, 'that we have already met. It was very unfortunate. I feel like apologising, but it was not really my fault.' It had not been Actaeon's fault.

'I always forget about the locking of bathroom doors,' said Miss Devi. 'It comes of having my own private suite on land. But we are surely above these foolish taboos.'

'I hope so,' said Hillier.

'Typewriters, typewriters,' crooned Theodorescu. 'I have always felt that our house should have a distinctive typeface, very large, a sort of variant of the old black-letter. Would it be possible to write in Roman and Arabic letters on the one instrument?' he asked Hillier.

'The difficulty there would be to arrange things so that one could type from both left to right and right to left. Not insuperable. It would be cheaper to use two typewriters, though.'

'Very interesting,' said Theodorescu, searching Hillier's face, it seemed, with one eye, two eyes not being necessary. Alan Walters was now standing alone at the bar, sulking over a new tomato-juice which Hillier this time hoped contained vodka, a large one.

'He knows nothing about it,' he mumbled. It was recognised that he had been a rude boy; the grown-ups had turned their backs on him. 'Yost and Soule,' he muttered to his red glass. 'He knows nothing about them. Silly old Jagger is a Yost Soule, a lost soul, ha ha ha.' Hillier didn't like the sound of that. But Theodorescu was large enough to be able to be kind to the lad, saying:

'We have not yet seen your beautiful sister this evening. Is she still in her cabin?'

'She's a Yost Soule, like Jagger here. She reads about sex all the time, but she knows nothing about it. Just like Jagger.'

'You may have tested Mr Jagger on the history of the type-writer,' said Theodorescu urbanely, 'but you have not tested him on sex. Nor,' he added hurriedly, seeing Alan open his mouth on a deep breath, 'are you going to.'

'Jagger is a sexless spy,' said the boy. Hillier reminded himself that he was not here to be a gentleman, above such matters as impertinent and precocious brats. He went close to the not over-clean left ear of Alan and said to it, 'Look. Any more nonsense from you, you bloody young horror, and I'll repeatedly jam a very pointed shoe up your arse.'

'Up my arse, eh?' said Alan very clearly. There were conven-tionally shocked looks at Hillier. At that moment a white-coated steward, evidently Goanese, entered with a carillon tuned to a minor arpeggio. He walked through the Soho pub like a visitor from a neighbouring TV stageset, striking briskly the opening right-hand bars of Beethoven's 'Moonlight' Sonata.

'Ah, dinner,' said Theodorescu with relief. 'I'm starving.'

'You had a large tea,' said Miss Devi.

'I have a large frame.'

Hillier remembered that he had asked for a place at Miss Devi's table, which also would mean Theodorescu's. He was not sure now whether it had really been a good idea. Sooner or later Theodorescu's sheer weight, aided by Master Walters's shrill attrition from another point, however distant, in the dining-saloon, would bruise and chip the Jagger disguise. Besides, he knew he had made himself uglier than he really was, and he couldn't help wanting to be handsome for Miss Devi. Foolish taboos, eh? That's what she'd said.

THREE

'YOU THINK IT GOOD, the cuisine?' asked Theodorescu. The dining-saloon was very far from being like that fried-egg-on-horsesteak restaurant that, in Hillier's post-war London days, had stood just across the street from the Fitzroy. Conditioned air purred through the champagne light and, only a little louder, stringed instruments played slow and digestive music from a gallery above the gilded entrance. The musicians all seemed very old, servants of the Line near retirement, but they made a virtue of the slow finger movements that arthritis imposed on them: Richard Rodgers became noble, processional. The appointments of the dining-saloon were superb, the chairs accommodating the biggest bottom in comfort, the linen of the finest Dunfermline damask. Theodorescu's table was by a soft-lit aquarium; in this, fantastic fish—haired, armoured, haloed, spined, whiptailed— gravely visiting castles, grottos and gazebos, ever and anon deliv- ered wide-mouthed silent reports to the human eaters. There were just Theodorescu, Miss Devi and Hillier at the table. The Walters family, Hillier was mainly glad to see, were seated well beyond a protective barrier of well-fleshed and rather loud- talking tycoons and their ladies. Mainly but not wholly glad: Miss Walters seemed to look very delightful in a shift dress of flame velvet with a long heavy gold medallion necklace. She was read- ing at table, and that was wrong, but her brother sulked and her father and stepmother ate silently and solidly, Mrs Walters urging further helpings on her dim but gulous husband.

So far Hillier had joined Theodorescu in a dish of lobster medallions in a sauce cardinale. The lobster had, so the chief steward had informed them, been poached in white wine and a court-bouillon made with the shells, then set alight in warm pernod. The saloon was full of silent waiters, many Goanese, some British (one, Wriste's winger-pal, had come up to whisper 'Ta for the Guinness'). There was no harassed banging and clat- tering through the kitchen doors; all was leisurely.

'I think,' said Theodorescu, 'you and I will now have some red mullet and artichoke hearts. The man who was sitting in that place before you was not a good trencherman I tend to feel embarrassed when my table companions eat very much less than I: I am made to feel greedy.' Hillier looked at Miss Devi's deft and busy long red talons. She was eating a large and various curry with many side-dishes; it should, if she ate it all, last her till about midnight. 'I think we had better stay with this champagne, don't you?' said Theodorescu. It was 1953 Bollinger; they were already near the end of this first bottle. 'Harmless enough, not in the least spectacular, but I take wine to be a kind of necessary bread, it must not intrude too much into the meal. Wine-worshipping is the most vulgar of idolatries.'

'You must,' said Hillier, 'allow me to have the next bottle on *my* bill.'

'Well now,' said Theodorescu, 'I will make a bargain with you. Whoever eats the less shall pay for the wine. Are you agreeable?'

'I don't think I stand a chance,' said Hillier.

'Oh, I think that nauseous boy has impaired your self-confidence. At table I fear the thin man. The fat laugh and seem to cram themselves, but it is all so much wind and show. Are you at all a betting man?'

'Well—' In Hillier's closed tank a sort of fermentation was taking place; a coarse kind of *Schaumwein* of the spirit made him say; 'What do you have in mind?'

'Whatever sum you care to name. The Trencherman Stakes.' Miss Devi tinkled a giggle. 'Shall we say a thousand pounds?'

Could that, should he lose, be charged to his expenses, wondered Hillier. But, of course, it didn't apply. A cheque signed by Jagger was only a piece of paper. 'Done,' he said. 'We order the dishes alternately. All plates to be thoroughly cleaned.'

'Splendid. We start now.' And they worked away at the red mullet and artichoke hearts. 'Slowly,' said Theodorescu. 'We have all the time in the world. Speaking of champagne, there was some serious talk—in 1918, I think it was, the second centenary of the first use of the name to designate the sparkling wines of Hautvillers—some talk, as I say, of seeking canonisation for

Dom Pérignon, champagne's inventor. Nothing came of it, and yet men have been canonised for less.'

'Very much less,' said Hillier. 'I would sooner seek intercession from Saint Pérignon than from Saint Paul.'

'You're a praying man, then? A believer?'

'Not exactly that. Not any longer.' Careful, careful. 'I believe in man's capacity to choose. I accept free will, the basic Christian tenet.'

'Excellent. And now, talking of choosing—' Theodorescu beckoned. The chief steward himself came across, a soft-looking ginger-moustached man. Hillier and Theodorescu ordered ahead alternately. Hillier: fillets of sole Queen Elizabeth, with sauce blonde; Theodorescu: shellfish tart with sauce Newburg; Hillier: *soufflé au foie gras* and to be generous with the Madeira; Theodorescu: avocado halves with caviar and a cold chiffon sauce. 'And,' said Theodorescu, 'more champagne.'

They ate. Some of the nearer diners, aware of what was going on, relaxed their own eating to watch the contest. Theodorescu praised the red caviar that had been heaped on the avocado, then he said:

'And where, Mr Jagger, did you receive your Catholic education?'

Hillier needed to concentrate on his food. 'Oh,' he said, at random, 'in France.' He had given away too much already; he must maintain his disguise. 'At a little place north of Bordeaux. Cantenac. I doubt if you'd know it.'

'Cantenac? But who doesn't know Cantenac, or at any rate the Château Brane-Cantenac?'

'Of course,' said Hillier. 'But I'd understood that you weren't a wine man. The Baron de Brane who made Mouton-Rothschild great.'

'A strange place, though, for a young Englishman to be brought up. Your father was concerned with viticulture?'

'My mother was French,' lied Hillier.

'Indeed? What was her maiden name? It's possible that I know the family.'

'I doubt it,' said Hillier. 'It was a very obscure family.'

'But I take it that you received your technical education in England?'

'In Germany.'

'Where in Germany?'

'Now,' said Hillier, 'I suggest *filet mignon à la romana*, and a little butterfly pasta and a few zucchini.'

'Very well.' The chief steward was busy with his pencil. 'And after that some roast lamb *persillée* and onion and gruyère casse-role with green beans and celery julienne.'

'And more champagne?'

'I think we might change. Something heavier. '55 was a great year for clarets. A Lafite Rothschild?'

'I could ask for nothing better.'

'And for you, my dear?' Miss Devi had eaten a great deal, though not all, of her curries. She wanted a simple crème brûlée and a glass of madeira to go with it. She had had her fill of cham-pagne: her eyes were bright, a well-lighted New Delhi, no smoul-dering jungles. Hillier grew uneasy as, while they awaited their little fillets, Theodorescu bit hungrily at some stick-bread. It might be bluff: watch him. The dining-saloon was emptying at leisure: in the distance a dance-band was tuning up; the aged fid-dlers had departed. The diners nearest the contestants were less interested than before: this was pure gorging, their full stomachs told them; the men were, behind blue smoke-screens, now satisfying hunger for the finest possible Cuban leaf. The Walters family was still there, the girl reading, the boy inhaling a balloon-glass, the wife smoking, the husband looking not very well.

'Whereabouts in Germany?' asked Theodorescu, cutting his fillet. 'I know Germany. But, of course, I know most countries. My business takes me far and wide.' I have been warned, thought Hillier. He said:

'What I meant was that I studied typewriters in Germany. After the war. In Wilhelmshaven.'

'Of course. A great naval base reduced to a seaside centre of light industries. You will probably be acquainted with Herr Luttwitz of the Olympia Company.'

Hillier took a chance, frowning. 'I don't seem to remember a Herr Luttwitz.'

'Of course, stupid of me. I was thinking of a quite different company altogether.'

'And what,' asked Hillier, when the roast lamb came—he could tell it was delicious, but things would soon be ceasing to be delicious—'is your particular line of business?'

'Pure buying and selling,' shrugged Theodorescu massively. Was it imagination, or was he having difficulty with that forkful of onion and gruyère casserole? 'I produce nothing. I am a broken reed in the great world—your great world—of creativity.'

'Pheasant,' ordered Hillier, 'with pecan stuffing. Bread sauce and game chips.' Oh, God. 'Broccoli blossoms.'

'And then perhaps a poussin each with barley. And *sauce béchamel velouté*. Some spinach and minced mushrooms. A roast potato with sausage stuffing.' He seemed to Hillier to order with a pinch of defiance. Was he at last feeling the strain? Was that sweat on his upper lip?

'That sounds admirable,' said Hillier. 'Another bottle of the same?'

'Why not some burgundy? A '49 Chambertin, I think.'

The eating was growing grimmer. Miss Devi said: 'I think, if you will excuse me, I shall go out on deck.' Hillier rose at once, saying:

'Let me accompany you.' And, to Theodorescu, 'I'll be back directly.'

'No!' cried Theodorescu. 'Stay here, please. The ocean is a traditional vomitorium.'

'Are you suggesting,' said Hillier, sitting again, 'that I would play so mean a trick?'

'I'm suggesting nothing.' Miss Devi, turning before going through the vomitory of the dining-saloon, smiled rather sadly at Hillier. Hillier, without half-rising, gave her a little bow. She left. 'Let us push on,' frowned Theodorescu.

'I don't like this talk of pushing on. It's an insult to good food. I'm thoroughly enjoying this.'

'Enjoy it, then, and stop talking.'

Enjoying it doggedly but with a lilt of potential triumph, Hillier suddenly heard a crash, a flop, a groan, and little screams from, he now saw, the Walters table. The head of the head of the family had cracked down among the fruit-parings, upsetting cruet and coffee-cups. A stroke or something. A coronary. The stewards who, as the dining-saloon emptied, had been discreetly closing in to watch the eating contest, now converged, with the remaining diners, on to the Walters table, a sudden boil on the smooth skin of holiday. Both Hillier and Theodorescu looked down guiltily at their near-empty plates. A steward ran off for the ship's doctor. 'Shall we,' said Hillier, 'call it a draw? We've both done pretty well.'

'You yield?' said Theodorescu. 'You resign?'

'Of course not. I was suggesting we be reasonable. Over there a horrible example has been presented to us.' The ship's doctor, in evening dress of the mercantile marine, was shouting for the way to be cleared.

'It's time we moved on,' said Theodorescu. He called the chief steward. 'Bring,' he said, 'the cold sweet trolley.'

'This gentleman's in a pretty bad way, sir. If you don't mind waiting a minute—'

'Nonsense. This isn't a hospital ward.' It looked like it, though. A couple of orderlies had come in with a stretcher. While Mr Walters, snoring desperately, was being placed upon it, a Goanese steward trundled the cold sweet trolley along. Mrs Walters was weeping. The two children were nowhere to be seen. Mr Walters, in cortège, was carried out. Theodorescu and Hillier very nearly had the dining-saloon to themselves. 'Right,' said Theodorescu. 'Harlequin sherbet?'

'Harlequin sherbet.' They served each other.

'I think,' said Theodorescu, 'a bottle of Blanquette de Limoux.'

'What an excellent idea.'

They got through their sweets sourly. Peach mousse with sirop framboise. Cream dessert ring Chantilly with zabaglione sauce. Poires Hélène with cold chocolate sauce. Cold Grand Marnier pudding. Strawberry marlow. Marrons panaché vicomte. 'Look,' gasped Hillier, 'this sort of thing isn't my line at all.'

'Isn't it? Isn't it, Mr Jagger? What is your line then?'

'My teeth are on fire.'

'Cool them with some of this nectarine flan.'

'I think I shall be sick.'

'That's not allowed. That is not in the rules.'

'Who makes the rules?'

'I do.' Theodorescu poured Hillier a wonderful chill tumbler of frothing Blanquette. Hillier felt better after it. He was able to take some chocolate rum dessert, garnished with whipped cream and Kahlua, also some orange marmalade crème bavaroise, loud with Cointreau. 'How about some apple tart normande with Calvados?' asked Theodorescu. But Hillier had an apocalyptical vision of his insides—all that churned mess of slop and fibre, cream sluggishly oozing along the pipes, the flavouring liqueurs ready to self-ignite, a frothing inner sea of souring wine. A small Indian township could have been nourished for a day on it all. This was the West that Roper had deserted. 'I give up,' he gasped. 'You win.'

'You owe me one thousand pounds,' said Theodorescu. 'I wish to be paid before we reach Yarylyuk. No. I may leave the cruise before then. I wish to be paid before noon tomorrow.'

'You can't leave before Yarylyuk. It's our next port.'

'There are such things as helicopters. Much depends on certain messages I may receive.'

'You can have a cheque now.'

'I know I can have a cheque now. But what I want is cash.'

'But I haven't any cash. At least, not that amount.'

'There's plenty in the purser's safe. You have, I take it, traveller's cheques or a letter of credit. Cash.' He now lit a cigar as unshakily as if he'd merely dined on a couple of poached eggs.

Then he walked out of the dining-saloon dead straight. Hillier ran, pushing against him. That traditional vomitorium.

FOUR

'AND HOW,' ASKED HILLIER somewhat guiltily, 'is your husband?' He felt vaguely responsible for Mr Walters's coronary; he had propagandised for gluttony instead of, after at latest the *filet mignon*, standing up to denounce it in a Father Byrne–type sermon. But he had thought he stood a good chance of winning a thousand pounds, a useful sum for his retirement. Now he had to pay out all that in cash and he couldn't do it. At any rate, the money had been demanded, with the grace of a brief moratorium. He felt, though, with a spy's intuition, that it might not really come to that. The first thing was to find out more about Theodorescu. That was why he was here, on the touchline of the dance, drinking Cordon Bleu mixed with crème de menthe—a reef of crushed ice below—at the simple graceful metal bar of the open-air recreation deck. He was looking for Miss Devi. It was proper anyway, quite apart from pumping her for information, to want to see Miss Devi on this delicious Adriatic summer night with its expensive stellar and lunar show put on for the dancing tycoons and their women. He would, alternatively, have liked to see something of Miss Walters, but her father was very ill, there were questions of decency.

But Mrs Walters seemed above such questions, knocking back large highballs while her husband snored desperately in the sickbay. Hillier was able to see her more closely now, even to glance with shamed favour into the deep cut of her midnight blue straight satin, a gauzy stole of evening blue loose on her shoulders. Her hair was a frizzed auburn, not too attractive; she had a mean heart-shaped face with eyes she narrowed in a habit of cunning; her ears were lobeless and jangled no rings. She was no more than thirty-eight. She said now, in a contralto surprisingly unresonant: 'He brought this on himself. That's his third stroke. I warn him and warn him but he says he's determined to enjoy life. Look where enjoying life has put him.'

'In a decently-run order of things,' said Hillier sententiously, 'the pleasures of wealthy age would be reserved for indigent youth.'

'You kidding?' said Mrs Walters. A vulgar woman perhaps at bottom. 'He was brought up on bread and jam, he says. Weak tea out of a tin can. Now he's got the better of bread, he reckons, owning all these flour-mills. Those children of his, believe it or not, have not eaten one slice of bread since the day they were weaned. He won't have bread in the house.' All the time she talked, she looked distractedly beyond Hillier, as though expecting someone.

'But,' repeated Hillier, 'how *is* your husband?'

'He'll recover,' she said with indifference. 'They've been injecting things into him.' And now she flashed brilliantly, swaying her hips minimally, as a sort of paradigm of a fancy man approached—a man who, Hillier felt, must, beneath the green dinner-jacket, the pomade, talc, cologne, after-shave lotion, anti-sweat dabs in the oxters, have a subtle and ineradicable odour of cooking-fat. They were both vulgar: let them get on with it.

Hillier strolled away from the bar, drink in one hand, one hand in side-pocket, pleased that the thought of cooking-fat did not make him feel queasy. He had given most of the monstrous dinner to the sea—quietly, in a quiet corner near some lifeboats. It had all tasted of nothing as it came up, one flavour cancelling out another. Now he felt well, though not hungry. Gazing benevolently at the dancers, who were performing some teen-age hip-shake, jowls shaking in a different rhythm, he was happy to see that Miss Devi was on the floor, partnered by a junior ship's officer. Good. He would ask her for the next dance. He hoped it would be something civilised, in which bodies were clasped firmly against each other. These new youngsters, who could have all the sex they wanted, were very sexless really. Their dances were narcissistic. They were trying to make themselves androgynous. Perhaps it was the first stage in a long process of evolution which should end in a human worm. Hillier had a vision of human worms and shuddered. Let us have plenty of sex while it is still there. I warn him and warn him but he says he's determined to enjoy life. Mrs Walters and her fancy man had gone off somewhere, perhaps towards the lifeboats. Why were lifeboats aphrodisiacal? Perhaps something to do with urgency. Adam and Eve on a raft.

The hip-shaking stopped, dancers returned to their tables. Miss Devi was alone with the junior ship's officer. He, a mere servant, could easily be seen off. Hillier waited, watching the two suck up something long through straws. The band-leader, who seemed very drunk, said: 'This next one would be for the oldsters, if there were any oldsters here.' Everything laid on, even flattery. The band started to play a slow fox-trot.

Miss Devi seemed quite pleased to be asked to dance by Hillier. 'I rather regret that silly wager now,' said Hillier as they did feather-steps. 'I don't mean because I lost—that's nothing—but because it was a sort of insult to India. I mean, look at it as a sort of tableau in a play by Brecht or somebody—two Western men gorging, a thousand pounds on it, and India watches, sad-eyed, aware of her starving millions.'

Miss Devi laughed. Her slender body, strained back in the dance, was delicious in his arms. Hillier, as he often did when close to a desirable woman, began to feel hungry. 'Starving millions,' she repeated, with a sort of cool mockery. 'I think that we all get what we want. Having too many children and not farming the land properly—that's as much as to say "I want to starve".'

'So you don't go in for compassion, pity, things of that sort?'

She thought about that, dancing. 'I try not to. We should know the consequences of our acts.'

'And if a mad stranger breaks into my house and knifes me?'

'It's pre-ordained, willed from the beginning. You can't fight God's will. To pity the victim is to resent the executioner. God should not be resented.'

'It's strange to me to hear you talking about God.' She looked coldly at him, stiffening. 'I mean here, on a luxury cruise, dancing a slow fox-trot.'

'Why? Everything's in God—slow fox-trot, saxophone, the salted peanuts on the bar. Why should it be strange? The universe is one thing.'

Hillier groaned to himself: it was like Roper talking, except that Roper wouldn't have God. 'And the universe has only one law?' he said.

'The laws are contained in it, not imposed. Whatever we do, we obey the law.'

'What does Mr Theodorescu say when you talk like that?'

'He tends to agree with me. He accepts the primacy of the

will. We should do what we want to do. Never nurse unacted desires.'

Good. 'And if we desire a person, not just a thing?'

'There must be a harmony of wills. Sometimes this is pre-destined. Usually it has to be contrived out of one person's desire. It's the task of the desirer to bring about a reciprocal desire. That's perhaps the most Godlike function a human soul can take on. It's a kind of creation of destiny.'

As logic this made little sense to Hillier, but he wasn't going to tell her that. Nor did he just yet propose to swoop down to the practical and personal application of her theory. Plenty of time, all the night before you. Switch on the oven and stack the dishes in the warming-drawer. 'You yourself,' he said, 'whose desirabil-ity is not in question, must have had this reciprocity wished on you many times. And in many countries.'

'Some countries more than others. But I have little time for social life.'

'Mr Theodorescu keeps you pretty busy?'

'Oh, what a terrible sour note that was.' She screwed up her face delectably. 'That saxophone-player seems to be drunk. What did you say? Oh, yes, pretty busy.'

Hillier now saw the steward Wriste, smoking, watching the dancing from a far door. He had put on a shirt and spotted bow-tie for the evening. Catching sight of Hillier, he waved cheerily but discreetly, opening his mouth with a kind of toothless joy. Hillier said: 'Typing and so on? I've been working on the design of a cheap lightweight electrical typewriter. You can carry it about and plug it into a lamp-socket.'

'We're dancing,' said Miss Devi, 'under the starry Adriatic sky, and all you can think of to talk to me about is typewriters.'

'The universe is one thing. God and typewriters and drunken saxophonists. What sort of business does Mr Theodorescu do? Mr Theodorescu is also part of the universe.'

'He calls himself an entrepôt of industrial information. He buys and sells it.'

'And is he always paid in cash?'

She didn't answer. But 'Look,' she said, 'if you're trying to find out whether Mr Theodorescu and I have a *personal* relationship, the answer is no. And if you're going to ask me to use my *personal* influence to get your debt rescinded, then the answer is again no. People shouldn't gamble with Mr Theodorescu. He always wins.'

'And supposing I refuse to pay him?'

'That would be most unwise. You might have an unfortunate accident. He's a very powerful man.'

'You mean he'd harm me physically? Well then, perhaps I'd better get in first. I can fight as dirtily as the best of them. I think a gentleman ought to be willing to accept the cheque of another gentleman. Mr Theodorescu wants cash and is ready to engineer unfortunate accidents. I don't think Mr Theodorescu is a gentleman.'

'You'd better not let him hear you say that.'

'Where is he? I'll say it to his face with pleasure. But I suppose he's flat out on his bunk or in his luxe suite or whatever it is.'

'Ah, no. He's in the radio-room, busy with messages. Mr Theodorescu is never ill. He can eat and drink anything. He is, I think, the most virile man I know.'

'Sorry,' said Hillier to a couple he'd nearly bumped into. And, to Miss dancing Devi, 'Yet he's not virile enough to want to draw you into a reciprocal nexus of desire.'

'You use very pompous words. Mr Theodorescu is interested in a different kind of sex. He has exhausted, he says, the possibilities of women.'

'Does that mean that the precocious Master Walters will have to watch out?'

'He is also the discreetest man I know. He is very discreet about everything.'

'My tastes are normal. I don't need so much discretion.'

'What do you mean?' But, before he could answer, she surveyed his face with cat's eyes. 'It seems to me,' she said, 'that you are for some reason trying to make yourself ugly. The face I am looking at doesn't seem to be your face at all. You are perhaps a man of mystery. That young and forward boy doesn't believe you have anything to do with typewriters. A minute ago you were too quick to bring typewriters into our discourse, as though you were trying to convince yourself that typewriters are your professional concern. Why are you here? Why are you taking this voyage? Who are you?'

'My name is Sebastian Jagger. I'm a typewriter technician.' Hillier sang those words gently in a free adaptation of Mimi's aria in the first act of *La Bohème*. This did not clash with the music of the fox-trot. The pianist, who seemed as drunk as his leader, was doing something atonal and aleatoric; meanwhile drummer and bassist assured the dancers that this was still the dance they had started off to dance. 'I've been doing some work for Olivetti. I'm returning to England for a time, but I'm taking a holiday first.'

'I would like to strip you,' she said, her eyes deliciously malicious, 'and see what sort of man you really are.'

'Let us,' said Hillier gallantly, 'have some reciprocal stripping.'

The music suddenly, except for the pianist, stopped. A

glowingly healthy though tubby man with grey curls, evening dress and dog-collar was standing on the players' rostrum. 'My friends,' he intoned with easy loudness. The pianist came in with a recitative accompaniment but then was hushed. The congregation listened, arms still about each other as in a love feast. 'It has been suggested to me that we end now. As most of you will know, one of our fellow-passengers is in the sickbay. Our revelry is, apparently, all too audible there. The worst is feared, I fear, for the poor man. It would be reverent and considerate to end the evening quietly, perhaps even in meditation. Thank you.' He got down to some light applause. The band-leader called:

'You've had it, chums. Proceed quietly to your homes and do nothing naughty at street-corners.'

'I think,' said Miss Devi, her left arm still lightly about Hillier, 'you're being insolent.'

'You're a great one for the forms, aren't you?' said Hillier. 'You admire discretion, you resent insolence. An indiscreet God had the insolence to make me what I am. What I am you are more than welcome to find out. At leisure. Stripping,' he added, 'was the process you had in mind.'

'I shall lock my cabin door.'

'You do that. You lock it.' Hillier's stomach growled with hunger. Miss Devi's arm was still about him. He slowly dislodged it. 'That silver ring-thing on your nose,' he said. He tweaked it and she started back. 'Keep it on,' he said. 'Don't, whatever else you do, take off that.' She raised her head high as though with the intention of placing a water-vessel on it, sketched a small spitting gesture, and then, with Aryan dignity, made her way off through the dispersing crowd.

Wriste was still on the periphery. His friend the winger was

with him, a lean, burnt, sardonic man in early middle age, still dressed as for the dining-saloon. 'I thought you was doing all right there,' said Wriste. 'Ta for the Guinness,' said the winger once more, leering. Hillier said:

'I want food brought to my cabin.'

'You've got to hand it to him,' nodded the winger. 'Unless, of course, he's just showing off.'

'All passengers' wishes must, providing they seem reasonable, be acceded to without question,' said Wriste primly. 'What can I get for you, sir?'

'Crustaceans, if you know what those are. No garnishings, but don't forget the red pepper. A painfully cold bottle of Sekt.'

'Right, sir. And the number of the cabin you have in mind, if you don't know it already, is fifty-eight. Gorblimey,'" said Wriste old-fashionedly, 'how the poor live.'

FIVE

IT WAS NOT POSSIBLE to proceed to that cabin with any degree of furtiveness, even though the hour was very late and the corridor-lights had been dimmed. The snores along the corridor were so loud that Hillier found it hard to believe them genuine; soon doors might fly open and outrage be registered from under curlers and out of mouths with their dentures removed. As an earnest of this, Wriste suddenly appeared at the end of the corridor to say 'Good luck, sir' as though Hillier were going in to bat. And Master Walters, in endragoned Chinese brocade dressing-gown, was pacing like a prospective father, puffing a Black Russian in a Dunhill holder. Hillier, remembering that 'father' was a relevant word here, asked kindly if there was any news.

'News?' The face, for all the precocity, was very young and blubbered. 'What news would there be? As a man sows so shall he reap. Arteriosclerosis. He knew he was bringing it on.' There seemed to be a flavour of Miss Devi's callous philosophy in all this.

'One can't always be blamed for the state of one's arteries.' said Hillier. 'Some people are just lucky.'

'If he dies,' said Alan, 'what's going to happen to Clara and me?'

'Clara?'

'My sister. That other bitch can take care of herself, which is just what she's doing. My father wouldn't listen to reason. I told him not to re-marry. We were doing very nicely on our own, the three of us. And everything will go to *her*, everything. She hates us, I know she does. What will happen to us then?'

Snores answered. 'Modern medical science,' said Hillier lamely. 'It's amazing what they can do nowadays. He'll be right as rain in a day or two, you'll see.'

'What do you know about it?' said Alan. 'What do you know about anything? Spying up and down the corridor, as I can see, spy as you are. If he dies I'll get her. Or you can get her, being a spy. I'll pay you to get her.'

'This is a lot of nonsense,' said Hillier loudly. A voice from a cabin went shhhhhh. As he'd thought, there were people awake. 'We'll talk about this in the morning. But in the morning every-thing will be all right. The sun will shine—it will all be a bad dream, soon forgotten. Now get to bed.'

Alan looked at Hillier, who was naked under a bathrobe.

'That's two baths in half a day,' he said. Thank God, the boy still had some innocence in him. 'At least you're a very clean spy.'

'Look,' said Hillier, 'let's get this absolutely clear. I'm *not* a spy. Have you got that? There *are* spies, and I've actually met one or two. But I'm not one of them. If you could spot me as a spy, I can't very well be a spy, can I? The whole point of being a spy is that you don't seem to be one. Have you got that now?'

'I bet you've got a gun.'

'I bet you've got one too. You seem to have everything else.'

The boy shook his head. 'Too young for a licence,' he said. 'That's my trouble—too young for everything. Too young to contest a will, for instance.'

'Too young to be up at this hour. Get to bed. Take a couple of sleeping-tablets. I bet you've got those too.'

'You don't seem,' said Alan, 'to be too bad of a bloke, really. Have you got children?'

'None. Nor a wife.'

'A lone wolf,' said Alan. 'The cat that walks alone. I only wish you'd be straight with me. I'd like to strip the disguise off and find out what you really are.'

Miss Devi again. 'Tomorrow,' said Hillier. 'Everything will seem different tomorrow. Which is your cabin?'

'That one there. Come in and have a nightcap.'

'Many thanks,' said Hillier. 'But I have some rather urgent business to attend to.' He writhed as with bowel pain.

'That's all the eating,' said Alan. 'I saw that and I heard about the rest of it. Don't trust that man,' he whispered. 'He's a foreigner. He can't kid me with his posh accent.' And then, in an officer-tone: 'All right. Off you go.' And he returned to his cabin. Wriste had also gone. Hillier padded to Cabin No. 58. As he had expected, the door was not locked. He knocked and at once entered. Again as he had expected, Miss Devi said: 'You're late.'

'Delayed,' gulped Hillier. Miss Devi was lying on her bunk, naked except for her silver nose-ring. 'Unavoidably.' She had loosened her hair and her body was framed in it as far as the knees. Her body was superb, brown as though cooked, with the faintest shimmer of a glaze upon it; the jet-black bush answered the magnificent hair like a cheeky parody; the breasts, though full, did not loll but sat firmly as though moulded out of some celestial rubber; the nipples had already started upright. She reached out her arms, golden swords, towards him. He kicked off his slippers and let his bathrobe fall to the floor. 'The light,' he gasped. 'I must put out the—'

'Leave it on. I want to see.'

Hillier engaged. *'Araikkul va,'* she whispered. Tamil? A southern woman then, Dravidian not Aryan. She had been trained out of some manual, but it was not that coarse *Kama Sutra*. Was it the rare book called *Pokam*, whose title Hillier had always remembered for its facetious English connotation? What now began was agonisingly exquisite, something he had forgotten existed. She gently inflamed him with the *mayil* or peacock embrace, moved on to the *matakatham*, the *poththi*, the *putanai*. Hillier started to pass out of time, nodding to himself as he saw himself begin to take flight. Goodbye, Hillier. A voice beyond, striking like light, humorously catechised him, and he knew all the answers. Holy Cross Day? The festival of the exaltation of the Cross, September 14th. The year of the publication of *Hypatia*? 1853. The Mulready Envelope, The Morall Philosophie of Doni, the Kennington Oval laid out in 1845,

The White Doe of Rylstone, Markheim, Thrawn Janet, Wade's magic boat called Wingelock, Pontius Pilate's porter was named Cartaphilus the wandering Jew. When did Queen Elizabeth come to the throne? November, 1558. Something there tried to tug him back, some purpose on earth, connected with now, his job, but he was drawn on and on, beyond, to the very source of the voice. He saw the lips moving, opening as to devour him. The first is the fifth and the fifth is the eighth, he was told by a niggling earth-voice, but he shouted it down. He let himself be lipped in by the chewing mouth, then was masticated strongly till he was resolved into a juice, willing this, wanting it. *Mani, mani* was the word, he remembered. The *mani* was tipped, gallons of it, into a vessel that throbbed as if it were organic and alive, and then the vessel was sealed with hot wax. He received his instructions in the name of man, addressed as Johnrobert-jameswilliam (the brothers Maryburgh playing a fife over Pompeii, Spalato, Kenwood, Osterley) Bedebellbliar: *Cast forth doughtily!* So to cast forth in that one narrow sweet cave would be to wreck all the ships of the world—Alabama, Ark, Beagle, Bellerophon, Bounty, Cutty Sark, Dreadnought, Endeavour, Erebus, Fram, Golden Hind, Great Eastern, Great Harry, Marie Celeste, Mayflower, Revenge, Skidbladnir, Victory. But it was the one way to refertilise all the earth, for the cave opened into myriad channels below ground, mapped before him like the tree of man in an *Anatomy*. The gallons of *mani* had swollen to a scalding ocean on which navies cheered, their masts cracking. The eighty-foot tower that crowed from his loins glowed whitehot and then disintegrated into a million flying bricks. He pumped the massive burden out. Uriel, Raphael, Raguel, Michael, Sariel, Gabriel and Jerahmeel cried with sevenfold main voice, a common chord that was yet seven distinct and different notes. But, miracle, at once, from unknown reservoirs, the vessel began to fill again.

'*Madu, madu!*' she seemed to call. It was then now to be the gross way of the south. She bloated herself by magic to massive earthmother, the breasts ever growing too big for his grasp, so that his fingers must grow and he grow new fingers. The nipples were rivets boring through the middle metacarpal bones. His soreness was first cooled then anointed by the heat of a beneficent hell that (Dante was right) found its location at earth's centre. He was caught in a cleft between great hills. He worked slowly, then faster, then let the cries of birds possess his ears—gannet, cormorant, bittern, ibis, spoonbill, flamingo, curassow, quail, rail, coot, trumpeter, bustard, plover, avocet, oystercatcher, curlew, oriole, crossbill, finch, shrike, godwit, wheatear, bluethroat. The cries condensed to a great roar of blood. The cabin soared, its ceiling blew off in the stratosphere and released them both. He clung, riding her, fearful of being dislodged, then, as the honeyed cantilena broke and flowed, he was ready to sink with her, she deflating herself to what she had been, her blown river of hair settling after the storm and flood.

But even now it was not all over. The last fit was in full awareness of time and place, the mole on the left shoulder noted, the close weave of the skin, the sweat that gummed body to body. The aim was to slice off the externals of the *jaghana* of each, so that viscera engaged, coiling and knotting into one complex of snakes. Here nature must allow of total penetration, both bodies lingam and yoni. 'Now pain,' she said. Her talons attacked his back; it was as if she were nailing him to herself. When she perceived his sinking, she broke away—viscera of each retreating and coiling in again, each polished belly slamming to, a door with secret hinges. She gave his neck and chest the sounding touch, so that the hairs stood erect, passed on to the half-moon on the buttocks, then the tiger's claw, the peacock's foot, the hare's jump, the blue lotus-leaf. She was essaying the man's part, and now she took it wholly, but not before Hillier had nearly swooned with the delectable agony of a piercing in his perineum so intense that it was as if he were to be spitted. She was on him then, and though he entered her it seemed she was entering him. He seemed raised from the surface of the bed by his tweaked and moulded nipples. He in his turn dug deep with plucking fingers into the fires that raged in the interlunar cavern, and soon what must be the ultimate accession gathered to its head. With athletic swiftness he turned her to the primal position and then, whinnying like a whole herd of wild horses, shivering as if transformed to protoplasm save for that plunging sword, he released lava like a mountain in a single thrust of destruction, so that she screamed like a burning city. Hillier lay on her still, sucked dry by vampires, moaning. The galaxies wheeled, history shrieked then settled, familiar sensations crept back into the body, common hungers began to bite. He fell from her dripping as from a sea-bathe and, as also from that, tasting salt. He sought his bathrobe, but she grabbed it first, covering herself with it. She smiled—not kindly but with malice, so that he frowned in puzzlement—and then she called:

'Come in!'

And so he entered, still in evening clothes, huge, bald, smiling. Mr Theodorescu. 'Ah, yes,' he organ-stopped. 'Accept only this brand. The genuine article.' The S burned on wet nakedness;

it was too late now to attempt to hide it. 'Mr Hillier,' beamed Theodorescu. 'I thought it must be Mr Hillier. Now I definitely know.'

SIX

'YES,' SAID THEODORESCU, 'now I definitely know.' He was carrying, Hillier now noticed, the kind of stick known as a Penang lawyer. 'You, of course, Miss Devi, have known a little longer. That branded S tells all. Soskice's work, a cruel operator. The face of Hillier still unknown, but that signature snaking all over Europe, revealed only to the debagger—and your enemies, Mr Hillier, do not go in for debagging, not having been educated in British public schools—to them, I say, or to a lady with the manifold talents of Miss Devi here.'

'I was a bloody fool,' said Hillier. 'There's no point in my denying my identity. Look, I feel as though I'm having a medical. Can I put something on?'

'I think not,' said Theodorescu. Miss Devi still had Hillier's robe about her; she was also sitting on her bunk, so that Hillier could not tug a sheet or blanket off. Hillier sat down on the cabin's solitary chair, set under the porthole. To his left was a dressing-table. In those drawers would be garments. Even now, the prospect of wearing one of Miss Devi's saris or wisp of her underwear met a physical response he had to hide with both hands. Again, in one of those drawers might be a gun. He risked putting out a hand to a drawer-handle, tugged, but the drawer was locked. 'It is better, Mr Hillier, that you sit there *in puris naturalibus,* delightful coy phrase. Let us see you as you are. Dear dear dear, how scarred your body

has been in war's or love's lists. But I would like to see the face. Pads of wax in the cheeks, I should imagine; the mouth-corner drawn down in a sneer—by simple stitching? Is that moustache real? Why do your eyes glitter so? Never mind, never mind. The time for talk is short. Let us talk then.'

'First,' said naked Hillier, 'tell me who you are.'

'I operate under my own name,' said Theodorescu, leaning against the wardrobe. 'I am utterly neutral, in the pay of no power, major or minor. I collect information and sell it to the highest—or shall I say higher?—bidder. I see only two men, usually in Lausanne. They bid according to the funds their respective organisations render available. It is a tolerably profitable trade, relatively harmless. Occasionally I make a direct sale, no auctioning. Well, now. Would you, Miss Devi, be good enough to dress? We will both look the other way, being gentlemen. And then I'd be glad if you'd proceed at once to the radioroom. You know what message to send.'

'What is all this?' asked Hillier. 'Something about me?'

Miss Devi rose from her bed, bundling up sheets and blankets as she did so. These she threw, a billow of white and brown, on to the space between Theodorescu and the cabin-door, so that Hillier could not get at them. Theodorescu then stepped gracefully aside, that she might take garments from the wardrobe. She chose black slacks and a white jumper. Hillier, naked, no gentleman, watched. She drew on the slacks without removing the bathrobe. Then she removed and threw it among the sheets and blankets, making Hillier gulp with the nostalgia of shared passion. She pulled the sweater on. Her hair, still flowing, was trapped in it. She released it with a long electric crackle. Hillier gulped and gulped. Theodorescu had kept his eyes averted, looking through the porthole at the deep Adriatic night. Miss Devi smiled at nothing, thrust her feet into sandals, then silently left. Theodorescu came to sit heavily upon the bunk. He said:

'You will have guessed what the message is. You are, if my informants in Trieste have not lied, now on your final assignment. I do not know what the assignment is, nor do I much care. The fact is that you will not be landing in Yarylyuk. Miss Devi is informing the authorities—in a suitably cryptic form they will know how to interpret—that you are on your way. They will be awaiting you on the quayside. I am not doing this for money, Mr Hillier, for, of course, you will not be landing. There will be men waiting for Mr. Jagger or whatever new persona you might consider assuming, and they will find nobody answering your description. They may, of course, find it necessary to strip one or two of the male passengers, looking for a tell-tale S. Those who are *are* stripped—and they will not be many, most of our *compagnons de voyage* being old and fat—those who *are* will not be object: it will be a story about adventures in a brutal police-state to retail over brandy and cigars back home. You would, if you were to stay on board instead of landing, also be in some slight danger. For these dear people are efficient at winkling out their quarry, as you well know. Visitors are allowed aboard, in the interests of the promotion of international friendship. This port of call is the sweet-sour sauce of the whole meaty trip. A British meal, British whisky, a few little purchases in the ship's gift-shop—these are encouragements to keep the Black Sea open to British cruises. There will be people wandering the ship looking for you, Mr Hillier. There may even be police-warrants, trumped-up charges. The Captain will not want too much trouble.'

'You do talk a lot,' said Hillier.

'Do I? Do I?' Theodorescu seemed pleased. 'Well, I'd better come to the point or points, had I not? Tomorrow a helicopter will be picking up Miss Devi and myself. We shall be sailing quite near the island of Zakynthos. You are cordially invited to come with us, Mr Hillier.'

'Where to?'

'Oh, I have no one headquarters. We could spend a pleasant enough time, the three of us, in my little villa near Amalias.'

'And then, of course, I would be sold.'

'Sold? *Sold?* Could I not sell you now if I wished? No, Mr Hillier, I trade only in information. You must be a repository of a great deal of that. We could take our time over it. And then you could go, free as the air, well-rewarded. What do you say?'

'No.'

Theodorescu sighed. 'I expected that. Well, well. The delights that Miss Devi is qualified to purvey are, as you already know, very considerable. Or rather you do not yet know. You've had time to touch only their fringes. Women I do not much care for myself—I prefer little Greek shepherd-boys—but Miss Devi— this I have been assured of by some whose judgement I respect on other matters of a hedonistic kind—Miss Devi is altogether exceptional. Think, Mr Hillier. You're retiring from the haz- ardous work of espionage. What have you to look forward to? A tiny pension, no golden handshake—'

'I'm promised a sizeable bonus if I do this last job.'

'If, Mr Hillier, if. You know you won't do it now. Soon you will not say even "if". I offer you money and Miss Devi offers herself. What do you say to that? I am not likely to be less gener- ous in my own bestowals than Miss Devi is in hers.'

'I could think better,' said Hillier, 'if I had some clothes on.'

'That's good,' said Theodorescu. 'That's a beginning. You talk of thinking, you see.'

'As for that, I've thought about it. I'm not coming with you.'

'Like yourself,' said Theodorescu, 'I believe in free will. I hate coercion. Bribery, of course, is altogether different. Well, there are certain things I wish to know now. I shall pay well. As an earnest of my generosity I start by rescinding the debt you owe me. The Trencherman Stakes.' He laughed. 'You need not pay me the thousand pounds.'

'Thank you,' said Hillier.

As if Hillier had really done him a favour, Theodorescu pulled a big cigar-case from his inner pocket. At the same time he allowed to peep out coyly bundles of American currency. 'Hundred-dollar bills, Mr Hillier. "C's", I think they call them. Do have a cigar.' He disclosed fat Romeo and Juliets. Hillier took one; he'd been dying for a smoke. Theodorescu donated fire from a gold Ronson. They both puffed. The feminine odours of Miss Devi's cabin were overlaid with blue wraiths of Edwardian clubmen. 'Do you remember,' said Theodorescu dreamily, 'a certain passage in the transports you seemed to be sharing with Miss Devi—an excruciatingly pleasurable one, in which it seemed that a claw sharpened to a needle-point pierced a most intimate part of your person?'

'How do you know about that?'

'It was arranged. It was a special injection, slow-working but efficacious. A substance developed by Dr Pobedonostev of Yuzovo called, I believe, B-type vellocet. That has entered your body. In about fifteen minutes you will answer any question I put to you with perfect truth. Please, please, Mr Hillier, give me the credit for a little sense, more—a little honesty, before you say that this is sheer bluff. You see, you will not fall into a trance, answering from a dream, as with so many of the so-called truth-drugs. You will be thoroughly conscious but possessed of a euphoria which will make concealment of the truth seem a crime against the deep and lasting friendship you will be convinced subsists between us. All I have to do is to wait.'

Hillier said, 'Bastard,' and tried to get up from the chair. Theodorescu immediately cracked him on the *glans penis* with his Penang lawyer. Hillier tried to punch Theodorescu, but Theodorescu parried the blow easily with his stick, puffing at his cigar with enjoyment. Hillier then had time to attend to his privy agony, sitting again, rocking and moaning.

'It is because I believe in free will as you do,' said Theodorescu, 'that I want you to answer certain questions totally of your volition. The first question is for five thousand dollars. It is rather like one of these stupid television quiz-games, isn't it? Note, Mr Hillier, that I needn't pay you anything at all. But I've robbed you of your chance of a bonus and I must make amends.'

'I won't answer, you bastard.'

'But you will, you will, nothing is more certain. Is it not better to answer with the exalted and, yes, totally *human* awareness that you yourself are choosing, not having information extracted from you with the aid of a silly little drug?'

'What's the first question?' asked Hillier, thinking: I needn't answer, I needn't answer, I have a choice.

'First of all, and for five thousand dollars, remember, I want to know the exact location of the East German escape route known, I believe, as Karl Otto.'

'I don't know. I honestly don't know.'

'Oh, surely. Well, think about it, but think quickly. Time is short for you, if not for me. Second, for six thousand dollars, I wish to be told the identities of the members of the terrorist organisation called Volruss in Kharkov.'

'Oh, God, you can't—'

'Wait, Mr Hillier. I haven't said anything about selling this information to the Soviet authorities. It's a matter of auctioning. So it's essential that, on top of this particular disclosure, you also reveal the code that I need to contact them. I understand it's a matter of putting a personal message in your British *Daily Worker*. The only British newspaper allowed in the Soviet Union, as you know, hence invaluable for conveying messages to those disaffected and vigorous bodies which are so annoying—though perhaps only annoying as a mosquito-sting is annoying—annoying, I say, to the MGB. I doubt it their representative will outbid the émigré sponsors of Volruss.'

Hillier, who now felt no pain, who no longer saw any embarrassment in his nakedness, who felt warm and rested and confident, smiled at Theodorescu. An intelligent and able man, he thought. A good eater and drinker. A man you could have a bloody good night out with. No enemy; a mere neutral who was wisely making money out of the whole stupid business that he, Hillier, was opting out of because the stupidity had recently become rather nasty. And then he saw that this must be the drug beginning to take effect. It was necessary to hate Theodorescu again, and quickly. He got up from his chair, though smiling amiably, and said: 'I'm going to get my bathrobe, and you're not bloody well going to stop me.' Theodorescu at once, and without malice, cracked both shins hard with the Penang lawyer. Pain flowed like scalding water. 'You fucking swine, Theodorescu,' he gritted. And then he was grateful to Theodorescu for turning himself into the enemy again. He was a good man to be willing to do that. He saw what was happening; he saw that he would have to be quick. 'Give me the money,' he said. 'Eleven thousand dollars.' Theodorescu whipped out all his notes. 'Karl Otto,' he said, 'starts in the cellar of Nummer Dreiundvierzig, Schlegelstrasse, Salzwedel.'

'Good, good.'

'I can only name five members of Volruss in Kharkov. They are N. A. Brussilov, I. R. Stolypin, F. Guchkov—I can't remember his patronymic—'

'Good, good, good.'

'Aren't you going to take this down?'

'It's going down. This top button in my flies is a microphone. I have a tape-recorder in my left inside pocket. I was not scratching my armpit just then. I was switching it on.'

'The others are F. T. Krylenko and H. K. Skovaioda.'

'Ah, a Ukrainian that last one. Excellent. And the code?'

'Elkin.'

'Elkin? Hm. And now, for twelve thousand dollars, the exact location—*exact*, mind—of Department 9A in London.'

'I can't tell you that.'

'But you must, Mr Hillier. More, you will. Any moment now.'

'I can't. That would be treason.'

'Nonsense. There is no war. There is not going to be any war. This is all a great childish game on the floor of the world. It's absurd to talk about treason, isn't it?' He smiled kindly with the huge polished lamps of his eyes. Hillier started to smile back. Then he stood up again and lunged at Theodorescu. Theodorescu himself stood and towered high. He took both of Hillier's punching hands gently in his, still savouring his cigar. 'Don't, Mr

Hillier. What's your first name? Ah, yes, I remember. Denis. We're friends, Denis, friends. If you don't tell me at once for twelve thousand dollars, you will tell me in a very few minutes for nothing.'

'For God's sake hit me. Hit me hard.'

'Oh no. Oh dear me no.' Theodorescu spoke prissily. 'Now come along, my dear Denis. Department 9A of Intercep. The exact location.'

'If you hit me,' said Hillier, 'I shall hate you, and then when I tell you I shall be telling you of my own volition. That's what you want, isn't it? Free will.'

'You're approaching the crepuscular zone, but you've not yet entered it. You'll be telling me because you want to tell me. See, here is the money. Twelve thousand dollars.' He fanned the notes before Hillier's swimming eyes. 'But be quick.'

'It's off Devonshire Road in Chiswick, W.4. Globe Street. From Number 24 to the dairy at the end. Oh, God. Oh, God forgive me.'

'He'll do that,' nodded Theodorescu. 'Sit down, my dear Denis. A pleasant name, Denis. It comes from Dionysus, you know. Sit down and rest. You seem to have nowhere to put this money. Perhaps I'd better keep it for you and give it you when you have clothes on.'

'Give it me now. It's mine. I earned it.'

'And you shall earn more.' Hillier grabbed the money and held it, like figleaves, over his blushing genitals. 'It's a pity you won't come with Miss Devi and me tomorrow. But we'll find you, never fear. There aren't very many places you can retire to. We shall be looking for you. Though,' he said thoughtfully, 'it's quite conceivable that you will come looking for Miss Devi.'

Abject shame and rising euphoria warred in Hillier. He kept his eyes tight shut, biting his mouth so as not to smile.

'You're not a good subject for B-type vellocet,' said Theodorescu. 'There are certain powerful reserves in your bloodstream. You should now be slobbering all over me with love.'

'I hate you,' smiled Hillier warmly. 'I loathe your bloody fat guts.'

Theodorescu shook his head. 'You'll hate me tomorrow. But tomorrow will be too late. You'll sleep very soundly tonight, I think. You won't wake early. But if you do, and if Miss Devi and I are not yet helicoptering off to the isles of Greece at the time of your awakening, it will be futile to attempt to do me harm. I shall be with the Captain on the bridge most of the morning. Moreover, you have nothing with which to do me harm. I took the precaution of entering your cabin and stealing your Aiken and silencer. A very nice little weapon. I have it here.' He took it from his left side-pocket. Hillier winced but then smiled. He nearly said that Theodorescu could keep it as a present. As if he had actually said that, Theodorescu put it back, patting the pocket. 'As for the ampoules you had in the same stupid hiding-place—it was stupid, wasn't it? So obvious—as for those, you can keep them, whatever they are. Perhaps lethal—I don't know. I found your hypodermic in one of your suitcases. I took the precaution of smashing it. It's best to be on the safe side, don't you agree?'

'Oh, yes, yes,' smiled Hillier. 'How did you get into my cabin?'

Theodorescu sighed. 'My dear fellow. There are duplicates in the purser's office. I said I'd lost my key and I was made free of the board on which the duplicates hang.'

'You're a bloody good bloke,' said Hillier sincerely.

Theodorescu, looking down on Hillier by the porthole, heard the door behind him open. 'Miss Devi,' he said without turning. 'You've been rather a long time.'

'I have, have I?' said Wriste in a girlish voice. He pouted, toothless, towards turning Theodorescu. 'What you doing with him there? He'll catch his death sat like that.'

'He likes to sit like that, don't you, Denis?'

'Oh yes, yes, Theo, I do.'

'Just because a bloke's had a bit of a dip in the jampot,' said Wriste, 'there's no call to get vindictive and sarky. She said she was your secretary. Now we know better, don't we?'

'This,' said Theodorescu, 'is a lady's cabin. You've no right to enter without knocking. Now please leave.'

'I'll leave all right,' said Wriste. 'But he's coming with me. I can see what you've been doing, beating him to a pulp with that bloody stick. Just because your bit can stand his weight better than yours.'

'I shall report you to the purser.'

'Report away.' Wriste saw that Hillier had money grasped tight at his groin. 'Oh,' he said, 'that's possible. I hadn't thought of that. Has he,' he asked Hillier, 'been giving you cabbage to let him bash you about a bit?'

'Not at all,' said Hillier, smiling truthfully. 'Nothing like that at all. He gave me this money for giving him—'

'He had it under the pillow,' organed Theodorescu. 'That's where he had it. All right, take him away.' He picked up the bathrobe from the floor and threw it at Hillier.

'Thank you so very much, Theo. That's awfully kind.'

'I'll take him away all right,' said Wriste, 'but not on your bleeding orders. Come on, old boy,' he said to Hillier as to a dog. 'Why did he have it under the pillow?' he beetled at Theodorescu. 'There's something about all this that I don't get.'

'He doesn't trust anybody,' cried Theodorescu. 'He won't go anywhere without his money.'

'He can trust me,' said Wriste, taking Hillier's hand. 'You trust me, don't you?'

'Oh, yes. I trust you.'

'That's all right, then. Now let Daddy put you to bed.' He led his charge out. Hillier smiled, just starting to drop off.

SEVEN

A WHOLE MAHAMANVANTARA later, he was shaken gently awake. 'Come on, sir,' coaxed Wriste, 'if you don't eat your breakfast now you won't feel like lunch.' Hillier could smell coffee. He ungummed his eyelids, then retreated from the light a space so as to make a more cunning and cautious entry into it. He knew that he ought to expect to feel dry-mouthed, headachy, sore-limbed, but he did not yet know why. Then, knowing why, he found himself feeling well and surprisingly energetic. The energy had been pumped in for some urgent purpose. What was it? He was, he noted, in his Chinese pyjamas, the 'happiness' ideogram stitched on the breast pocket. On his bed-table he saw money, foreign money. The bearded face of an American president looked sternly at him. Dollars, a lot of dollars. He remembered. Oh, God. 'Oh, God,' he groaned aloud.

'You'll feel better after this lot,' said Wriste. 'Look.' He arranged pillows behind Hillier, then, as Hillier sat up, placed the

tray before him. Frosted orange-juice; a grilled kipper; bacon and
devilled kidneys and two fried eggs; toast; vintage brandy marmalade; coffee. 'Coffee?' said Wriste. He poured into a cup as big
as a soup-bowl from two silver jugs. Hillier's tissues soaked in the
healing aromatic warmth. Healing? It was not his body that
required healing. The mingled coffee and milk were a little too
light for Miss Devi's colour. A television camera lurched on to
last night, presenting it brightly lit and in full detail.

'That man,' he said. 'That woman. Have they gone yet?'

Wriste nodded. 'Quite a little diversion it was. A helicopter
whizzing over the recreation-deck and a ladder coming down and
then these two going up. I thought his weight would drag the
bloody thing down, but it didn't. Light as a fairy he went up, luggage and all. He waved to everybody. Oh, and he left a sort of a letter for you.' Wriste handed over an envelope of an expensive silky
weave. It was addressed, discreetly, to S. Jagger Esq. 'Some of
these tycoons looked a bit sheepish. That's real big business, that is,
when a helicopter comes to take you off in the middle of a cruise.'

Hillier read: 'My dear friend. The offer still stands. A letter
sent to Cumhuriyet Caddesi 15, Istanbul, will find me. Miss Devi
sends her palpitating regards. Keep out of harm's way when the
ship reaches Yarylyuk. Seek sanctuary in the Captain's private
lavatory or somewhere. The authorities were grateful for the
warning. They cabled their gratitude and promise of a tolerably
substantial emolument in Swiss francs. Apparently there is a scientific conference on at the Chornoye Morye Hotel. Redoubling
of precautions. What a devil you are! You must not die, you are
too useful. Affectionately, R. Theodorescu.'

'Bad news is it, sir?'

'Abuse,' invented Hillier. He put the letter in his pyjama-pocket, drank off his icy fruit-juice and began the kipper. Wriste, sitting on the bed, pouted as if to suck in more. Hillier obliged. 'That money is in payment of a gambling debt,' he improvised. 'He's a big man for betting. He bet me I couldn't make Miss Devi.'

'And then he got nasty, did he?'

'A bit. A very nasty customer. It's a good thing you came in when you did. What made you come in?'

'I seen this Indian bint sending off a cable. I wondered a bit about that, seeing as you was supposed to be making a sesh of it, as I thought. I thought this big fat bastard could get nasty. So I came along and could hear him on to you.'

'I'm very grateful,' said Hillier. 'Would two hundred dollars be of any use?'

'Thank you, sir,' said Wriste, swiftly pocketing three hundred. 'A queer sort of a bugger in more ways than one. He was after that young lad, you know, the one that knows it all. Patting him and that. I don't know whether he got anywhere. Too clever for him that lad, maybe. But he gave this lad a present before he went. I seen him do that, patting him. A nice little parcel in the ship's-store gift-wrapping. But this lad didn't open it, least I didn't see him. Too upset he is. His dad's had it, they say. Won't be long now.'

'And how is the prospective widow?' Hillier forked in devilled kidneys.

'Nice way of putting it, sir. Crying her eyes out whenever she thinks of it, then going off for a sly snog with this Spanish confectioner bloke. At least that's what they say he is.'

'And the daughter?'

Wriste showed the whole stretch of his hard gums, top and

bottom. 'I thought that would come into it sooner or later. You're a man with a purpose in life, you are, I'll say that for you, that you are. A purpose. She lies there on her bunk, reading away. Horrible hot stuff it is, too, all this sex. But sad, you can tell she's sad. Well, it's a horrible damper to throw on what should be all what they call pleasure, but there'll be an empty place at their table from now on. You're welcome to it if you'd like to have it fixed. Them two gone now, and you won't want to be noshing all on your tod.' He looked hungrily at the American president, pouting.

'Would a hundred be of any use?' Hillier paid out this time, then put the wad into his pyjama-pocket, where Theodorescu's letter lay. He had finished his breakfast, and now the pocket seared his heart with guilt. It was time to be thinking about things. His watch said twelve-twenty. Wriste removed the tray; Hillier lighted a Churchill Danish. Wriste said:

'You won't be wanting lunch till about two. You take your time, no hurry about cleaning up here. So I'll be seeing you later.' And he left.

Treason, treason, treason. Treason and treachery. But he had had no choice. Or rather he had had no choice but to make a choice. Could he send warning cables of his own now? Not to Karl Otto's guardians nor to Volruss. It was safer to leave things as they were. How about Department 9A? Hillier had a vision of two shadowy men at either side of a table in a hotel room in Lausanne, Theodorescu between them, on the table before him an envelope. Gentlemen, who will make the first bid? And where would the bidding stop? Taxpayers were taxed to the hilt; millions were poured down the drain on obsolescent aircraft and missiles and warheads. Let them bid, let them pay out. *And where would the bidding stop?* Hillier palpated the wad of a few thousand at his breast. He felt bitter towards Theodorescu. Chickenfeed. He would get that bloody bonus, he would bring back Roper.

How? No longer as Jagger. No longer as anyone. D. Wishart, sanitary engineer; F. R. Lightfoot, pediatrician; Heath Verity, the minor poet; John James Pomeroy-Bickerstaff, IBM-man; P. B. Shelley, Kit Smart, Matchless Orinda—all would have an S on the left flank. He was known for that, the S-man, all over Europe, then. Theodorescu, whom he himself had had no occasion to know, knew all the time. He, Hillier, had been better known than he had known of. His time of usefulness as a spy must be over, known as he was. All he had now was information, quick to grow obsolete with the obsolescence of its referents. Could he set up on his own, a rival to Theodorescu? But Theodorescu had Miss Devi. He wanted Miss Devi now, lying there, writhing in his pyjamas. He looked again at Theodorescu's letter. Cumhuriyet Caddesi 15, Istanbul. That was somewhere near the Hilton. Should he? But, in thrall to Miss Devi, he would be Theodorescu's gibbering instrument, no more.

He got out of bed, stripped to the warm noon, and examined for the nth time the S on his flank. It was burnt deep; the dead skin like a luminous plastic. It could not be disguised, however cunning the cosmesis. He dressed quickly, as to hide the problem from sight, giving himself a cat-lick and a once-over with his Philishave. Then he took a swig of Old Mortality and water and went out on deck. It was a glorious blue day, Ionian, no longer Adriatic. In the distance, to port, lay Southern Greece—Kyparissia? Philiatra? Pylos? Tomorrow they would be in the Aegean, dodging through the mess of islands. Then Marmara's womb, through the vagina of the Dardanelles. Then the Bosphorus,

then the Pontus Euxinus—Kara Dengis to the Turks. The Black
Sea. Would his grave be there? He shivered in the sun. Black
black black. The sea that supported no organic life below one
hundred fathoms. Five enough for him. He thought he saw
Roper, twitching, hiccuping. Why? I was wrong, I was wrong, O
Jesus Mary Joseph help me. I take back all I said. I want to go
home. Home? For a dizzy moment Hillier puzzled over the word,
wondering what it meant. It spelt itself out for him against the
Ionian noon. He saw it as four-fifths of a Russian word.
HOMEP—*nomyer*—number. Home had something to do with a
number, a number he felt he ought to know, since it was the clue
to going home. It was urgent, this matter of a bloody number. In
what way urgent? Had it not come to him last night and had he
not tossed it away like an old cloakroom ticket? He was not
merely slack; he was corrupt.

There was a fair amount of noon drinking going on on deck,
passengers looking out at Greece with Pimms and Gordon's and
Campari in their mottled paws. Hillier went to the bar on the
recreation-deck and drank very quickly a Gordon's and tonic,
then a vodka and tomato-juice, then a very large Americano.
Think think think. He saw himself carried safely ashore in the
guise of a dead man, Wriste one of the bearers. The uniformed
thugs stood to attention and saluted the corpse. He looked more
closely and saw it was really a corpse. Roper wept. *You've let me
down you bastard*. He wept with self-pity.

Hillier wondered seriously, in his depression, whether he had
a worm inside him. His breakfast seemed a whole dawn away. He
went into the dining-saloon, seeing tycoons and their women in
shorts. Wriste had arranged things. The chief steward pulled
back his chair at the table of the Walters family. The children

looked pale and peaky. Mrs Walters was holding her mouth-corners down with an effort, occasionally dabbing dry eyes. She sent away a near-untouched plate of goulash with evident regret. No, she would have nothing else. Well, perhaps a little macédoine of fresh fruits soaked in Southern Comfort, topped up with champagne. We must keep our strength up. The children sincerely ate nearly nothing. And, added Mrs Walters, some Irish coffee, very strong.

'What news?' asked Hillier softly, as if already at the funeral. This girl—Clara, wasn't it? Was that her name?—was really delightful with her delicate boxer's nose and hair you wanted to eat, insomniac arcs, blue blushes, under her brown eyes. She was wearing an orange and black shift dress with diagonal stripes, a little black stole careless on her lap. She was neither reading nor eating, merely mashing up the buttock of a meringue with a pastry-fork. She was indifferent to Hillier's presence. The boy, in a newspaper shirt, ate a honey mousse in tiny spoonfuls. The woman answered Hillier. She said:

'They don't think he'll last the day out. Very low. In a coma. But he's had his life, that's a consolation. He's had all he ever wanted. We must try and look on the bright side.' Suiting the words, she attacked her macédoine.

'What's going to happen,' said Alan, 'to Clara and me?'

'We've been through all this before. What happens to any children when their father dies? Their mother looks after them, doesn't she?'

'You're not our mother,' said Alan truculently. 'You don't care a bit about us.'

'Not before this gentleman, please.' This woman could have a nasty temper, Hillier saw that. He ate some boned veal loin *en croúte* with a noodle soufflé and julienne of young carrots and celery. He drank a '49 Margaux. The girl suddenly cried:

'Nobody cares. You sit here stuffing yourselves and nobody cares. I'm going to my cabin.' Hillier's heart melted for her as she got up, so youthfully elegant, and made her way out with young dignity. Poor, poor girl, he thought. But he had things to ask. He asked:

'This may seem a callous question, but what do you propose to do when the time comes?'

'How do you mean?' said Mrs Walters, her macédoine-filled spoon arrested in mid-passage.

'Funeral arrangements. One has to think of these things. Transportation. Burial. Chartering an aircraft. Getting him home.'

'You can't charter aircraft in Russia,' said the boy. 'You'd have to take the State Line. Aeroflot, I think it is.'

'I hadn't thought about all this,' said Mrs Walters. Instinctively she looked about her for a man, her fancy man. But she stopped looking. Fancy men are for fancy things. 'It's all a nuisance, this is. What ought we to do?'

'Bury him at sea,' said Alan, 'with a Union Jack wrapped round him. That's how *I'd* like to be buried.'

'I don't think that's usual,' said Hillier, 'not when you're so close to a port. The done thing is—' He noticed that Clara had left her little black stole behind; it had sunk to the floor on her sudden rising. He carefully footed it towards himself, then held it between his ankles. She would get it back quite soon.

'The done thing is what?' asked Mrs Walters.

'To see the purser about seeing the carpenter about a coffin. To see the purser anyway. They may have coffins in stock. A cruise like this must encourage coronaries. Or perhaps you ought to get the ship's doctor to sort things out. I'm afraid I've not had any experience of this sort of business.'

'Well, why do you start telling us all about it, then?'

'It's ghoulish,' said Alan, 'that's what it is.' It was, too, agreed Hillier to himself. Ghoulish was what it was. 'It's as though you don't want to give him any hope at all.'

'One ought to be prepared,' said Hillier. 'John Donne, Dean of St Paul's, had his coffin made well in time and used to sleep in it. Sometimes thinking about a person being dead gives them a new lease. Like Extreme Unction. Like an obituary printed prematurely.'

'I don't want to hope,' sniffed Mrs Walters over her Irish coffee. 'I want to face facts, even though they *are* painful.'

'*You* were being a bit ghoulish, weren't you?' said Hillier to Alan. 'That business of the Union Jack, I mean.'

'It's different,' said Alan. 'More like heroism. The death of Nelson I was thinking of.'

Hillier ate his dish of asparagus with cold hollandaise. 'Any help I can give,' he said. 'Any help at all.' The difficulty would be getting the genuine corpse overboard. He'd need help. Wriste? Some plausible story to Wriste about that swine Theodorescu stealing his passport and he just had to get into Yarylyuk to see a man about a Cyrillic typewriter. It would mean a thousand dollars or so. Better not. He could do it on his own, prising the coffin open and fireman's lifting the groaning cadaver to the nearest taffrail. Man overboard. He'd have to go over with dead Mr Walters so that there should be someone live to be rescued. But the corpse would float perhaps. Lead weights? Hillier groaned as he fancied that corpse would groan.

The Walters boy and woman prepared to leave. 'Are you going to the sickbay now?' asked Hillier. He was; she was going to have a large brandy in the bar, needing it, she said, the strain terrible. 'A nice present, was it?' said Hillier to Alan. 'From Mr Theodorescu, I mean.'

'It's all right,' said Alan. 'Just what I needed.' They went. Hillier had some pears porcupine. Then some Lancashire cheese and a bit of bread. Then some coffee and a stinger. He felt he needed to build himself up.

He had no hesitation about going to Clara Walters's cabin, displaying to all the world the innocence of his purpose. He listened at the door before knocking. A sort of sobbing was going on in there, he thought. When he gently knocked, with a steward's discreetness, the voice that bade him enter was denasalised by crying. Going in, he found her just sitting up from using the whole length of the bunk for grief, knuckling an eye dry with one hand, roughly smoothing her hair with the other. 'It's only me,' said Hillier. 'I've brought this. You left it in the dining-saloon.' She raised her face to him, all young and blubbered, taking the stole in distracted thanks. 'And,' he said, 'forgive me for seeming so callous. Eating like that, I mean. With such appetite, that is. I couldn't really help being hungry though, could I?'

'I know,' she said. rubbing her cheek against the stole. 'He's not *your* father.'

'A cigarette?' He always kept a caseful for offering to ladies. Men had to be content with his coarse Brazilian cigars.

'I don't smoke.'

'Very wise,' said Hillier, pocketing the case. 'I had a father though, like everybody else. I know what it's like. But his death didn't affect me right away. I was fourteen when it happened. A

month after the funeral I was afflicted with a very peculiar ailment, one that didn't seem to have anything to do with filial
grief.'

'Oh?'

'Yes. It was spermatorrhea. Have you ever heard of that?'

Interest glowed faintly. 'It sounds sexual,' she said without
pudeur.

'Well, it happened in sleep but without dreams. It was seed-
spilling functioning in a void. Night after night, sometimes five
or six times a night. It always woke me up. I felt guilty, of course,
but the guilt seemed to be the end, not the by-product. Is there
anything about that in any of your books?' He went towards the
bunk, so as to read the titles of the little library she had ranged on
the shelf just above it: *Priapus—A Study of the Male Impulse;
Varieties of the Orgasm; Pleasures of the Torture Chamber;
Mechanical Refinements in Coition; A Dictionary of Sex; Clinical
Studies in Sexual Inversion; The Sign of Sodom; Infant Eros*——
And so on and so on. Dear dear dear. A paperback on her bunkside table—a blonde in underwear and her own blood—would
have been provocative to a man less satyromaniacal than Hillier;
these books were more like fighting pledges of her purity,
archangels guarding her terrible innocence. Hillier sat on the
bunk beside her.

'Look some time for me,' he said. 'You're evidently more
learned in sexual matters than I am. But the psychiatrist I went to
told me that it was an unconscious assertion of the progenitive
impulse, something like that. Mimesis was a word he used. I was
acting out my father but turning him into an archetype.
Whatever that means,' he added.

She had listened to him with her lips slightly parted. Now she clamped them together and turned their corners down, frowning, dissatisfied. 'I don't know anything,' she said. 'It's all big words. I've tried to understand but I can't.'

'There's plenty of time. You're still very young.'

'That's what they keep telling me. That's what they told me in America. But Alan's younger than me and he was on one of those big quiz shows and he knew all the answers. I'm ignorant. I've not been properly educated.'

She seemed, bouncing on the bunk in petulance, to bounce herself nearer to Hillier. It would be so easy, he thought, to put my arm round her now and say: 'There there there.' And she was ready for crying on the shoulder of a mature and understanding man. But the books above him shouted their battle-slogans: *Yoni and Lingam; Sex and Death among the Aztecs.* 'What were you doing in America?' he asked.

'It was what they called New Milling Techniques. Mother was dead and they said he ought to get us away for a time. But he thought it would be sinful to take a holiday just then, with her hardly cold in her grave as he put it, and so we went for the New Milling Techniques.'

'And were the New Milling Techniques all right?'

'That's where he met *her*,' she said. 'This one. In America but she's not American. She'd been married to an American, in Kansas it was, and he'd divorced her and he said, my father said, she was a breath of home.'

'So she married him?'

'That was it. *She* married *him*. For his money.'

'Have you any uncles or aunts or cousins or things?'

'Things,' she said. 'There are some *things*. That's all you can call them. And they all went to Auckland, wherever that is. And they do something with kauri pine, whatever that is. There's something called a fossil gum.' For some reason, she got ready to cry on this last term, and now Hillier had to put his arm gently about her in what he thought of as a schoolmasterly way. 'They export, it,' she now frankly wept. Hillier asked himself what it ought to be. The other arm round, a gentle kiss on the rather low forehead (a protection against too much knowledge, not female animality), then the wet cheek, then the unrouged mouth-corner? No, he could not. He caught a picture of the father snoring towards his death in the sickbay. He felt sickened. Always ready to use people as if they were *things,* that's all you can call them, and they all went to Auckland.

'Auckland's in New Zealand,' he said. 'It's said to be rather nice there.' That made her cry worse. 'Listen,' he said. 'You and your brother come and have tea with me in my cabin. We'll have a good tea. You've both eaten so little. About half-past four. Would you like that? I have things to tell you, interesting things.' She looked at him with brown eyes awash. He marvelled at himself, Uncle Hillier inviting youngsters to tea. And this delicious grief of hers could so easily be coaxed towards the gentlest and most comforting of initiations. He would not do it; she was not a nubile girl now but a tearful daughter. 'Tell Alan, will you? Tell him I want to let you both into a secret. It seems to me that you're people to be trusted.' Was *he* one to be trusted, though? The books thought not: *The Perfumed Garden* had sharp suspicious eyes peering through the flowers. 'So you'll come, will you?' She nodded several times. 'And now I've got to go.' He essayed a chaste kiss on her frontal lobes; she did not turn away. Like dogs the books snarled at him as he left.

He went to the sickbay. He told the orderly on duty there

that he'd broken his hypodermic. 'I'm diabetic,' he said. 'Perhaps I could buy one from you.' But he was given one with the fine generosity of a ship at sea. 'How is the old man?' he whispered. No real change, he was told; he might last a long time yet. 'As far as Yarylyuk?' Quite possibly. They could get him ashore. Russian hospitals were good. 'He may live then?' You never could tell. Hillier was relieved at that: one fantastic scheme could be crossed off. There would have to be some playing by ear. Engage first, strategies after. Back in his cabin he restored, with much pain, his face to the face of Hillier. It was the expression more than the physiognomy that was adjusted. Jagger was the name of a function rather than a person. But he must keep the pseudonym. Jagger for the journey, Hillier for home. Home for the elderly, home for inebriates, home for retired spies. As for 'home' *tout court*, he had still to puzzle out a meaning.

EIGHT

'YOU'VE CHANGED the colour of your eyes,' marvelled Clara. She had changed her clothes—cotton tartan slacks with a plain green T-shirt. Alan was still in his newspaper shirt: a headline—THIS MAN MAY KILL POLICE WARN—looked sternly at Hillier. 'You've got rid of that that grey moustache,' approved the boy. 'Better. A lot better.' He folded his arms, obscuring the headline. Hillier, as tea-mother, poured. Lemon for both of them: highly sophisticated. He himself took cream and sugar. Wriste had wheeled in a fair variety of tea-foods—sandwiches, Kunzle pastries, scones, crumpets in a hot dish, a chocolate Swiss roll and a Fuller's walnut cake. 'A sandwich,' Hillier offered. 'Gentleman's Relish. Salmon. Tomato and sardine. Cucumber.'

'We don't eat bread,' they duetted in canon.

'Yes, I knew about that. You ought to try some. A new experience. A *nouveau frisson*. Go on, be devils.' But they wouldn't risk it; they chose sweet things, nibbling. 'The decline of a civilisation,' taught Hillier, 'is figured in the decline of its bread. English bread is uneatable. Some of the London wealthy have a bread airlift from France. Did you know that? No. The bread on ships is baked properly, not boiled. One has an image of civilisation being maintained on little ships plying from nowhere to nowhere.'

'They'd still have to have our flour,' said Alan.

'How is he?' asked Hillier.

'Plying from nowhere to nowhere. No change. *She,*' said Alan bitterly, 'has quarrelled with that wop type man. A kind of Norwegian type man has been teaching her to dive. Golden muscles and that.'

'Fond of men, is she?'

'She's got this one back home. That's her steady one. And Dad pretended to know nothing about it. He feels he needs to trust somebody. A wife is a person you trust.'

'Have you a wife?' asked Clara.

'No,' answered Alan. 'Nor children. He's on his own. Going around in disguises and then taking them off. That man Theodorescu told me all about you,' he said to Hillier.

'Did he?' said Hillier without fear.

'He called you a womaniser.' Clara looked interested. 'He

gave me a camera as a present,' said Alan. 'A new Japanese type. A Myonichi, it's called. He said it would make an amusing hobby for me to go round recording you womanising.'

'Perhaps he's jealous,' said Hillier. 'He can't do any womanising.'

'No,' said Alan. He shifted on his chair as in slight pain. 'Or won't.' He turned to his sister in sudden contempt. 'You and your books about Sodom. Sex on paper instead of a bed.'

'It's the safest kind of sex,' said Hillier. 'Did Mr Theodorescu say anything else about me?'

'He didn't have much time for talking. He had to helicopter off to a takeover bid or something. But he didn't have to tell me anything really, because I know you're a spy.'

'That always seems a dirty word,' said Hillier, pouring more tea. 'I much prefer "secret agent".'

'That's what you are then?' said Clara.

'Yes. That. It's a job like any other. It's supposed to call for the finest qualities in a man. You know—bravery, skill, cunning, supreme patriotism.'

'And womanising,' added Alan.

'Sometimes.'

'Why are you telling us?' asked Clara.

'He had to sooner or later. Me, anyway. He knew I knew. So,' said Alan, 'you're throwing yourself into our hands.'

'In a way, yes. I need friends. That man Theodorescu has wirelessed the Soviet police. My cover has been blown sky-high, as they say. Whatever disguise I assume I can be identified by an ineffaceable mark on my body.'

'A birthmark?' asked Clara.

'A deathmark, rather. I was most cruelly branded. It was one of my many adventures,' said Hillier modestly. He ate a cucumber sandwich.

'Wait,' said Alan. He went to the door and peered out. 'Nobody eavesdropping.' He came back. 'You're being careless. Are you sure this cabin isn't bugged?'

'Pretty sure. But it doesn't matter. I've got to land in Yarylyuk whatever happens. It means contriving something when we get there. What I mean is that I'm expected. But they know I know I'm expected. They expect me to be among the passengers, but they don't expect me to go ashore. They know I'm not a fool and they know that I know that they're not fools either. My danger will be on this ship. That's why I'm going ashore.'

'But,' said Alan, 'they will know that too. I mean, they'll always be one jump ahead.' And then: 'I always knew that Theodorescu man wasn't to be trusted. A queer smell came off his body. This ship seems to be full of spies.'

'Not *full* exactly.'

'But one thing we don't know,' said Alan, 'is who you're spying for. How do we know that you're not spying for the other side and that the danger comes from spies on our side who are disguised as spies on their side? Or police. Or something.' He accepted a Kunzle cake. 'That you're trying to get back to Russia with secret information and somebody working for our side is already waiting to come aboard and get rid of you?'

'Much too complicated. The whole thing could, theoretically, spiral to an apex where the two opposites embrace each other and become one, but it doesn't work like that in practice. There's a British scientist attending a conference at Yarylyuk—a man I used to be at school with, strangely enough—and my job is to get him on board and take him back to England. It's as simple as that. It's nothing to do with spying.'

The brother and sister thought that over, warily eating Kunzel cakes. Clara's eyes shone gently but Alan's were hard. Alan said: 'Where do we come into this?'

'You believe me, then?'

Clara nodded with vigour; Alan said, off-handedly: 'Oh yes, we believe you. But what do you want us to do?'

'I don't want *you*,' said Hillier sternly to Alan, 'to start blurting about my being a spy any more, especially when I may seem to be doing strange things. If I seem to be acting oddly, and if anybody starts to get suspicious, then it's your job to find excuses for me. I want you to be around, both of you, when I try to do what I have to do to get off this ship. Diversions. Anything. You, my boy, should be equal to contriving the most fantastic of devices.'

'You talk like one of my books,' giggled Clara nervously. 'Most fantastic of devices. In Argentina or somewhere it is. Knobs and spikes and things.'

'Keep off sex,' said Alan, 'just for five minutes, *please*. This is serious stuff.'

'Let's not keep off sex altogether,' said Hillier. 'You, Clara, are a girl of considerable beauty.' Clara simpered prettily; Alan bunched up his mouth and made whistling noises. 'I want you to make use of it, if need be, for diversionary purposes. The odd ogle, the provocative glance. You know the sort of thing.'

'It's not in any of my books,' she said, frowning.

'No, I suppose not. Your books all start at a stage beyond provocation.'

'Will you go in armed?' asked Alan.

'There's absolutely no point. Besides, that man Theodorescu stole my gun, you know.'

'I didn't know.'

'But the carrying of a gun is merely talismanic in this sort of affair. Once you start shooting you infallibly get shot.'

'Phallic,' said Clara. 'Not always,' said Alan. Both ate more cakes, thinking; they had recovered their appetites. 'Well, now,' said Alan. 'Is there anything more you want from us?'

'Yes. What we call the terminal message. If I don't return to the ship I shall want you to send this to London. A cable.' He handed over a slip of paper.

Alan frowned at it and then read it aloud, though in a whisper. *'Chairman, Typeface.* That isn't much of an address.'

'Never mind. It'll get there.'

'Contact unmade. Jagger. Hm. And that means what?'

'It means they've got me.'

'Death?' said Clara softly. 'It means they'll kill you?'

'I don't know what more it means except that they've got me. That's enough. Somebody may come and try to get me out. But it means the closing of a dossier. Anyway, this is my last assignment. I don't think anybody at home will really care.'

'It's a hard life,' said Alan, as though it had been his life too.

'It's the life I chose.'

'But what's it all for?' asked Clara. 'Agents and spies and counter-spies and secret weapons and dark cellars and being brainwashed. What are you all trying to do?'

'Have you ever wondered,' said Hillier, 'about the nature of ultimate reality? What lies beyond all this shifting mess of phenomena? What lies beyond even God?'

'Nothing's beyond God,' said Alan. 'That stands to reason.'

'Beyond God,' said Hillier, 'lies the concept of God. In the concept of God lies the concept of anti-God. Ultimate reality is a dualism or a game for two players. We—people like me and my counterparts on the other side—we reflect that game. It's a pale reflection. There used to be a much brighter one, in the days when the two sides represented what are known as good and evil. That was a tougher and more interesting game, because one's opponent wasn't on the other side of a conventional net or line. He wasn't marked off by a special jersey or colour or race or language or allegiance to a particular historico-geographical abstraction. But we don't believe in good and evil any more. That's why we play this silly and hopeless little game.'

'You don't have to play it,' said Alan.

'If we don't play it, what else are we going to play? We're too insignificant to be attacked by either the forces of light or the forces of darkness. And yet, playing this game, we occasionally let evil in. Evil tumbles in, unaware. But there's no good to fight evil with. That's when one grows sick of the game and wants to resign from it. That's why this is my last assignment.'

'It's doing good, I should have thought,' said Clara. 'You're getting a British scientist out of Russia.'

'I'm removing him from the game,' said Hillier, 'that's all. A chessman off the board. But the game remains.'

'I think,' said Alan weightily, offering a Black Russian to Hillier, 'we ought to stick together, the three of us.' Unwontedly, Hillier accepted the cigarette and a light from the flaming Cygnus. 'We can have dinner in one of those special little dining-rooms. I'll go and arrange that.'

'Won't it look too much like a conspiracy?' asked Hillier, amused but touched.

'So it will be. A conspiracy against *her*. You talk about good and evil not existing much any more, but *she's* evil.'

'I thought it was just men she wanted. Young men. Sex, I mean.'

'A sex goddess. That's how she sees herself. A tatty old sex goddess.'

November goddess in your. Hillier went to the wardrobe and felt in the back pocket of his dress trousers. 'Here's something you can help with,'" he said. 'Try and decipher that. It's not very important, just a kind of joking farewell message from the Department. But try it. You ought to be good at that sort of thing.'

Alan took the folded paper, gently concave from Hillier's sitting on it, and took the giving of it as a dismissal. 'Come on, Clara,' he said. 'Well see you at dinner, then.'

'I think not tonight. Thanks all the same. I'll have some dinner in my cabin. And then a bit of self-communion.'

'That sounds religious,' said Clara.

'It *is* religious,' said her brother. 'Everything he's told us is religious.'

PART III

ONE

THE FLOUR KING SNORED ON, WITH INCREASING FEEBLENESS, towards his own black sea. Kraarkh kraarkh. Their *memento mori* tucked away, the voyagers tucked in. The *Polyolbion* dodged among the Cyclades. Kraarkh. The ham had been cooked in equal parts of chicken stock and muscatel, sliced to the bone, each slice spread with chestnut purée, ground almonds and minced onion. Covered with puff pastry, browned, served with a sauce Marsala. Kraarkh. Milos, Santarin. Roast chicken Nerone, with potatoes romana. Siphnos, Paros. Here the Nereids sing, their hair as gold as their voices. Tournedos truffés with a sauce bordelaise. Kraarkh. On Sikinos the Nereids appear with donkey or goat hoofs. Steak au poivre aflame in brandy. Master Walters frowned over the coded message. ZZWM DDHGEM. Kraarkh. Ariadne's island. Pommes Balbee. Kythnos, Syros, Tinos, Andros. EH IJNZ. Parian marble, wine, oil, gum-mastic. Kraarkh. Hominy grits. Egg nog ice cream. OJNMU ODWI E. Kraarkh. The Northern Sporades. Sherry bisque. OVU ODVP.

Kraarkh. Veal cutlets in sour cream. To starboard, Mytilene, then the Turkish mainland. Kraarkh. Miss Walters, excited by what was to come, quietened her nerves with a sex-book. The *Polyolbion* delicately probed the Dardenelles. *Swell the march.* Kraarkh with olive potatoes and juniper berries. *Of England's story* with kraarkh and courgettes.

Hillier kept to his cabin because of Clara Walters. This was no time for cramming that honeycomb into his mouth. Spare bread and cheese and bottled ale fed that mouth which spent much time testing its Russian accent, reacquiring facility. Wriste was worried: was he perhaps not well? Wriste sat with him some-times while he ate, telling tales of when he was a muckman in Canberra, a brutal stretch in jail in Adelaide, sheilas on Bondi Beach. The salt of the earth, Wriste. *Of England's story.* Kraarkh. The Sea of Marmara. A mere wave at Istanbul to port: they would be visiting Istanbul on the way back. The Bosporus, Beykoz to starboard. Kraarkh. He was still alive, a mere vat of feebly bubbling chemicals. He might last till Istanbul. It would be easier there to arrange his transport to a British crematorium. The ship moved firmly towards the Crimean peninsula. Yarylyuk smiled equivocally ahead.

Nightfall; landfall. The evening was all plush, studded with Tartar brilliants; the air like soft and snaky Borodin. Some instinct told Hillier to greet his danger in underpants and dressing-gown. His L-shaped cabin was on the port side; from the light or deck-window above the washbasin he could see the harbour nuzzle up without himself being seen. He was in the dark, really in the dark. The horror was that he had no plan. He faced his fate, the fat laughers on deck their fun. There was always something inimical about the approach of land after long days at sea, even when that land was home, whatever home was. It was like the intrusion of the sforzandi of hearty visitors into the quiet rhythms of a hospital ward, or like the switching on of a raw electric bulb as the cosy afternoon of toe-toasting in the shadows, by the hypnotic cave of a Sunday fire, became church-going evening. The quay lights of Yarylyuk were naked enough; the go-downs were ugly with smashed windows. A dog barked somewhere in comforting international language. Tamburlaine and his sons, shabby in washed-out worker's blue, looked up at the British ship: cruel Tartar faces with *papirosi* burning under ample moustaches. There was a shouting handling of ropes. Hillier heard the gangplank thud down. Some of the passengers cheered. He tried to think beyond the piled packing-cases, trolleys, oil-slicked stones, cracked windows, YARYLYUK in Cyrillic lettering and yellow neon glowing from a roof, to the distant hills, cypress, olive, vine, laughing teeth—sempiternal innocent life, clodhopping dances and flowery folk festivals. He tried, gulping, to think beyond the uniformed and capped smokers, arms akimbo, doing the rump-cleft-freeing knees-bend as they watched and waited. There would be unofficial lights—villas and workers' holiday hostels—to left and right of this way in for foreigners. There would be little boats and regatta yachts with flags. A couple of uniforms strolled into his view. Perhaps they were not so clever here as in Moscow; perhaps Theodorescu's message had been misunderstood or not taken too seriously. These were, surely, decent ordinary *militsioners* who wanted no trouble—a British whisky in the ship's bar rather, a pen or camera or doll in Tudor silk. Their roubles would be acceptable; British shore visitors would want roubles; no trouble with roubles, no rouble-trouble.

Three jaunty Slavs, not Tartars, passport-stamping men in uniform, stamped past Hillier's light, talking loudly. All intending shore visitors, it had been loudspeakered earlier, must report with their passports to the bar on C-deck. And would there be stripping for the thinner men in a commandeered cabin near by? A coachload was to be sped to the Hotel Krym, where there would be a feast of Crimean oysters, salmon, sturgeon, seethed kid, ripe figs and wine as sweet as ripe figs. Hillier started as his door was suddenly opened, letting in light from the corridor. 'You're in the dark,' said young Alan. His Black Russian announced itself. Hillier drew the runnered curtain across his view of Yarylyuk. 'You can switch on,' he said. Alan was in a decent dark blue shore-going suit with a polka-dot bow-tie. At once Hillier realised why he himself was near-naked. Yarylyuk was going to give him a uniform. 'I've cracked this code,' said Alan.

'Never mind about that now. Where's your sister?'

'She's just finishing dressing. She'll be here in a minute. Look, about this code. The November goddess is Queen Elizabeth I. She came to the throne in November, 1558.'

'1558?' That had something to do with Roper. The family-tree on the wall in Didsbury, Manchester. The ancestor who died young for his faith. 1558: an Elizabethan martyr. 'I'm beginning to see,' said Hillier. 'A binary code, is it?'

'If you mean alternate letters belong to alternating systems, yes. In one system the first letter is the fifth, in the other the fifth letter is the eighth. It's quite simple, really. But I haven't had time to do it all. They call you by a different name. I suppose it stood to reason your name couldn't be Jagger. It begins: DEAR HILLIR. That's a foreign-sounding name. Are you sure,' he said accusingly, 'you've been telling us the truth?'

'They may have spelt it wrong. It should be Hillier.'

'I didn't get much further than that. But it's full of apologies, as far as I can see. They're sorry about something or other.'

'Perhaps the amount of my terminal bonus. Anyway, I can have a look at it later. Thanks. You'd do well in this game.' There was a knock at the door and Clara walked in. She looked ravishing. Hillier knew he had been right to go into retirement this last day and more, subsisting on bread and cheese and Russian. Infirm of purpose. She was in a cocktail dress of silver lamé with cape back and treble pearl-diamanté collar necklace, her shoes of silver kid. Perfume of an older woman clouted Hillier's nostrils, making him salivate. He yearned for her. Damn work. Damn death. 'How is he?' he asked.

'About the same.'

'And that bitch,' said Alan evilly, 'is going ashore with that muscled Scandinavian bastard, God curse them both.'

'Language, language,' reproved Clara. She shook her head in sorrow at him and then went to sit on Hillier's bunk. Her knees showed; Hillier knew, but did not show, an accession of agony. He said briskly:

'To business. I want a Russian police uniform and I want it now. This means that a policeman will have to be lured in here—'

A loud complaint came from the corridor: 'Making me bloody strip for a short-arm inspection. If that's the condition for going ashore I'm staying on board. Bloody Russkies.' A cabin-door slammed. So Theodorescu's prediction was being fulfilled: a very capable, though bad, man.

'Lured?' said Alan. 'How lured?'

'You have two techniques available. If one fails, try the other. You, my boy, take that camera on deck. The Japanese one—'

'Japanese one?' He looked puzzled.

'Yes, yes. The one you say Theodorescu gave you. Take it without the case, though—' There was a knock at the door. It was Clara who raised her finger to shushing lips. 'Come in,' shouted Hillier bravely. He would bare his chest to bullets; he knew when he was beaten. Wriste peered in, then entered. He was smart for a shore visit, the grey suit natty enough for London, the tie—a vulgar touch that went with the toothless jaws—mock-Harrovian. He said:

'Not dressed yet? Still not feeling so good?' He saw Clara sitting on the bunk and did a Leporello-type leer. 'All right, forgive me butting in, but there's two blokes in the bar asking for you.'

'Russians?'

'Yes, but nice blokes both. Laughing and joking, speak lovely English. They said something about typewriters.'

'And they asked for Jagger.'

'More like Yagger. I just happened to be there getting my passport stamped. I didn't say more than that I'd look to see if you was in.'

'Well, I'm not. Say I've gone ashore.'

'Nobody's gone ashore yet. They've got some kind of FFI thing going on in one of the cabins. A very thorough lot, the Russians. Looking for drugs hidden up people's arseholes, perhaps. I beg your pardon, miss. I do most definitely beg your pardon. I really and most sincerely apologise for what I said then. I just forgot myself. I do most definitely—'

'You've heard of industrial espionage,' said Hillier. 'The Russians are better at it than anybody. Slip me a mickey and then gouge out all my technical secrets. Say,' he said, inspired, 'that I

left the ship with a certain Mr Theodorescu. You saw that helicopter. A lot of people did. Tell them that.' Wriste discreetly slid
his thumb along his finger-ends, three times, rapidly. 'Here,'
Hillier sighed. He dug out a hundred-dollar bill from his bunkside table drawer. 'And don't let me down.'

'You, sir? You're my pal, you are. And I'm really sorry, miss.
Sometimes my tongue just carries me away—'

'What's FFI?' asked Alan.

'Free From Infection,' said Wriste promptly. 'We used to have
it coming back off leave.'

'How about now?' asked Hillier. 'This business now, I mean?'

'That's the funny thing,' said Wriste. 'They didn't want
everybody. Just a selected few. They could see I was honest.' He
struck a pose and leered. Then, wagging his hundred-dollar bill,
he cakewalked out.

'Yes,' said Alan. 'You said something about a camera.'

'Find a solitary policeman and offer it for five roubles. That's
mad, of course, but never mind. Just hold up five fingers and say
rubl. He ought to slaver over a chance like that. And then say
you've got the case in your cabin, no extra charge.'

'How do I say that? I don't know any Russian.'

'You disappoint me, you do really. Use gesture. He'll understand. Then bring him in here. He'll be quite willing to come.
Any chance to snoop. He won't be suspicious of you, a mere
youngster. There won't, of course, be any camera-case. There'll
just be me.'

'And supposing it fails?'

'If it fails we bring Plan Number Two into operation. Or
rather Clara does.'

'What does Clara do?'

'You offer a camera, Clara offers herself.' The two drooped and became what they were, children. They widened shocked and fearful eyes at Hillier. 'It's an act,' said Hillier rapidly. 'Just that, no more. Just a bit of play-acting. Nothing can happen. I shall be here in that wardrobe, waiting. But, of course,' he ended, as they still looked at him dumbly and reproachfully, 'you can't really fail with the camera trick.'

'But how do I do it?' asked Clara.

'Do I really have to tell you that? I thought you were interested in sex. All you have to do is to sway seductively and give him a bold look, what they call the old come-hither. You're supposed to know all that instinctively.' Ridiculously, Hillier demonstrated. They didn't laugh.

'All right, then.' Alan didn't look too happy. 'I'll go and start Plan Number One.'

'And the very best of luck.' Alan went out hanging his head. 'Well,' said Hillier to Clara, 'that's deflated him a bit, hasn't it? Not quite so cocky as he was.' He considered sitting beside Clara on the bunk, but then thought better of it. He took the nearest chair instead, crossing his legs, disclosing a bare hairy one beyond the knee, swinging it. There were women, he knew, who pretended that male knee-caps could be sexy. Clara didn't look at it; she looked at him. She said:

'Alan hasn't got a camera.'

'What?'

'He's never had a camera. He's never been interested in photographing things.'

'But he got one as a present. He said so.'

'Yes. I couldn't understand why he lied. If he'd got one he

would have shown it me. He certainly wouldn't have hidden it. What he got from that man he hid.'

'Oh, God. Why didn't he say? This is no time for having secrets from each other.' That touched something in her—not sexology but *True Romances*. Hillier again considered sitting beside her.

'Why don't you forget all about it?' she said. 'It's just not worth it, is it? Killing and spying and kidnapping. Men. A lot of children.'

'Would you like a lot of children?'

'Oh, fancy asking a question like that now. There'd be time for questions like that if you weren't mixed up in all this stupidity. We could have a nice voyage.'

'We shall have a nice voyage when I've finished the job. I promise you. We'll read your sex-books together and drink beef-tea at mid-morning. Or perhaps we'll throw your sex-books overboard.'

'You're laughing at me.'

'I'm not,' said Hillier, not laughing. 'I'm deadly serious.' And then he thought: seriously dead; a serious case of death; prognosis purgatory. He wanted to live. The vowel shifted. A fat letter for a thin one. It seemed a long time since Wriste had talked about his typing sister. 'I think,' said Hillier, deadly serious, 'I could talk about love.' No man, uttering that word outside the heat of urgent need, could ever fail to be embarrassed by it. It was a con-man's word. But with women, even more with girls, it was different. Clara went roseate and looked down at the Line's carpet. Hillier had to give the word a meaning satisfactory to himself. The love he proposed, still marvelling at himself, was the only genuine kind: the incestuous kind. 'I mean it,' he said. 'Love.' And as an earnest of meaning it he covered his knees with his dressing-gown, imagining himself glued by honour to his chair.

'You shouldn't have said it,' flushed Clara. 'Not to me. We don't know each other.'

'It's not a word in your sex-books. If I'd proposed fellation you'd have taken it in your stride. Love. I said love.'

'I mean, there's the difference in our ages. You must be old enough to be my father.'

'I am. Soon you'll be needing a father. And I still say love.'

'I shall have to—what's the word?—*lure* him into my own cabin,' she mumbled, still looking down. 'It'll be—what's the word?—more plausible. You don't think ahead, that's your trouble. You just think of hitting him and taking his uniform. There's the time after that. A dirty old man breaking into a young girl's cabin—'

'You needn't choose an old one.' Love. He loved this girl.

'And then when you've gone off wearing his uniform I can scream till somebody comes and then I can say he took it off himself for what purpose everybody will know and then I *lured* him and got him off his guard and hit him— What would I hit him with?'

'With the heaviest of your sex-books.'

'*Seriously.*' She tamped with excitement. 'What are *you* going to hit him with?'

'With his gun.'

'Oh.' The proscenium arch had come down. The maniac on the stage had leapt into the audience. 'I hadn't thought he'd be carrying a gun.'

'These men will not be village bobbies. I won't hit him too

hard, just enough to give him an injection of PSTX. That pro-duces an effect of great intoxication. If he's already out he'll probably stay out. Splendid. He came in drunk and undressed and then you clonked him with a stiletto heel—do that, you must do that—and then—'

'Then I bundled his clothes out of the porthole to make things more difficult for him. Including the gun.' She was ashine with eagerness to get down to the job of luring a strange man in.

'You're a beautiful and desirable and clever and brave girl,' said Hillier gravely, 'and I love you. And in jail or labour-camp or salt-mine I shall go on loving you. And even when the bullet bites I shall love you.' It all sounded preposterous, like love itself.

'But you'll be coming back. You will come back, won't you?'

Before he could answer, the door opened. Alan came in, very hangdog. 'No luck,' he mumbled. 'Nobody wanted to buy a cam-era. So I tried a Parker pen, and they didn't want that either. Nor some shirts. Not even my dinner-suit.'

'I don't think,' said Clara, 'young boys wear dinner-suits in Russia.'

'I did my best,' said Alan defiantly. 'I'm not much good at this sort of thing. I'm sorry.'

'Never mind,' said Hillier, kindly, in love. 'It stands to reason that you still have a lot to learn. Let Clara and me take over now.'

'I think I'll go ashore,' said Alan. 'There's this big coach wait-ing at the dock-gates.' He paused, waiting in vain to be told to be careful. 'I'll be careful,' he said, doubtfully.

'Act Two,' announced Hillier. 'A change of *venue*, but not really of scene. I'll throw those sex-books of yours through your porthole,' he told Clara. 'We don't want anybody to say you encouraged him.'

TWO

THERE WAS TIME for Hillier to make delicate love to Clara's cabin, an extension of herself. First, though, he put out his tongue at the sex-books, bundled them, struggling to be free, in his arms, and then hurled them out into the starboard night. The illiterate sea took them as indifferently as a Nazi bonfire. Then he padded round with tiny steps, stroking hairbrushes against his hands and face (prickly male kisses, but proxies of hers), sniffing her unguents and pancake make-up and too-mature perfume. There were stockings on the chair, of a gunmetal colour, and he tried to strangle himself with them, at the same time chewing the dampish feet. She took size nine. He hesitated about burying his face in the underwear in the drawer or taking a drink of tap-water from a shoe that poked out from beneath the bed (size four). The calm of an army was the anger of a people. Love, for the moment, must be the purpose blazoned on a war-poster, not the tremor of the trigger-finger. It was time to be getting into that wardrobe.

He had to crouch in it, among her dresses. These, being the external or public she, could not excite him as much as what had lain against or soothed or scented or stimulated her skin. But he kissed the hems of her invisible garments and prayed, not at all to his surprise, less to the goddess who manifested herself to the world in them, so many discardable bodies, than to that devil Miss Devi who had racked his nerves with lust and left them weakened and exposed (flagellated into sainthood) to more spiritual influences. Through the chink of the infinitesimally ajar wardrobe door he saw just such a bunk as that on which he had suffered and enjoyed Dravidian transports. He set Miss Devi upon it in the lotus position, *multibrachiate*, and prayed his thanks for those fires of purgatory through which he had been permitted to pass to reach the *beatrical* vision. Then he wiped her out before she became human again and lay on the coverlet, waiting for him.

Time passed, and he wondered whether he had done right to expose this shining one, Clara, to even the play-acting of whoredom. But it would not be the postures of professional seduction that would excite so much as the evident innocence of their unhandy imitation. The man she would bring in here would be a bad man, no doubt of it, and would deserve what he was going to get. Then he thought about love and wondered whether any woman who was loved at all realised how excruciating were those intensities of devotion. The troubadours and con-men had debased the language, and the physical act reduced one to a paradigm of animality. Seek to possess the body of the loved one and you might as well be in a brothel. The act could not be ennobled into a sacrament in the way that bread could be transubstantiated. You could cram bread into your mouth at breakfast, spitting out crumbs as you talked about the sermon, but before that you had taken an insipid wafer, no nutriment in it, and muttered 'My Lord and my God'. And you believed you were heard. With love you had to take breakfast and sacrament together and could not, at the moment of revelation, cry 'My lady and my goddess'. Or if you could, you knew that there would be nobody to hear you.

Hillier suffered from cramp, crammed in among the odorous dresses. He opened the wardrobe door and prepared to loosen up his limbs, and then he heard footsteps approaching. He crammed himself in again, a mouthful of bread, and literally heard his heart hammer, out of phase with the footsteps. The cabin-door opened, my Lord and my God, she had bloody well done it. He saw drab police-uniform, the dull shine of a holster, riding-boots, and retracted to thirty or more slivers by the intermittency of his view, her silver lamé dress. How much could he bear? That belt and holster had to come off, but would she be unflustered enough to get him to unbuckle it now before those hard police-fingers mauled and probed? What Hillier saw he saw in slices, but he heard clearly enough the hoarse one Russian word: 'Razdyevay—razdyevay—' He widened the chink and saw too much—the rip of the dress at the shoulder, a Slav rape of the West, the fat red neck and the coarse stubble above it, the rank of the man (by God, she had done well, his brain coldly noted, noting insignia he had forgotten how to interpret but knew were above the badge of a lieutenancy, noting too, as he saw the blunt face in profile, a couple of rows of medal-ribbons and despising the man for this deflection from purpose but also loving him for being human enough to be deflected and then hating him for that lust that was all too human and was grunting and grinning in gold and stained ivory towards the one intolerable desecration). Clara, very fearful, already dishevelled as after a whole night's forced abandon, looked across the bearing-down shoulder towards her salvation in the wardrobe. Hillier looked out at her an instant, pointing desperately towards the holster. She at once began to try to loosen the man's tunic and he, grinning 'Da, ya dolzhen razdyevat'sya', rose from her, unbuckled his belt and threw it to the floor, then started to unbutton clumsily. To Clara he said, as before: 'Razdyevay—razdyevay—' The verb to undress, in its intransitive and reflexive forms, was one she ought to remember, thought Hillier madly, crouching hidden again. Now, in his shirt, the man made for her with fingers spread as for wrestling, and Hillier took his chance.

'*Khorosho,*' he said, pointing the gun (it was a heavy police *Tigr*, one of the new issue) and thumbing open the stiffish safety-catch. '*Vstavayetye, svinyah.*' It was back to that afternoon with the *Westdeutsche Teufel*, though in a more satisfactory language. The shirted man addressed as pig was slow in standing up; he seemed even desirous of clinging to Clara for protection. But now, in a genuine officer-voice, Hillier called him a leching bitch-get, and told him to come over to the *gardyerob*, he himself arcing away from it, and to stand with his fat pig-guts and lavatory-face facing it. The man obeyed, rumbling and spitting, though, disquietingly, his rather fine brown eyes looked with some warmth on Hillier: it was as though it were a pleasant capitalist relaxation—like drinking Scotch or listening to jazz—to be caught in a mere *boudoir* predicament. 'This,' said Hillier in kind Russian, 'will not hurt much.' He cracked the gun-butt on the man's stubbled occiput. To his surprise, there was no response. He cracked harder. The man, with mammy-singer's arms, tried to embrace the wardrobe and then, the skirr of eight finger-nails drawing old-time music-staves on the two wooden sides as he went down, he went down.

Hillier turned to Clara. He was shocked but wretchedly excited to see so much shoulder exposed and even an upper quadrant of her right breast. She seemed all right, though, not frightened any more. 'I'll buy you a new dress, my darling,' he groaned. 'I promise you.' She said:

'You didn't hit hard enough. Look.' The man seemed to prepare to raise himself with one hand-press from his prone moaning. Hillier gave him the gentlest of butt-thumps and, with a sigh of content, the man subsided. Hillier said:

'I hope you'll see me dress again. Often. But in future in my own clothes. Give me a hand with these boots. Too big for me, but never mind.' Then came the breeches. Under them Hillier saw, with pity, patched drawers. He struggled into the uniform, panting. 'How do I look?'

'Oh, *do* be careful.'

'Now his belt. Where's the cap? Ah, behind the door. Treating the place as his own, the *svinyah*.' The breeches were roomy, but the tunic would hide all bagginess. 'I'd better pad myself out a bit.' He stuffed Clara's bath-towel in his chest. 'And now.' He took the loaded syringe from his dressing-gown breast-pocket, squirted a sample at the air, then, in the man's bare fore-arm, plunged the rest deep and rough. Some rilled along the skin, meeting russet hairs. Then, to both their astonishments, the man came to.

He came to suddenly, as if from a fairy-tale kiss. He re-entered consciousness in a state of robust drunkenness, blinking, lip-smacking, then smiling. His liberated under-mind began a drunken Russian monologue to which Hillier listened fascinated: 'Dad in bed mother warm snow on ground said hot tea now no samovar hit Yuri hard on snout Lukerya cry tears freeze give cold boiled beetroot juice dad drunk.' He tried to get up, gazing with love on Hillier. Hillier, with a new idea, said to Clara:

'Where's your stepmother's cabin?'

'Along here, we're all along here together.'

'Old Nikolayev school hit hard not know how long river.'

'Go and see if it's locked. If it is, get the duplicate key from the purser's board. But hurry.' She took from the door-hook a lit-tle fur cape. She couldn't go out with a torn dress. Hillier loved her.

'Salgir longest river Crimea but very short. South slopes Yaila

mountains very fertile.' He repeated it: *'Ochin plodorodnyiy.'*
Then he tried once more to get up. Hillier pushed him gently
down. 'Behind shed summer day Natasha skirt up big belly she
show I not show she show I not show.' Well, thought Hillier, he
was beyond that *pudeur* now. 'She show I not show she show I
show.' At last. 'Old Nikolayev see hit hard on snout tell dad dad
hit hard on bottom.' A lot of hitting in that distant Crimean boyhood. Clara panted back in.

'There's that place where they make tea at the end of the corridor. There are keys there. I've opened up. Is that right?'

'Good girl. Delightful, excellent girl.' Hillier raised the smiling burbler to his feet without difficulty. 'Lean on me, old man. A
nice long sleep, *tovarishch*. You're going to beddybyes.'

'In her bed?'

'Why not? It'll be a nice surprise for her.'

The burbling had changed to song: 'Whish, little doggies, off
you go. Over the crisp and silver snow.' A song of the Northern
Crimea, probably, the south being free from the referred terrors
of the steppes. Think of those men in Balaclava helmets. Think
of Florence Nightingale. The corridor was empty. There was no
trouble at all about propelling him to the bed of Mrs Walters.
'Mama is sitting by the stove. In her samovar tea, in her bosom
love.' The room, sniffed Hillier, was redolent of sex. *V grudye
lyubov.* In her bosom love. Soon there was no more song, only
healthy snoring.

'I must get ready to go now,' said Hillier.

She raised her face. This time the man in that uniform was
very gentle.

THREE

IT WAS THE DIFFERENCE between the eucharist and what the breadman delivered. Crammed, like bread, into tunic and trouser pockets, were the Innes beard and the Innes passport, the ampoules and syringe (needle capped for protection), dollars from Theodorescu and black-market roubles from Pulj, a packet of White Sea Canal from the dead-out police-officer, as well as his card of identity (S.R. Polotski, aged 39, born Kerch, married, the dirty swine). The *Tigr*, safety-caught, snarled from his hip. He marched down the gangplank noisily, barking jocular Russian at the young constable at its foot ('Bit of all right here, son. Bags of wallop and some very nice-looking tarts. Any sign of any suspicious characters, eh? No, I thought not. Load of cods-wallop that report was. All right, carry on, carry on') and, having play-punched the bewildered youth on the chest, he marched off towards the ramp that led up to the little terminal. It was nicely dark on the quay, only a few working-lamps staring imbecilically, but it was brighter inside the terminal, though the customs-hall was in shadow, not being in use. A girl was serving beer at a little bar, the only customers Tartar dock-labourers; there was another girl at a souvenir kiosk, doing no trade. Near the landward door were a couple of constables, smoking. They stiffened when they saw Hillier, ready to throw him a salute, but he waved at them jollily as he marched through, singing. He sang S.R. Polotski's song about the little doggies in the snow, lah-lahing where he had forgotten the words. One of the constables called to his back: 'Find anybody, comrade captain?' but he sang over his shoulder: '*Niktooooh*, false alarm.' And then he clomped down steps, entering a little area of bales and packing-cases and a few parked lorries. The night was delicious and smelt of strawberries. A light wind blew straight down from the mother land-mass, a reminder that the Kremlin was up there, despite the subtropical nonsense of warmth and oranges on that little southern uvula.

It was darker than it ought to be by the dock-gates and guard-room. If Hillier were what he pretended to be he would do some-thing about that: not easy to check true face with passport parody in that light. A man in uniform with a rifle, shabby as a leftover from the Crimean War, came to attention for Hillier. In the guardroom two men played cards, one of them moaning about the deal. A very simple game, without guile; the comrades were hopeless at poker. A third man was, with sour face, mixing some-thing with hot water in a jug. Hillier marched through. It struck him that there ought to be a police-car somewhere, but he inhaled and exhaled with a show of pleasure to the empty street that led out of dockland: he was walking for his health. On either side of the street were little gardens, grudgingly lighted to show cypress and bougainvillea and lots of roses. On a bench inside the right-hand garden a young couple sat, furtively embracing. That did Hillier's heart good. Deeper within the garden someone cleared his throat with vigour. A dog barked, miles away, and set other dogs barking. These, and the smell of roses touched (or did he imagine this?) with the zest of lemons, were pledges that life went on in universal patterns below the horrors of power and language. Hillier had to find the Chornoye Morye Hotel. He thanked distant Theodorescu for that bit of information about Roper's whereabouts. He was supposed, of course, to know very well where that hotel was. But even police-officers could be strangers in a town. Indeed, the stranger they were the more they were respected. He marched on.

He was aware of fertile champaigns to the north, and hills beyond those: country scents blew down, unimpeded by traffic-smells. But at the end of the street which led from the docks he saw traffic and heard trolley-hissing and clanks. Trams, of course. He had always liked trams. He saw no unpredestined traffic: this blessed country with its shortage of motor-cars, where a drunk could lie down between kerb and tramlines and not be run over. Hillier arrived at the corner and looked on a fine boulevard, very Continental. The trees were, he thought, mulberries, and their crowns susurrated in the breeze. It was not late, but there were not many people about, only a few lads and girls, dressed skimpily for summer, aimless in pairs or groups. Of course, there would be an esplanade somewhere, looking out at winking lights on the water. Perhaps a band played the state-directed circus-music of Khatchaturian from a Byzantine iron bandstand, people around listening, drinking state beer. He hesitated, wondering which way to turn.

He turned left, and saw that a souvenir-shop was open, though it had no customers. In the ill-lit window were *matrioshkas*, wooden bears, cheap barbaric necklaces and Czech enamel brooches. There were also china drinking-mugs and Hillier frowned at these, sure he had seen them somewhere before, though not, so far as he could remember, on Soviet territory. On each mug a woman's face had been crudely painted: black hair screwed into a bun, the eyes wrinkled in evil smiling, the nose and chin conspiring to frame a cackle of age. Where the hell had that been? It came to him: some watering-place in Italy where the medicinal waters (magnesium sulphate? heptahydrated?) were grossly purgative, the bitter draught served sniggeringly in a mug like these, with, however, a younger, more beautiful, Italianate face. And, yes, the legend had been: '*Io sono Beatrice chi ti faccio andare*'. A low joke: I am Beatrice who makes you go. Straight out of Dante, that line, but she had been leading him up to the glory of the stars, purgatory one of the stages not the terminus. Now this had something to do with him, Hillier, but what?

He knew right away. It was Clara, clear bright one. He was becoming respiritualised, made aware of an immortal soul again after all these many years. And yet his dirty body could not be purged for her through this one last adventure, a breath-held entry into the flames then out again with his salvaged burden. It was not enough: *domina, non sum dignus.* A thousand clumps of pubic hair had tangled and locked in his, of all colours from Baltic honey to Oriental tar. His flesh had been scored by innumerable teeth, some false. And he had gorged and swilled, grunting. And then consider the lies and betrayals to serve a factitious end. He shook his head: he had not been a good man. He needed, in a single muscular gesture, to throw that luggage of his past self (blood-and-beer-stained cheap suitcases full of nameless filth wrapped in old *Daily Mirrors*) on to the refuse cart which, after a single telephone-call, would readily come to his gate, driven by a man with brown eyes and a beard who would smile away a gratuity (This is my job, sir). He was creaking towards a regeneration.

He turned to look at the street. From a closed shop which called itself an *atelier* a man came out limping. He wore an open-necked dirty shirt and khaki trousers. His face was lined but he was not old. A tram clanked eastwards, almost empty. To the man he said, '*Pozhal'sta, tovarishch. Gdye Chornoye Morye?*'

'You are making a joke? The Black Sea is all behind you.' He made a two-armed gesture as of throwing the sea there out of his own bosom.

'Stupid of me.' Hillier smiled. 'I mean the Black Sea Hotel.'

The man looked closely at Hillier. He had a faint smell of coarse raspberry liqueur. 'What is this?' he said. 'What's the game? Everybody knows where that is. You're not a real police-man, asking that question. You're what I'd call a *samoʒvanyets.*' Impostor, that meant. The woman who kept the souvenir-shop was at the door, listening. Hillier groaned to himself. He blustered:

'Don't insult the uniform, *tovarishch.* There's a law against that.'

'There's a law against everything, isn't there? But there are some laws we're not going to have. Secret police masquerading as ordinary police. What will they think of next? If you're trying to get me to incriminate myself you've got another think com-ing.' He was loud now. A young couple, blond giant and dumpy brunette, stopped to hear, the girl giggling. 'Where are you from? Moscow? You don't sound like a Yarylyuk man.'

'You're drunk,' said Hillier. 'You're not responsible for what you're saying.' And he took a chance and began to walk towards the few rags of red left in the west. In the unfamiliar big boots, he stumbled against a broken bit of paving. A child had appeared from nowhere in the gutter, a girl with a snot-wet upper lip. The child laughed.

'Not too drunk,' cried the man, 'to know when I'm being got at. I've nothing to hide. There, you see,' he told everybody. 'He didn't want the Black Sea Hotel after all. He's going the opposite way.' Hillier walked quickly past a redolent but empty fish-restaurant, a shuttered state butcher's, and a branch of the Gosbank that looked like a small prison for money. 'Getting at us,' called the man. 'All we want is to be left alone.' All I want too, thought Hillier. He crossed diagonally to a side-street opening, totally unlighted, and got himself out of the way. Here a hill began. He trudged up broken cobbles, looking for a right turning. On either side were mean houses, in one of which a blue television screen did a rapid stichomythia of shot and dialogue, the window wide open for the heat. The other houses were dead, perhaps everyone out on the esplanade. Hillier wanted to be left alone, but he felt desperately left alone. The right turning he found was an alley full of sodden cartons, from the feel underfoot, with squelchy vegetable refuse sown among them. Hillier plopped gamely eastwards to a tune of cats fighting. There should, he knew, be a moon in first quarter rising about now. To his far left there was the scent of a hayfield: the country started early here. At one point he heard a husband-and-wife quarrel, apparently in a backyard: *'Korova,'* the husband called the wife, also *'Samka'*, very loud. He turned right into a street which had tiny front gardens with roses in them, and then he was on the boulevard again, the mulberries stirring in a fresh breeze. He came to a sign which said *Ostanovka Tramvaya*. There were three people waiting.

'So,' said a remembered voice, 'you're up to your tricks again, are you? Creeping up on me nastily with your spying tricks. And if I say I'll tell the police you'll say that you are the police. This,' he told the embracing couple waiting with him, 'is what I call a *samozvanyets*. He thinks to disguise himself by wearing a police uniform, but I'm up to all his tricks. All right,' he said to Hillier, 'what if I do work at the Black Sea Hotel? It's the big ones you ought to be after, not poor devils like us working in the kitchen. We don't get the chance, not that I'd take it if I got it. I've always kept my nose clean, I have. Ought to be ashamed of yourself, you ought.' Hillier did a resigned barmy-take-no-notice shoulder-shrug for the open-mouthed couple (open-mouthed, he then saw, because they were chewing American gum). The tram rattled up, its trolley sparking. It was a single-decker.

'The next thing you'll be saying is you don't know the fare,' said the man, comfortably seated opposite Hillier. 'Go on, say it.'

'I don't know the fare.'

'What did I tell you?' he announced in triumph to the five passengers. 'Well, it's ten kopeks. As you knew all the time, *samoʐvanyets.*'

The conductress ignored Hillier's proffer. The police, then, travelled free. She was a sort of bread-and-butter pudding of a girl, in a uniform that fitted deplorably.

'That's right,' said the man. 'One law for the rich, another for the poor. Moscow,' he sneered. 'Why can't they leave us alone?'

Hillier gathered a lungful of breath and shouted: *'Zamolchi!'* To his surprise the man *did* shut up, though he grumbled to himself. 'Going there now, are you?' asked Hillier, more kindly. 'To the hotel, I mean.'

'I'm not saying anything,' said the man. 'I've said too much already.' He took from his hip-pocket a very old-looking magazine called *Sport* and started to read a full-page photograph of a high-jumper with gloomy intentness. Hillier lighted a White Sea Canal, first twisting the cardboard mouthpiece, and looked out of the window. The tram turned right off the boulevard into a narrow street of pretty stucco houses with bougainvillea prominent in the front gardens. A street-lamp showed one clump of the flower up clearly, a glow of red and lilac petaloid bracts. Again that blessed world beyond politics. The tram turned left, and there beyond on the right was the sea with lights winking. There was no esplanade. Instead there were workers' holiday hostels in garish primary colours, each with its private beach. In one a dance was swinging away to out-of-date music, corny trumpet and saxophone in unison on *You Want Lovin' But I Want Love*. Was that distinction possible in Russian? The tram stopped.

'As you well know,' said the man opposite, tucking away his *Sport*, 'we're here.' He let, or made, Hillier get off first.

The Chornoye Morye Hotel was on the left, away from the beach but with a winding path through a rich but ill-tended garden. Its name was on a board, floodlighted. The architecture was good Victorian English seaside, a sort of Blackpool Hydro with striped awnings. Hillier was disturbed to find plain-clothes men, bullish, thuggish, patrolling near the ornate entrance. But, of course, a temporary requisition. A scientific conference, big stuff, state stuff, the S-man, despite negative reports from the docks, perhaps really at large. That damned man was behind him, saying: 'There you are. Real police. They'll see through you. They'll know you for what you are, *samozvanyets.*' Hillier blazed. He turned on the man, grasped him by his dirty kitchen-worker's collar and pulled him into an arbour of cypress and myrtle and begonia. He said:

'This gun I have is not just for show. I shall use it on you without hesitation. We can't have filthy little nobodies like you getting in the way of vital state business.'

'I'll confess everything.' The man gibbered. 'It was only two cartons. The head waiter's in it up to his eyeballs.'

'English or American?'

'*Lakki Straiyk*. Two cartons. I swear. Nothing else.'

'Let me see you go straight to the kitchen entrance. Any non-sense at all and I shan't think twice about shooting.'

'And the *Direktor's* in it. Watches. Swiss watches. Give me time and I'll make out a full list of names.'

'Go on.' Hillier butted him with his gun-butt. 'Get in there an and nothing more will be said. But if I hear that you've been talk-ing any more nonsense about impostors—'

The man snivelled. 'It's back to the days of Stalin,' he said. 'All bullying and threatening. It was different when we had poor old Nikita.'

FOUR

THIS MAN WAS a nonentity, yes, a *nichtozhestvo*, but nonentities talked more than entities; what he said in the kitchen (probably scullery) would be transmitted very quickly to the office of the *Direktor*. A sort of copper sniffing after smuggled fags. Chewing-gum too, perhaps. A thug in a cheap suit, the right jacket-pocket weighted down, rotated his jaws as he said to Hillier, with little deference, 'Any news? Any sign of anybody?' From within the hotel came noise and a faint percussion of glasses clinked in toasts: here's to you; here's to me; here's to Soviet science.

'False alarm,' said Hillier. Another thug came up, a Baltic type, to peer at Hillier as though, which he couldn't, he couldn't quite place him. 'There's a Doctor Roper here,' said Hillier, 'an Englishman.'

'*Da, Doktor Ropyr, Anglichanin*. Trouble at last, eh?'

'Why should there be trouble?' Hillier proffered his White

Sea Canals and took one himself. He was dying for a real smoke, one of his filthy Brazilians. Thank God he'd brought some with him. Later, talking quietly with Roper, he would have one. 'There's no trouble that I know of. Something to do with his papers, that's all. A matter of routine.'

'Ah, *rutina*.' The first thug shrugged. Hillier was welcome to go in if he wanted. The other thug said:

'*Moskva?*'

'That's right, Moscow.'

'You don't talk like a Moscow man.' Nor like a Yarylyuk one either. You couldn't win.

'I,' said Hillier, 'am an Englishman who speaks very good Russian.' That went straight to their hearts. They waved him in, puffing laughter through their *papirosi*.

The entrance-hall was shabby and pretentious. There were a couple of noseless stone goddesses sightlessly welcoming, both eroded as by November rain, their glory gone. The carpet had, in places, worn down to a woofless warp; in other places there were holes, the biggest one outside the gentleman's *tualet*. An old man in uniform chewed his beard outside the lift-gates, though the lift was labelled *Nye Rabotayet*—Out of Order. He was sticking to his post, all he had. The dining-room was straight ahead, full of what Hillier took to be Soviet scientists. Most seemed rosy and happy: this seaside convention was doing them good. They were seated, in fours and sixes, at tables with little flags of provenance, though surely all must now be convivially stirred up, making nonsense of all divisions outside of palpable ethnology. Hillier squinted through the smoke: limp pennants for the Ukrainian, Azerbaijan, Georgian, Uzbek, Kazakh, Tajik, Kirghiz, Turkmen Soviet Socialist Republics, but blaring banners (several) for the

Russian Soviet Federative Socialist Republic. Time was short.
That scullion nonentity might already be at work. Where was
Roper? Hillier dredged the Slav, Lithuanian, Moldavian,
Armenian, Ostyak, Uzbek, Chuvash, Chechenet roaring and
toasting commingling for an Anglo-Saxon face. The trouble was
that no one would stay still. No sense of guilt stirred by the presence of a police uniform, the scientists quaffed to each other
(Budvar beer, Russian champagne, Georgian muscatel, vodka
and konyak by the hundred-gramme fiasco) in amiable contor-
tions—arms linked at the elbow, close bodily embraces so that
each drank the other's, alternate cheek-smackings between
draughts. Some of the scientists were ancient and giggled naughtily in their cups, beards framing wet lips framing few or no teeth.
Where the hell was Roper? Hillier grabbed a white-coated waiter
with a spilling tray, young, cocky, his Mongol hair in a cock-crest.

'*Gdye Doktor Ropyr?*'

'*Kto?*'

'*Anglichanin.*'

The waiter laughed and nodded towards the far end of the
dining-room. There was a glass door there that seemed to lead to
a garden. '*Izvyergayet,*' he said gaily. Being sick, was he? That
seemed typical of Roper somehow. Hillier marched towards that
door.

A string of fairy-lights with gaps in the series was draped
among the cypresses: surely a scientific conference ought to be
able to do better than that. Otherwise it was dark, the moon still
unrisen. Hillier urgently whispered: 'Roper?' There was a
response of hiccups, somehow Russianised: *ikota, ikota, ikota.*
Wherever he was, he was outside the square of light that came
from the window. Hillier flicked his lighter, thought he might,

while he was at it, have a coarse Brazilian, so lit up one. Better, much better. 'Roper?' A man came up with an electric torch, a new thug, so Hillier doused his light. The man sprayed the police uniform with his beam then, satisfied, grunted and spotlighted a hiccuping shape on a stone garden-seat. 'You,' laughed the man, 'are the Englishman who speaks very good Russian.' Either he was one of the hotel-entrance thugs or else the joke had spread quickly. 'Here is another Englishman whose Russian is not so good.'

'Go away,' said Hillier. 'We want to talk.'

Roper, by the sound of it, was sick. 'Oh, Jesus, Mary and Joseph,' he prayed, in English.

'*Amin,*' said the Russian in Russian. Then he said: 'If you want to talk, go to the massage-hut there. Wait, I'll switch on the light for you. Shall I bring strong coffee?'

'That's kind,' said Hillier, uneasy that things were going so well.

'*Ikota,*' went Roper. '*Ikota ikota.*' And then, at the end of a little path of myrtle and roses, disclosed by the walking torch, bright light, as of an interrogation-chamber, suddenly shone. Hillier took Roper's arm.

'*Kto?*' asked sick Roper, with a very English vowel.

'*Politsia. Rutina.*'

'Oh God,' said Roper in English. 'I meant no harm walking out like that. I can't take it like they can. I wasn't trying to be insulting.'

'*Chto?*'

'*Nichevo,*' said Roper. 'Bloody blasted *nichevo*. I think I'm going to be sick again.' He retched, but *nichevo* came up.

'Perhaps,' said the thug, 'vinegar would be better than coffee.'

In the full light of the hut his face showed most unthuggish: it had something of the helpful shop-assistant in it.

'Coffee,' said Hillier. 'And thank you. But take your time about it. Shall we say in about ten minutes?'

'Ikota ikota.' Hillier kept his face averted from Roper as they entered the light.

'Ten minutes,' agreed the man, and went off.

'Now,' said Hillier in English. 'How do you feel now, Roper?' He looked full on him and was appalled by the ageing of the face. The tow hair was patchily grey; there was a twitch near the right eye. Roper looked up and stopped hiccuping. He said:

'Funny. I was thinking of you only the other day.' He tottered towards one of the four army cots on which, Hillier presumed, massage was done after ball-games on the beach, and lay on it, eyes closed. He got up swiftly and blinked. 'The bottom of the bed started coming up. The only thing that hasn't. Matric English,' said Roper. 'The Authorised Version of the Book of Job. For the literature, not the religion. And you said that Eliphaz and Bildad and Zophar were a proper bloody lot of Job's comforters.'

'Strange you should remember that.'

'Oh, I've been remembering a lot of things lately.'

'Strange you should remember the names. I'd completely forgotten them. Where does that door lead to?' There was a door at the back of the hut. Hillier opened it and looked out. There was faint light now, the moon rising. He saw a high stone wall, full of crannies. Beyond the sea shook its tambourines.

'I read the Bible a lot,' said Roper. 'The Douay Version. It's not so good as the Authorised. The bloody Protestants have always had the best of everything.' He closed his eyes. 'Oh God.

It's the bloody mixture that does it. They've all got iron stomachs, this lot.'

'I've come to take you home, Roper.'

'Home? To Kalinin?' He opened his eyes. 'I see you're in the police now. Funny, I should have thought they'd put you to spying or something. God, I do feel bad.'

'Don't be a fool, Roper. Wake up. You may have gone over to the Russians, but I haven't. Wake up, you bloody idiot. I'm still in the same game. I'm taking you back to England.'

Roper opened his eyes and began to shake. 'England. Filthy England. Kidnapping me, is that it? Taking me back to prison and making me stand trial and then hanging me. You're a traitor, whatever-your-name-is, I can't-remember-your-name, you're in the bloody conspiracy, it's been going on for four hundred years and more. Get out of my sight, I'll scream for help, you bastard.'

'Hillier. Remember? Denis Hillier. If you even attempt to scream I'll—Never mind. Look, Roper, there's no question of kidnapping. I've brought letters with me. Nobody's going to do anything to you. You're needed back in England, it's as simple as that. There's a quite fantastic offer here in my pocket. The trouble is, I haven't time for nice cosy easy gentle persuasion. I've got to get you out of here now.'

Roper opened his mouth as to scream but then started retching and coughing. 'That bloody huh huh cigar of yours. I could smell it all over the huh huh huh house when I went home that day. And after huh huh that she left. Poor little huh huh huh girl.' He started to sweat. 'I think I want to be—' Hillier surveyed him without favour: a middle-aged man with an acquired Russian dumpiness, dressed in a dark blue shiny Russian suit, bagged and stained, its tailoring evoking an earlier age, a nonentity to whom was strapped a large mad talent. He pointed a gargoyling mouth to the concrete floor. Nothing came up, or down.

'Take deep breaths,' said Hillier gently. 'Nobody's going to make you do anything you don't want. Tell me what you've been doing all these years. Tell me what they've done to you.'

Roper breathed deep and rackingly, coughing up strings of spittle. 'I've been on fuel,' he said. 'Rockets. Cosmonauts. They've not done anything to me. They've left me alone.'

'No indoctrination?'

'Bloody nonsense. The scientific premises of Marxism are out of date. I told them that. They agreed.'

'Agreed, did they?'

'Of course they agreed. Self-evident. Look, I think I feel a bit better. Did that chap say something about coffee?'

'It's coming. But if you've seen through Marxism why the hell do you want to stay here? What's wrong with coming back to the West?'

'I spoke too soon. I feel awful again.'

'Oh, for Christ's sake snap out of it, man. Listen. They'll welcome you with brass bands when you get home. Can't you see, it'll be a marvellous bit of propaganda, apart from every-thing else. It's only a matter of getting over that wall. I've got a fake passport for you and a false beard—'

'A false beard? Oh, that's—that's—' He started to cough again.

'There's a British ship in the harbour. The *Polyolbion*. We'll be in Istanbul tomorrow. Come on, man. That wall looks easy.'

'Hillier,' said Roper soberly. 'Hillier, listen to me. I wouldn't go back to England not even if they paid me a hundred thousand pounds a year.' He paused as though he expected Hillier to say that it was roughly about that sum that was proposed in the letters he carried. Then he said: 'Its nothing to do with the government, believe me. It's to do with history.'

'Oh God, Roper, don't be so damned frivolous.'

'Frivolous you call it, frivolous? What's the name of that ship you've got out there?'

'The *Polyolbion*. But I don't see what that's—'

'It's the *Perfidious Polyolbion* it ought to be called. There are some very good historians here, let me tell you, and they take history seriously, not like your lot back in Perfidious Polyolbion. They went into that business of my ancestor who was killed for his faith. They've told me never to forget, and by God they're right. That bloody flowery tepid country where bygones are always bygones. I can see him now, flesh of my flesh, screaming in agony as the flames licked him, and everybody laughing and joking. And I'm supposed to forget about that and say it was all a big mistake and no hard feelings and let's shake hands and go and have a pint of tepid creamy English bitter in the local.'

'But it's true, Roper. We've got to forget history. It's a burden we've got to shed. We can't get anything done if we carry all that dead weight on our backs.'

'Martyrs stand outside history,' said Roper. 'Edward Roper's clock stopped at two minutes to four. Fifteen fifty-eight. Martyrs are witnesses for the light, even though their lights are put out and their clocks stopped. That poor burned man may have been on the wrong track, but at least he had the right dream. The dream of a world society with man redeemed from sin. He saw Europe breaking up into little mean squabbling nations, and then usury creeping in and capitalism and wasteful wars. He had a vision of wide plains.'

'The Russian Steppes?'

'Laugh if you like. You always were one for laughing. You've never had a serious thought in your life. You've gone over lock stock and barrel to the bloody English.'

'I *am* bloody English. So are you.' Hillier started. 'What's that noise?'

'Rain, that's all, just rain. Not the piddling little rain of England and the measly little bit of English sun. It's not like that here. Here it's all big stuff.'

Big stuff. Rain beat on the roof like the fists of a people's revolution. 'This rain is perfect,' said Hillier. 'This is just the weather for a get-away.'

'That's right,' said Roper. 'Capitalist intrigues and ambushes and spyings and wars. Guns and get-away cars. Disguises. If I went back to the West they wouldn't use me for the conquest of space. Oh, no. Has England ever tried to put a man into space? Don't make me laugh,' he said grimly.

'We can't afford it,' shouted Hillier. The rain was near-deafening.

'No,' shouted Roper back. He was looking a lot better. as if all he'd needed was rain. 'But you can afford to be in bloody NATO and have spies and ICBMs and—Here.' He fumbled in an inner pocket. 'Here, read this.' It was a curling photostat of something. 'Whenever I start weakening and thinking of the bloody village green and British tommies nursing babies and what they call justice and democracy and fair play—whenever I think of the House of Commons and Shakespeare and the Queen's corgis I have a look at this. Read it, go on, read it.'

'Look, Roper, we haven't got time—'

'If you don't read it I'll scream for help.'

'You're screaming already. Russian rain isn't on your side. What is it, anyway?'

'It's an extract from Hearne's *British Martyrs*. Not a book I'd ever met before. But they had it in Moscow. Read it.'

Hillier read: 'Edward Roper was drawn to the marketplace in a cart. A large crowd had collected and there were many children whom their parents had brought along for the bloody, or fiery, entertainment. When Roper appeared, dressed only in shirt and trunks and hose, a great cry was raised: Have at the caitiff, he is a blasphemer, death to heresy, to the flames with him, etc. Roper smiled, even bowed, but this was taken as an impudent mockery and it intensified the clamour of vilification. Men piled kindling round the stake; it would take quickly, for the weather had long been dry. Roper, still smiling, was pushed towards it, but he said in a voice clear and unwavering: "If I cannot avoid my fate then I will walk towards it with no rough impulsion. Leave me be." And so he made his way with steady step and unhandled by the gross ministers of his martyrdom to the waiting stake, arm of Christ's tree. Before they bound him to it, he took from the bosom of his shirt a single red rose and said: "Let not this emblem of Her Majesty and of the royal house which bore her perish with me. I pray that she and her kin and indeed all her subjects, however misguided and naughtily blind to the light, may escape the fire." Whereupon he cast the rose, a full-blown June one, into the crowd, which knew not what to do with it. If they rent and dispetalled it, as having lain in the breast of a heretic and traitor, that would have been a kind of *lèse-majesté*. They seemed anxious to rid themselves of it while leaving it unscathed, so it passed swiftly to the back of the mob, where one took it and it was not seen again, though it has been said that it was kept pressed as a token of martyrdom in a book of devotions later lost. Roper was now asked if he would make his peace with God before the kindling was touched with the brand that was ready and waiting. He said: "See how that flame dissolves in the sunlight. It is a sad thing to be leaving the sun, but I know that I shall dissolve, through the agony of my burning, into the greatest sun of all. As for prayer, I pray that the Queen and this whole realm be brought back, in God's good time, to the true faith whereof I am, though bad and unworthy, a steadfast witness." At that moment the sun disappeared into the clouds, and some of the mob grew frightened as if this was a portent. And then the sun emerged again and they renewed their shouts and jeers. Roper, bound to the stake like a bear, said gaily: "Let me taste your fire. If I cry out it will be but my body crying, not my soul. I pity my poor body, as Christ on the cross must have pitied his, and in a manner beg forgiveness of it. But it will be the true witness and these impending flames ennoble it. God bless you all." He composed himself to prayer and the kindling took quickly, the crowd groaning and shouting the while though some little children cried. The fire was built up speedily with dry twigs and branches and soon small logs, and the body of Edward Roper tasted the fire. He screamed high and loud as his garments blazed, then his skin, then his flesh. Then through the smoke and flames his disfigured head, the hair an aureole, was seen to loll. Mercifully soon his death was consummated. The mob waited, in a double sweat of sun and fire, till the roasted flesh and inner organs, including the stout heart, fell into the fire, hissing and cooking; they waited till the executioner crushed the blackened bones into a powder. Then they went home or about their business, and it was noted that many who had cried out on Roper the most loud were now reduced to silence. So it may have been that the work of a martyr or witness to the light was already beginning.'

Hillier looked up, inevitably moved. Roper said:

'Not all this Russian rain can quench those flames.' Hillier said:

'This took place in 1558, did it?'

'You know it did.' The rain had grown discouraged; the fists on the roof beat more feebly.

'And it seems to have taken place in summer.'

'Yes. You can see that from the rose and the sun and the sweat. Dirty English bastards, defiling a summer's day.'

'Well,' said Hillier, 'you bloody fool, it didn't happen in the reign of Queen Elizabeth I. Elizabeth didn't come to the throne till the November of 1558. The Queen that put your ancestor to death was Bloody Mary. You bloody benighted idiot, Roper. Curse your stupidity, you stupid idiot. Your ancestor was a witness for the Protestant faith.'

'That's not true. That can't be true.' Roper was very pale; the eye-twitch went like clockwork; he started to hiccup again: *ikota ikota.*

'You call yourself a bloody scientist, but you haven't even the sense to look up the facts. Your family must have been late converts, and then this story must have passed into their archives, all wrong, totally bloody wrong. Oh, you incredible idiot.'

'You're lying. Where's your *ikota* evidence?'

'In any reference book. Look it up tomorrow, unless, of course, your Russian pals have kindly falsified history for you. In any case, what difference does it make whether he was burned by a Catholic or a Protestant queen? It was still the foul and filthy English, wasn't it? You can still go on feeling bitter and fuelling rockets to point against the nasty treacherous West. But you're still a bloody unscientific fool.'

'But *ikota*—But *ikota ikota*—They've always said that Catholicism would have been on the right lines if it hadn't been for the religious *ikota* content. Capitalism they said was *ikota* a Protestant thing. I won't have it that he died for capitalism *ikota*. Something's gone wrong somewhere. Your history *ikota* books have gone all wrong.'

'What your pals do, Roper, is to choose an approach appropriate to their subject. They found the right one for you all right. And they knew you wouldn't have any historical dates among your scientific tomes. And, anyway, it won't alter things for you even now, will it? You're committed, aren't you, you silly bastard?'

Roper's hiccups suddenly stopped, but the twitch went on. 'I suppose you could say that Protestantism was the first of the great revolutions. I must think this out when I get time. Somebody said that somewhere, in some book or other, I can't remember the name. That world peace and the classless society could only come about through the death agony of an older order.'

'Oh, I can give you all that. Thesis and antithesis and synthesis and all that Marxist nonsense. Socialism had to come out of capitalism. It certainly couldn't have come out of Catholic Christianity. So you can still go on as you are, you bloody fool. Edward Roper can still go on being a martyr for a historical process that Mary Tudor was trying to hold back. You're all right, Roper. You don't have to alter your position. But don't talk to me about intellectual integrity and the importance of working from incontrovertible data. You came over here for reasons other than the martyrdom of poor bloody Edward Roper. That's just an emotional booster. You came over here because of a process that began with that German bitch. You needed a faith and you couldn't have any faith either in religion or what you used to call your country. It's all been quite logical. I even sympathise. But you're coming back with me, Roper. That's what I've been sent out for. This is my last job, but it's still a job. And I've always prided myself on doing a good job.'

'Bravo,' said a voice from the door. It had opened silently. 'But, and I'm genuinely sorry about this, nobody's going back with anybody. I too like to do a good job.' Hillier frowned, looking up at the man in the white raincoat who pointed, in an attitude of relaxed grace, a gun with a silencer attached. He thought he knew the man but he couldn't be sure. 'Wriste?' he said, incredulous.

'*Mister* Wriste,' smiled the man. 'The honorific is in order. My stewardship, Mr Hillier, is more exalted than you supposed.'

FIVE

'I THOUGHT,' SAID ROPER reproachfully, 'you were the man who was bringing us some coffee.'

'There was a man,' said Wriste. 'His carrying of coffee made him easier to hit. I may have hit him too hard. One always expects Russian skulls to be tough, but one forgets that the Soviet Union comprises many ethnic types. There must be some very delicate skulls, I should think, in a citizenry so various and far-flung. However, this man is sleeping—perhaps for ever, who knows?—in a bower of the most delicious roses. Red roses, Mr Roper.' He smiled.

'How do you know about red roses?' asked Roper.

'A gentleman called Theodorescu—Mr Hillier knows him well—has a Xerox copy of your autobiography. A work of no great literary merit, Mr Roper, but factually it is not uninteresting. One of the facts that Theodorescu has not, despite his collecting zeal, yet collected is the fact of my identity and office. I cleaned his cabin and found many enlightening things there. As for your autobiography, Mr Roper, I took the opportunity of photostatting some of the later pages. That business of the red-rosed martyrdom was touching but not relevant to my purpose. My purpose was to understand better the reason for what I have to do. I don't like being a mindless instrument. I like to know why the target chosen is the target chosen.'

'What's all this,' Hillier asked Roper, 'about an autobiography?'

'I admire you, Mr Hillier,' said Wriste. 'You should by rights be gaping at my transformation, unable to say anything at all. I admire you as I admire Mr Theodorescu—you're both tough-minded gentlemen not easily surprised. I think perhaps I shall have some small opportunity of admiring Mr Roper before Mr Roper too is laid among the red roses. He, like you, Mr Hillier, seems undisposed to tremble at my gun. And, talking of guns, be good enough, Mr Hillier, to unbuckle that belt and let it drop to the floor.'

'If I don't?'

'If you don't I shall inflict a painful, though not lethal, wound on Mr Roper here. That wouldn't be fair, would it?' Hillier undid the belt and let it fall. Wriste scooped it towards himself with his foot and then bent swiftly, his own gun-point ticking between Hillier and Roper, to draw the *Tigr* from its open holster and then ram it into his left raincoat pocket. He smiled warmly and said: 'We might as well all be seated. A man has a right to a certain minimal comfort before transacting a painful task, as indeed, have the men who complete the predicate of the transaction.' Hillier sat; Wriste sat; Roper remained seated; one bed only was empty. Hillier studied Wriste. The voice had changed to suit the measured pedantry of his language, which was not unlike that of Mr Theodorescu. There was, thought Hillier, always something of the schoolmaster in the secret agent. The patrician tone that Wriste additionally shared with Theodorescu was not, however, always found in schoolmasters. Wriste's Harrovian tie now seemed no longer a fake. Had he been to songs with Sir Winston Churchill, wondering, as he sang, what Sir Winston had saved the West for? Wriste now wore teeth. They were the finest false teeth that Hillier had ever seen. They were not merely irregular, they were gapped towards the left upper molars, there was a careful spot of decay on a lower canine, an upper incisor carried a glint of gold.

'Well,' said Hillier, 'it seems I was throwing my money away.'

'It wasn't going to be any use to you, Mr Hillier, not where you're going. Where are you going, by the way? Is there anything after death? I often attempt to engage in an eschatological discussion with what I euphemistically term my patients. Most seem frightened of something, else why should they (as they do, believe me, most of them) blubber so? One doesn't blubber for the loss of life—a few more slices of smoked salmon, an hour more of sun, a session of wick-dipping (forgive the vulgarity: it reminds me of burning the candle at both ends), a few more wine-bubbles up the nose. Perhaps all of us who are engaged in this sort of work—international intrigue, espionage, scarlet pimpernellianism, hired assassination—seek something deeper than what most people term life, meaning a pattern of simple gratifications.'

'I could have done with some coffee,' said Roper.

'I'm truly sorry about that,' said Wriste. 'No viaticum before the journey. But I think Mr Hillier might be allowed one of his shocking Brazilian cigars. Light up, Mr Hillier, rejoicing in the steadiness of your hand. To me the tremor is reserved: I can never approach that moment of truth unmoved.'

Hillier smoked gratefully. The rain had eased. He felt a peculiar peace though many regrets, the chief of which was about Clara. If he was going to be shot he was not going to be shot just yet: this interim was most precious, all responsibility put off, the ticking seconds essential drops of life's honey, the sweet gold of pure being. He looked almost gently on Wriste. And, of course, something would intervene to scotch the act; something always did. Oneself did not die; that, like the very quiddity of otherness, was for others.

'If you're thinking, Mr Hillier, that there will be a last-minute intervention of salvatory forces, I beg you to put off that hopeless, or hopeful, notion. There were three guards. I have dealt with all of them. In the hotel the junketing of scientists is at its height. There are exhibitions of frog-dancing. There is talk of bringing down the chambermaids to join in the revels. I gather there is something to celebrate—isn't that so, Mr Roper?'

'Breakthrough on the Beta Plan,' mumbled Roper. 'Look here, I think I've got a right to know what's going on. So,' he afterthought, 'has Hillier here.'

'You're quite right, you have a right. I'm here to kill both of you. Totally, let me make this clear, without personal vindictive-ness. I am, as I said, an agent—or, in deference to the myths of your shared religion, let me say an *angel*—of death. I shoot peo-ple for money, but I like to find out why (here's a Shakespearian touch for you) their names are pricked. That lends an intellectual interest. Now, Mr Roper, your death is a sort of pendent to Mr Hillier's. My primary assignment is to kill Mr Hillier. I was paid not in roubles nor in dollars but in sterling—good crisp notes I carry on my person at this moment. Who do you think paid me that money, Mr Hillier?'

'I can't even guess.'

'You *can* guess, but you don't wish to. The revelation would be too shocking. Nevertheless, let us have the totality of the moment of truth. You're going to die very bitterly, Mr Hillier. To be betrayed by the very people you have given your all to, in whose service you have grown gnarled and scarred and seared. That S on your body was a cruel touch. I've worked for Soskice. It's typical of the man. Still, I think you were adequately avenged. One less man for me to work for. I don't know, though. Others are coming up. That man Grimold promises well. The game goes merrily on.'

'Do you mean,' asked Hillier, beginning to feel that he could feel sick, 'that my own people instructed you to kill me?'

'I personally wasn't instructed. Panleth, our agency—delightful name, isn't it? Cosy, somehow. Kill all pan-germs with Panleth—Panleth passed on the assignment. It seems to me, having studied the matter, that there's neither wantonness nor ingratitude in the desire of your late friends to have you killed. I should think you were even given a sporting chance. Naturally, I had a look at that

letter I handed to you when you embarked at Venice. I couldn't
be bothered to decipher it, but I guessed at its content. I should
think there was an apology there for what was coming. There are
gentlemen in England now abed, sleeping sound in the knowledge that the decent thing was done. You should by rights have
spent your voyage puzzling out that message, but you decided to
dedicate it to a sort of fling. A last fling, as it happens. The pattern of things proves you were right to do that. I would have got
you anyway, though not perhaps here. You've had a final rich
spoonful of life. Gorblimey, sir,' he added, in his steward voice,
'that's a bit of a bleedin' understatement.' And, in the Harrow
voice, 'You can be thankful for that.'

'I still want to know *why*,' sweated Hillier.

'I think I can give the answer,' said Roper. 'You know too
much.'

'Too much for *what*?'

'You're being deliberately obtuse,' said Wriste. 'Too much to
be let loose into a retirement. Mr Roper is perfectly right. I
should imagine you've already sold information to Theodorescu.
That money on your naked lap—what a stupid story you told me
about a wager. Your generous hand-outs to me, incidentally,
seem to attest a sense of guilt. Anyway, were you to live you'd
sell more information or even give it away. That you were
brought up a Roman Catholic was always one thing against you.
You left your Church, but you'd probably go back to it in retirement. A sort of hobby, I suppose. As with Mr Roper here, that
old loyalty tended always to militate against another. You could
never be wholly patriotic. Add to this your known sensuality—
itself a kind of substitute for faith—and you have, I should have
thought, enough grounds for a quiet and regretful liquidation.

Think about it, Mr Hillier. Put yourself in the position of those English gentlemen who, when they're not on the golf-course, worry about security.'

Roper seemed less fearful than interested. He frankly leered his admiration of Wriste's lucidity of exposition. He said: 'Where do I come into this?'

'A pendent, as I told you. It was considered, for obvious reasons, better that Mr Hillier should be given his quietus on Soviet soil. You, Mr Roper, were never thought of as more than a mere pretext for getting Mr Hillier here. This will be unpalatable, I know. You are—and I have this on the highest authority—not wanted back in England.'

Roper, despite all he had spat out at Roper-burning England, now seemed to tamp down indignation. 'I'm not having that, you know.'

'Come now, think it over. You've already done your best work. Scientists, like poets, mature early and decay early. It is *young* scientists that are wanted. The stock fictional image of the grey-haired doddering genius being smuggled in or out is totally false. Your value to the Russians is mostly symbolic. The British are more concerned at the moment with luring Alexeyev over to the West than with reclaiming you.'

'Alexeyev?' went Roper. 'But Alexeyev's only a bloody kid.'

'It's the bloody kids that are needed,' said Wriste. The locution, in Wriste's pedantic tones, carried connotations of sacrifice. Ritual, it was all ritual. 'As for the moral implications of your defection, it's only a vocal minority in Parliament that's crying out for your head. A treason-trial would spill too much muck into the headlines. That muck has to be buried, not spread.'

Roper went crimson. Hillier asked: 'What muck?'

'I don't know the whole of it,' said Wriste. 'Those passages of Mr Roper's autobiography that I've read—'

'How did he get hold of that?' asked Roper in red anger. 'That bugger you mentioned—Theo something-or-other—'

Wriste shrugged. 'Apparently you've had a double agent snooping in your vicinity. Perhaps a lab-boy or room-cleaner or something. He sold a Xerox copy of your completed chapters to a man who sold it to a man who sold it to a man who sold it to Mr Theodorescu. Mr Theodorescu is voracious for information. Of course, a typescript—top copy or carbon—is valueless in any market other than the literary. It's holographs that are needed. Though to the student of human motivation, the chronicler of that specific kind that produces the traitor, your typescript isn't without interest. The trouble is that anybody with a moderately inflamed imagination could have written it. And your typescript seems to leave off, as though with fright, on the threshold of the really significant revelation. I should be interested to know why you embarked on this task at all.'

'It was suggested to me,' said Roper, mumbling again. 'Clarify my ideas. Examine myself. It was an exercise. But you still haven't said why—'

'I think all that's clear now, isn't it? The client I have to serve in respect of you, Mr Roper—'

'Look,' said Roper, 'I'm sick to death of this bloody *mister*. I'm *Doctor* Roper, got it? Doctor, doctor, *doctor*.' It was like a stoic cry out of Jacobean drama: *I am Duchess of Malfi still*.

'Alas, *Mister* Roper, your doctorate was taken away from you. It was publicly announced, I gather, but you personally evidently weren't informed. The senate of the university concerned announced that they'd discovered evidences of plagiarism.'

'That's a bloody lie.'

'Probably. But it was in the national interest that you should seem to be a fraud and a fake. The British public could sleep sound. A man of straw had gone over to the Russians. The news of your dedoctorisation, if that's the right term, never appeared in the *Daily Worker*, and certainly *Pravda* wouldn't mention it. You remained ignorant.'

'So did I,' said Hillier. 'A great deal of what you're saying grows more and more suspect.'

'As you please. But you, Mr Hillier, began to opt out of the modern world long before you sent in your resignation. You read mostly menus and the moles on whores' bellies. All this is unimportant. What I say now is far from unimportant. A certain cabinet minister, Mr Roper, became agitated when he learned, at a little dinner party in Albany, that you were to be forcibly repatriated. About the autobiography he knew nothing. I deduced that he feared revelations which would affect him privily if you should be brought to trial. I can guess at the nature of the revelations. If only you had gone further in your autobiography I should know absolutely how this high personage was involved in your career. But no matter. It was important, so far as he was concerned, that you should not return to England. He had made use of Panleth before. It was a matter of trying to make the last government fall. The government's majority was down to two; the member of a certain marginal constituency was known to be suffering from heart disease; Panleth arranged for the progress of that ailment to gallop to a premature consummation. When he learned, in the strictest confidence, that you, Mr Roper, were coming home, he contacted Panleth again. Hence my two assignments, their respective provenances quite independent, united only by place. Panleth is an efficient agency. It looks after its clients and consults their convenience. It takes only ten per cent.'

'Well,' said Roper, more cheerfully, 'you don't have to do the job, do you? You're going to kill Hillier, and Hillier won't be taking me—' He nearly said 'home'.

'Ah, that's not it.' Wriste head-shook sadly.

'You've got your money,' said Hillier. 'You said so. You don't have to kill either of us.'

'I've got *some* money,' said Wriste. 'Not all. You paid me at the beginning of your trip, Mr Hillier, and you were presumably going to pay me at the end. So with these two jobs. Before I can receive the balance—from Department X and Mr Y alike—I have to furnish evidence of the satisfactory fulfillment of the assignments. What I normally take back is a finger—'

'A *finger?*'

'Yes. For the fingerprints. Most of my patients are fingerprinted men. Agents and top-level scientists and so on, men with detailed dossiers. Strange, once you have a dossier you seem potentially to have committed a capital crime. This sort of punishment—' He waved his gun. 'It always hovers. When you've finished that cigar, Mr Hillier, the hawk must swoop.'

'You could,' said Roper, 'cut off a finger and let us go.' He spoke as dispassionately as if his body were a tree to be pruned.

Wriste again shook his head, more sadly than before. 'I've never yet performed an act of other than terminal surgery, though the request has been made often enough. No, gentlemen both, I have my honour, I have my professional pride. If either of you were ever to appear, fingerless but otherwise whole, walking the world smiling, my career would be at an end. Besides, there's a man called the Inspector.'

'Oh, my God,' groaned Hillier.

'Yes, the Inspector. Nobody knows his name, I doubt if any-one's ever seen him, I sometimes doubt whether he really exists. He is perhaps a mere personification of Honour. But it's conve-nient to believe in him. No, no, gentlemen, it's no good.' He took from an inside pocket a plush case, rather finely made, and clicked it open. 'I've never had occasion to use this before,' he said. 'See, there are grooves for two fingers. I have another case, rather well-worn, for the single digit. One man I know, very ambitious, uses a cigar-case, but that seems to me to be crude. I had this specially made by a man in Walthamstow, of all places. I said it was for the accommodation of amputated fingers, and he laughed.'

Hillier could not drag any more smoke from his Brazilian. He had five more in his pocket: what a waste. 'Well,' he said. Roper, as if to ensure that Wriste's token should not disgrace him, though dead, was busily biting his nails.

'Strange, isn't it?' said Wriste dreamily, pulling back the safety-catch. Hillier's eyes were drawn to the weapon; if he and it were to engage in the ultimate intimacy, he had at least to know its name. It was a Pollock 45, beautifully looked after. Wriste was a real professional, but there were elements of corruption in him. This personal interest in his victims would be the death of him, Hillier thought. 'Strange,' repeated Wriste, 'that in a minute or so you will both be vouchsafed the final answer. Religion may be proved all nonsense or else completely vindicated. And the Archbishop of Canterbury and the Pope of Rome cannot in the least profit from your discovery. Top secret. Locked drawers. A safe with an unbreakable combination. There may be a quattro-cento heaven, there may be a Gothic hell. Why not? Our aseptic rational world does not have to be a mirror of ultimate reality. Hell with fire and vipers and mocking devils for ever and ever and ever. At this moment I always survey my victims with a kind of awe. The knowledge they are going to possess is the only knowledge worth having. Would either of you gentlemen like to pray?'

'No,' cried stout Roper. 'A load of bloody nonsense.'

'Mr Hillier?'

Hillier swallowed on a vision of Clara. He had, even though retrospectively, defiled that image. His whores and victims marched, in swirling mist, over an endless plain, their formation S-shaped, pointing at him with three-fingered hands, lipless, noseless, only great eye-lamps staring. 'A form of words,' he muttered. 'No more.' He knew he didn't really believe that. Roper was a better man than he. 'Oh my God,' he recited, 'I am sorry and beg pardon for all my sins and detest them above all things—'

'Bloody nonsense,' cried Roper. He seemed determined, like Kit Marlowe, to die swearing. 'Cunting balderdash.'

'—Because they deserve Thy dreadful punishment, because they have crucified my loving saviour Jesus Christ—'

'Bumfluffing bleeding burking tripe. When you're dead you're finished with.'

'—And most of all because they offend Thine infinite goodness. And I firmly resolve by the help of Thy grace never to offend Thee again—'

'That's one resolution that will be fulfilled,' delivered Wriste.

'—And carefully to avoid the occasions of sin.'

There was a timid knock at the door of the little hut. Hillier's heart leaped. Never pray, someone—Father Byrne?—had once said, for the thing of immediate advantage. Wriste joined Roper in swearing, though more softly. Then he said: 'This is awkward. This I had not expected.'

'You talk too much,' said Roper, 'that's your trouble. You could have got this job over nicely if it hadn't been for all that yak.' It seemed a sincere reproof.

'A third,' said Wriste. 'Innocent, perhaps. A pity. Nothing in it for me. Totally gratuitous.' Brooding on the economics of death he pointed his gun at the door. 'Come in,' he called.

The door opened. A boy stood there, draped against the dying rain in a big man's jacket.

'Well,' said Wriste, in his steward's accent, 'if it ain't little Mister bloody Knowall. I'm truly sorry about this, son, but I don't see any way out. Come in, right in,' he gun-waved, using the patrician tones. 'How did you know we were here?'

Roper frowned on Alan Walters as though he had come to a class of his without registering for it. Alan said:

'A bit of a whiff of cigar-smoke. Not much, just a bit. I lost you.' He looked apologetically at Hillier. 'I lost you on the road. And then I looked in the hotel, but it's all filthy drunkenness there.'

'Clever boy,' purred Wriste. 'That stepmother of yours will be pleased to have you out of the way. I wonder if it would be prudent to seek a small emolument.'

'I was going to put *her* out of the way,' said Alan. 'This seems good territory for killing people. But then I thought: first things first. I always knew you were a phoney.'

'Oh, naturally. You know everything, don't you? Including the correct postures for pederastic gratification.'

'That had to be,' said Alan. 'It was the only way. There are some awful men in the world, you included. But you weren't clever enough. You told me you'd spent the war in an Australian prison. And the next minute you were talking about having an FFI when you came back off leave. I always knew you weren't to be trusted. You'd never do anything without getting money for it first.'

'I'm getting no money for this,' said Wriste. 'Take your hands from underneath that outsize jacket. Join them together. Close your eyes. Say your little boy's prayers. You can precede these gentlemen. The *antipasto,* the Italians call it. Theodorescu would like that. Come on, boy, we've wasted enough time as it is.'

'You bloody neutral,' cursed Alan. 'You're going where all the neutrals go.' Dull fire spat through the jacket, leaving a smoking hole. In great-eyed surprise Wriste grabbed, rebus, his wrist, cracked bone with blood taking breath to fountain out. He watched, almost with tears, his gun drip from his fingers and fall without noise on one of the massage-cots. Alan now had the Aiken, silencer and all, in the open. 'Now try this,' he said. He aimed at Wriste's pained surprise through the fumes of frying smoked bacon. He thudded fire at the nose and got the right eye. The eye leaped out on its string as in a surrealist montage. The socket leered as the blood prepared to charge, and then the whole face was black fluidity mounted on a falling body. The mouth, independent of the smashed brain, cried 'Cor' in Cockney. The left fingers, like rats in shipwreck, clawed at a cot, seeking to save themselves. Wriste's going down was leisurely, noisy, the body's indulging itself in its closing scene. There was a crack and the sound of spatter from the trousers. Then Wriste was only a thing.

'I think I'd better be sick,' said Alan. 'It's time somebody was sick.' He went and stood, like a naughty boy, in the corner. His shoulders heaved as he tried to throw up the modern world.

SIX

'IT'S BACK TO those days,' twitched Roper in distaste, fascinated by the well-dressed and Harrovian rubbish on the floor. Hillier knew which days he meant. 'There are people bent on making a butcher's shop of the whole world.' He did not mean Alan, on whom he twitched a wondering and nearly grateful look. To Alan Hillier said:

'Get some fresh air. There'll be time enough to say thank you. I won't say it now except just thank you. But go and get some fresh air.' The boy nodded, out of rhythm with his empty spasms, then opened the door and went out. He'd dropped the smoking Aiken on to the nearest cot, wiping his hands against each other, as though that, the corpse-maker, were itself the corpse. From the outer darkness came the noise of song and glass-crashing. 'And now,' said Hillier, when the door was closed again, 'we'll have to be quick.'

'We? What do you mean—we? This is none of my business.'

'Oh, isn't it? You've been concealing things from me, Roper. Going on about bloody martyrdom and red roses when all the time there was something else. What have you been doing with cabinet ministers? I'll find out, never fear. In the meantime, help me to get these trousers down.'

'Disguised as a steward, was he?' said Roper, not helping. 'You just never know, do you? Harmless-looking people waiting and watching, grinning and friendly but always ready to pounce. *Ikota ikota*,' he hiccuped as Hillier exposed dead Wriste's left flank. 'Ergh.' He screwed up his nose. 'What the hell *ikota* is all this for?'

'This,' Hillier said, 'is me out of the way. Me done for, finished. The ultimate opting-out.' He took out his pocket-knife and
then, digging deep, scored an S on Wriste's unresisting skin.
Then he lighted a *Handelsgold* Brazilian, the first of his posthu-
mous ones, puffing gratefully.

'It's a desecration,' said Roper. 'R.I.P. He's paid the price.'

'Not quite.' By rapid pumping with his breath, Hillier
inflamed the tip of the Brazilian to a red-hot poker-glow. 'This is
a very inadequate substitute for the real thing,' he said, applying
the first burn to the S-channel. 'But it will serve.' To the smoked-
bacon smell of the gun, still lingering, a richer more meaty aroma
began to be added.

'What the hell—*ikota ikota*—'

'Tonight,' said Hillier, 'in the L-shaped cabin we're sharing,
you'll see exactly what all this is about.'

'I'm not coming. What the hell have I to come for? Where
will *you* be going to, anyway?'

Hillier looked up and stared for four seconds. 'I just hadn't
thought,' he said. 'Of course, we haven't had time to take all this
in, have we?' He almost let the cigar go out. 'Good God, no.
We're both exiles, aren't we?' He bellowsed the end red again
and continued, delicate as a musician, his scoring.

'I'm home,' said Roper. 'This is where I live. The Soviet
Union, I mean. *I'm* not in exile.' He coughed at the smoke and the
smell of searing. 'I'm better off than you are.' And Hillier saw
himself from the wooden ceiling—in stolen Soviet police-
uniform, drawing an S in fire on a corpse with a ruined face, the
security-men watching at Southampton, at London Airport, just
to be on the safe side, the sawn-off token undelivered. 'Home,'
delivered Roper, 'is where you let things gather dust, where

things get lost in drawers and the waiter in the corner restaurant knows your name. It's also where the work's waiting.'

'And a woman waiting? Wife or daughter or both?'

'I've got over all that,' said Roper. 'What I mean is, in that old way. There are some very nice girls at the *Institut*. We have a meal and a drink and a dance. I'm not in need of anything.'

Hillier finished his pokerwork, dusting off bits of charred hair and skin. Then, without help from Roper, he pulled the trousers up and, grunting with effort and distaste, secured them to their braces. 'This raincoat will be useful,' he said.

'Defile the corpse and strip it, eh?' twitched Roper. 'Your work's very dirty work, Hillier. Not like mine.'

'Let's see what—' I'm entitled to this, thought Hillier, drawing out from the dead man's inner pocket a very fat wallet. Sterling, his own dollars, roubles. 'Roubles,' he showed Roper. 'Don't feel too secure when you talk about home. How do you know Wriste wasn't doing a job for Moscow as well as for those bastards I called my friends? A defecting scientist shot when a British ship was in port. You were going on about reading the Douay Version. Perhaps they know you'll be returning to religion one of these days—'

'Never. A load of balderdash.'

'Who can ever tell what he'll do in the future? Even tomorrow? For that matter, look at me tonight, making a good act of contrition.'

'I was ashamed of you,' twitched Roper.

'One of these days you'll be defiling your pure scientific thought with Christian sentimentality. Or getting out of Russia to kiss the Pope's toe, taking your formulae with you.'

'Look,' said Roper bluntly. 'Nobody's ever above suspicion.

Do you get that? Those drunks in there are just the same as I am.
It's just something you live with, but it's the same everywhere. It's
the same in bloody awful England. As for that thing there,' meaning brain-smashed, branded, robbed Wriste, 'he told the truth
about that bloke gunning for me in England. That's one thing he
told the truth about. That business about me being too old and losing my doctorate was just a lot of nonsense. But he was right
about the other thing. What I'm going to do now is get back to my
room and have a decent night's kip. I'll take a couple of tablets
first, I think. But I'm home, remember that. And I'm all right.'

'You very nearly weren't.'

'Nor were you.' He grinned for the first time that evening.
'Poor old Hillier. You're in a bloody bad way, aren't you? But
here's something that might be useful to you. You can get the
bastards with this.' And he took from his inner pocket a rather
grubby wad of paper scrawled in blue ink. 'This is the chapter
I've been working on. I don't think I want to push on with my
memoirs now. They served their purpose, clarified things. Here
you are, something to read on the voyage to wherever you're
going. Where *are* you going?'

'First stop Istanbul. I'll think things over there. And there's a
man I've got to see.' Hillier took the wad. 'You've become a great
one for giving me things to read. I had things for you to read—
letters. But that was a long time ago. Well, I suppose we'd both
better get out of here.'

'It was nice seeing you after all these years. You could, you
know,' Roper afterthought, 'stay here if you wanted. I should
imagine they'd find you useful.'

'That's all over for me. I'm retiring. I don't think I like contemporary history much.'

'Some aspects of it are very interesting.' He looked at the ceiling. 'Up there, I mean. Men in space. We'll be making the moon any day now.'

'A barren bloody chunk of green cheese. Well, you're welcome to it.'

The door opened and Alan rushed in, his face green cheese. 'There's a *thing* out there. Something crawling and moaning. It was trying to follow me.'

It was Roper who picked up the Aiken from the cot. 'Your friend here,' he told Alan, 'is finished with all this sort of thing. Leave it to me.' He strode bravely out in a night that, the baser smells of contemporary history now subsiding, was full of rain-wet flower-scents. Meanwhile Hillier looked down on the boy, that former horrid precocious brat, with compassion and a love referred from that other love. Whether, like a father, to hide the boy's distress in his arms was something he couldn't decide. He said:

'I think I can guess what the crawling thing is. There's nothing to be frightened about. Well.' he added, 'I let you in for more than you could have dreamed possible when you left Southampton. Should I say I'm sorry?'

'I can't think, I just can't think.'

Hillier, seeing Theodorescu leering inside him, went hard for an instant. 'And yet,' he said, 'you seduced yourself into becoming a member of the modern world.' He shuddered, watching the lecherous breathing bulk of Theodorescu descend on the thin young body. 'You must have wanted that gun very badly.'

'I didn't know it was yours. I swear. And all I wanted to do really was to frighten her.'

'In that vast dinner-eating crowd?'

'I thought I'd get her alone. What I really mean is I didn't think. I just didn't think.' He began to cry.

Hillier put his arms round the boy's shoulders. 'I'll look after you,' he said. 'You're my responsibility now. Both of you.'

Roper could be heard speaking bad Russian. There was also the noise of skirring feet, as though a man was being half-carried. Hillier went out to help. It was the guard, sorely thumped by Wriste but not killed. A skullcap of dried blood sat on his hair; on his soaked suit a few red rose-petals clung. Roper said, weightily through his panting, *Vot tam chelovyek*—there's the man.' The guard, open-mouthed, glazed, frowning in rhythm with his pain, saw but did not recognise. The shop-assistant's face looked bewildered, as if he had been unaccountably accused of short-changing. Wriste still had half a face. That half ought, by rights, to go. Perhaps that could be left to Roper. A totally faceless S-man was required. The guard wanted to lie down. 'And now,' said Roper, 'you two ought to get out of here. Leave everything to me now. One in the eye for old Vasnetsov and Vereshchagin in there. Drunk as coots and supposed to be in charge of security. A bit of a shambles all round. One in the eye all right, having to leave everything to an Englishman. We'll show them all yet.'

'See what I mean?' said Hillier. 'The old Adam coming out.'

'None of us is perfect. There's a bloke on this conference who says that the Ukrainians could knock spots off the Muscovites. The thing to do is to get on with the job.'

'I borrowed this jacket,' said Alan, taking it off, 'from a man asleep in the vestibule. Will you give it back to him?'

Roper took out a mess of old envelopes from the inner pocket. He snorted. 'This belongs to Vrubel. I'm going to have some fun here, I can se see that. I don't care much for Vrubel.'

'We'll have to get a tram,' said Hillier. His tunic seemed crammed with passports and money. 'When we've gone, would you mind completing the image—' He made a *coup de grâce* pantomime. Roper seemed to understand. 'With his,' he added. 'I'll have my own back.'

Roper surrendered the Aiken with a smirk of regret. 'Nice little job. I assumed you wouldn't be needing it any more.'

'It's unwise to assume anything. You should know that, being a scientist. I fancy I have just one final job to do. On my own account.'

'Well, it's been nice seeing you,' said Roper, as though Hillier had just dropped in from next door to enjoy an evening of referred crapula, fear, threats and assassination. To Alan he said: 'You've been a good boy,' as though he'd sat in the corner with cake and lemonade, causing no trouble. Then he twitched a cheery goodbye.

Going down the winding path to the coast-road, Hillier and Alan heard a very dull thud from the massage-hut. The S-man was now fully there. Alan shivered. Hillier tried to laugh, saying: 'Imagine you're in a novel by Conrad. You know the sort of thing: "By Jove, I thought, what an admirable adventure this is, and here am I, a young man in the thick of it."'

'Yes,' said Alan. 'A very young man. But ageing quite satisfactorily.'

Hillier saw trolley-sparks and heard, over the sea's swish and shingle-shuffle, the familiar rattle. 'By Jove,' he said, not in Conrad now but in Bradcaster after an evening at the cinema with Roper, running for the last tram, 'we'll have to—' They arrived breathless at the stop just as it began to rattle off. Hillier groaned under his breathlessness as he saw who was sitting opposite.

'So it's you,' nodded the man. 'And if you think it's a bit suspicious me going off early like this, well then, you can go on thinking. I didn't feel well. You shouldn't have done what you did, threatening me like that. And I see that all you've managed to pull in is that kid there. Easy, isn't it, taking kids to the police-station and getting them to talk.'

'What does he say about me?' asked Alan fearfully.

'All right,' said Hillier and, to the man, '*Zamolchi!*'

'That's all you can say, isn't it? But you won't say *zamolchi* to that kid there. Oh, no, you'll get him to talk. Well, he won't say anything about me because he doesn't know me and I don't know him. It's the higher-ups you ought to be going for, the head waiter and the *Direktor* and all that lot. All right, I've said my say.' And he took out his old copy of *Sport* and intently examined a photograph of a women's athletic team. But when the tram arrived on the boulevard with the mulberries and Hillier and Alan started to get off, he called:

'*Samozvanyets!*'

'What does that mean?' asked Alan.

'That's what *you* called me that evening in the bar. When you recognised that I knew nothing about typewriters. I think,' said Hillier, 'I'd better turn myself into a sort of neutral.'

'Don't say that.'

'Cap off and raincoat on. This is where my imposture starts to end.'

A boy and a bareheaded man in a white raincoat and riding-boots walked quickly down the rain-wet road that led to the dock-gates. Suddenly the quiet that should have cooed with sailors and their pick-ups erupted into mature festal cries and the roar and spit of an old motor. Its exhaust pluming, a crammed grey bus was going their way, though somewhat faster. 'It's our crowd,' said Alan, wincing on the 'our'. 'They've had their gutsing dinner. *She*'ll be there, bitch.'

'In that case,' said Hillier, 'we'll have to run again. She mustn't get on board before we do.'

'Why?'

'There will be a time,' puffed running Hillier. 'Be patient.'

The well-dined passengers were already leaving the bus by the time Alan and Hillier reached the gates. 'Too many figs,' said somebody. 'I warned her.' A woman, not Mrs Walters, was being helped off, green. There was a powerful tang of raw spirits being laughed around.

'There she is,' said Alan. 'Last off, with that blond beast.' They pushed into the heart of the passport-waving queue, Hillier still panting. Soon there would be no more of that, slyness and nimbleness and hatchets; he foresaw mild autumn sun, a garden chair, misty air flawed by the smoke of mild tobacco. He felt for a passport and found several. He was inclined to shuffle them and deal at random—bearded Innes; dead Wriste; *samozvanyets* Jagger; true, shining, opting-out Hillier: take one, any.

'By God,' said a man to Hillier, 'you've been attacking the fleshpots and no error.' He punched Hillier lightly in the peaked cap that was hidden under the belted raincoat. 'Nice pair of boots you've got there, old man,' said somebody else. 'Where did you pick those up? Look, Alice, there's a lovely bit of Russian leather.' People, including the guard at the gate, began to peer at Hillier's legs: a space was hollowed out round him, the better to peer. 'I don't feel at all the thing,' said the green woman. Hillier shoved in, showing a picture of himself. The gate-guard compared truth and image sourly, the speed of his comparison forming a slowish nod, then grunted Hillier through. He and Alan quickly inserted themselves into a complex of belching men but found their shipward progress too slow. They sped to the view of the ship, lighted, immaculate, safe, England. But England wasn't safe any more. At the foot of the gangway well-fleshed men and women, panting under a load of Black Sea provender safely stowed, were starting to labour up. Up there he saw no Clara smiling in greeting and relief. The rail was lined with jocular wavers, but Hillier remained careful, thrusting his nose, as into a blown Dorothy Perkins, into a fat back and keeping it there. 'Have a good time, sir?' asked a voice at the top of the gangway. It was Wriste's winger-pal. 'Ta once again for the Guinness,' he added. Hillier said to Alan: 'See you in Clara's cabin,' and then rushed towards the nearest companionway, seeking A-Deck. The ship hummed with emptiness, but it would soon fill with drink-seekers, thirsty for something dryer, colder, less fierily crude than what Yarylyuk could afford. He dashed down corridors of aseptic perfume and discreet light, at last finding his own. Here was Mrs Walter's cabin.

Inside, the bedclothes hardly rucked, snored a calm sleeper: S. R. Polotski, aged 39, born Kerch, married, the dirty swine. Hillier rapidly took off Wriste's raincoat, emptied the tunic of all that he owned or had acquired, then stripped to his shirt and pants. He neatly laid S. R. Polotski's uniform on the bedside chair and placed his boots at the foot of the bunk. Then, raincoat on again, the pockets stuffed, he went to his own cabin. He opened the door cautiously: there was no smell as of harmful visitors, only the ghost of Clara's too-adult perfume lingered. He poured himself the last of the Old Mortality and drank it neat. He regretted the end of that useful, though money-loving, shipboard Wriste, then he shuddered to think how easy it was to regard a human being as a mere function. Was that what was meant by being neutral—a machine rather than a puppet-stage for the enactment of the big fight against good, or against evil? He put on a lightweight suit, knotting the tie with care. He was going to see Clara. His heart thumped, but no longer with fear.

But it was with fear that he listened outside her door, his hand on the knob. Those rhythmical screams, inhuman but like the noises made by some human engine—the screaming machine that welcomes holiday gigglers to the sixpenny Chamber of Horrors. He went in. On the bunk lay Alan prone, screaming. Clara was sitting on the bunk with him, her hair disarrayed in distress, going 'Hush now, hush dear, everything will be all right.' Seeing Hillier with hard hardly-focused eyes, she said: 'You've done this to us. I hate you.' And she got up and made for Hillier with her tiny claws, scarlet-painted beyond her years as in a school parody of flesh-tearing. Hillier could have wept out the whole horror of life in a single concentrated spasm. But he grabbed her hands and said:

'We all have to be baptised. Both your baptisms have been heroic.'

From the corridor came louder screams than any of which Alan was capable. Full rich womanly outrage called. Alan was shocked into silence, listening, tear-streaked and open-mouthed. They listened all three. Poor S. R. Polotski, the dirty swine. Soon there were harsh male voices under the screams, two of them sounding marine and official.

'Unheroic,' said Clara as they heard protesting Russian somehow being kicked off. Her hands relaxed.

'Shall we,' said Hillier, 'have a large cold supper in my cabin? I'll ring for—Stupid of me,' he added.

'But that's the best way to look at him, I suppose,' said Alan. 'Just somebody nobody can ring for any more.'

SEVEN

From Roper's Memoirs*

THE TROUBLE WITH LUCY WAS she wanted to be in charge. She wanted to be a wife, but I already had one of those, wherever she was, and I didn't want another. It was all right Lucy coming to the house and giving it a bit of a tidy-up and insisting on getting laundry together and cooking the odd meal. That was all right, although the meals were always finicking what she called exotic dishes, vine-leaves wrapped round things and lasagne and what-not. It was better to have these working parties in the house (though what did I really want with a house now?) so that she could be sort of swallowed up among the others while we got on with this pamphlet about science in society. Some nights when we'd finished work and I tried to sneak off on my own saying I'd got to see somebody, she used to ask who I was going to see, and then I couldn't think who I was going to see, not knowing many

* Clara and Alan calmer now but sent to bed with a couple of sleeping tablets each. The *Polyolbion* throbbing away from Yarylyuk towards Istanbul. I have sent a radio message to the address given by T, namely Cumhuriyet Caddesi 15. Another steward answered my ring, saying Wriste unaccountably not reported back to ship. I sit here with the crabbed royal blue script of Roper and a new bottle of Old Mortality. All right, Roper, let's hear all about it.

people in London now except those we both worked with. All I
wanted was a quiet sandwich in a pub and then perhaps to go to
the cinema, all on my own. But sometimes I had to take work
home and then she said she'd cook something for me, so as not to
waste my time doing it myself, and she'd be quite content to sit
quiet, so she said, with a book. I saw that if I didn't watch out
we'd be on to sex, and that was something I didn't particularly
want, not with Lucy anyway.

Why not? I suppose she was attractive enough in her very
thin way, but I'd got used to a different sort of woman, bad as she
was. But the badness wasn't her fault, I kept telling myself. If
there'd been no woman in the house I wouldn't have been per-
petually reminded of Brigitte, reminded that is by contrast. I still
had something of Brigitte, namely photographs, and it was
because Lucy was around that I took to comforting myself with
photographs which recalled happier times—Brigitte on a rock at
the seaside posing as a sort of Lorelei, Brigitte wearing her frothy
décolleté evening dress, Brigitte demure in a simple frock. They
were a comfort sometimes to take to bed.*

It was when I went down with a bit of stomach trouble that
things got a bit out of hand. I rang up to say I wouldn't be coming to the lab and then I went back to bed with a hot water bottle.
It was I think gastric flu. I knew there was no way out of what
was going to happen that evening, but I felt too ill to care very
much. Well, she turned up at about five, having got off early and
everybody would wink and know why, and then she was in her
element, florence nightingaling all over the house in for some
reason her white lab coat. She gave me bicarb and hot milk and

* Oh no, Roper. You never even did that at school.

two hot water bottles (one of them was Brigitte's and as if Brigitte was being vindictive even in her absence it started to leak so I threw it out) and smoothed my Fevered Brow. She said I ought not to be left that night and besides there was the question of seeing how I was in the morning, so she insisted on making up the bed in the spare room. Naturally I was grateful but I knew there would be a Reckoning.

The Reckoning came three days later when I was feeling a good deal better and thinking of getting up. She said no, see how I was when she came back that evening and perhaps the next day something might be done about my getting up. It was a very cold day in late November and she returned from work shivering. I suppose I should never have suggested to her that she have a hot water bottle that night instead of me, me being very warm now, and I told her not to take the one that leaked. But she did, either by accident or design, perhaps the latter, and she came into my room to say that she couldn't possibly sleep in a damp bed. Well, there we were then. She just lay there and I just lay there as though we were side by side in lounging chairs on a crowded deck, then she said she still felt very cold and came closer. Then I said: You'll catch my flu. She said: There are things more important than catching flu. Before I knew what was happening we'd started. I suppose the sweating got rid of the last of the flu, and I sweated a long time.

I sweated a long time because I was able to just go on and on, nothing happening to me at all. It was like acting it on the stage. That school group photograph was just about visible in the light from the street lamp and I could see Father Byrne and Hillier and O'Brien and Pereira and the others very dimly. After an hour they must have got very bored with the performance. Mine, anyway. She thought it was marvellous and kept going oh oh darling oh I never knew it could be like this and don't stop. It was all right for her but there was nothing in it for me. I tried to imagine it was somebody else—a girl in one of the offices with the same black sweater on every day giving off a great aroma of stew and earwax but with huge breasts on her, a half-caste girl singer on the television whose dresses were cut very low so that the camera always deliberately tried to make her look naked, a big-buttocked woman in the local supermarket. All the time I was trying to avoid Brigitte but at last I had to bring her in and then it was different. At last I was able to bring it to an end and then she cried out very loud and afterwards said: Darling, was it as good for you as it was for me?

Somebody in some book on sex said that the biggest sin a man can commit with a woman is to do it and pretend you're doing it with somebody else. That seems to me very mystical. I mean, who knows you're pretending except you? Unless, of course, you're going to bring God into it. What the book should have said was the danger of calling the real woman by the name of the imagined one. But Lucy was very good about that. She even said: Poor darling, you must have loved her very much and she hurt you very badly, didn't she? And then she said: Never mind, when we're really together I'll make you happier than she ever could. And I'll never leave you. What Lucy meant was getting married. We're as good as married now, aren't we, darling, except that I'm still not Mrs Roper. She had a wedding ring though, her dead mother's she said it was, and she would use it as a kind of stimulator in bed, as though she thought that was why married women wore wedding rings.

But she couldn't drive Brigitte out. She was making me bring Brigitte back again. Every night. And she herself had brought all her clothes and little knick-knacks from her flat and then she gave up the flat. But I'd never asked her to come and settle in and share my bed, had I? It was what they call a liberty. But I couldn't tell her to get out, could I? One day she said that people in the Institute were talking and that it was about time I did something about a divorce. So then I went out and got drunk. I wasn't supposed to drink at all now. When Brigitte left I'd started to hit the bottle a bit, but it was Lucy who'd stopped all that. Beer for everyone else at those parties, lemon barley water for me. So it was a big disappointment for Lucy now when I staggered in after closing-time reeking of bitter beer (five pints) and whisky (five John Haigs, large), also *whiskey* in memory of Father Byrne (two small JJs). Why had I been thinking of Father Byrne? Perhaps because of the damnable sex, perhaps because I was homesick and had no home.* Anyway, when I staggered in I fell against things, and Lucy was *bitterly* disappointed. I staggered against a little table with a brown fruit-bowl on it, and in the brown fruit-bowl not fruit but a crouching cat made of blue china. I knocked this over, and the head came off the cat, and then Lucy cried, saying it had belonged to her mother. So I said nobody had asked her to bring it into *my* house and for that matter nobody had asked *her* to bring *herself* into *my* house, so she cried worse. She said nothing of walking out of the house with her bags packed, all she said was that I'd better sleep in the spare room that night and she hoped I'd have one hell of a hangover the next morning, which I did.

---

* You sentimental self-pitying bastard, Roper. You'll be back in the Devil yet, you mark my words.

From now on I didn't much care to go home in the evenings. Damn it, it was my home, or house anyway, and I had a good big damned slice of mortgage still to pay off. But I couldn't order Lucy out, having, in her view, taken advantage of her and allowed her to build up hopes as yet unfulfilled. And this business of it being the biggest sin a man could commit in bed with a woman made me, even though it was all nonsense, feel guilty towards her. I was turning her into a kind of thin Brigitte, although, to be fair to myself, it was always Lucy who made the first bed-move. So, although I was in my rights in regarding her as an intruder, I couldn't tell her to get out. But I wasn't going to marry her—oh no. I was still married. What I did most evenings now was to look for Brigitte.

I looked first of all in Soho. There were laws now which forbade prostitutes to parade the streets with little dogs on leads or to walk up and down with their handbags open, waiting for men to come along to tell them they'd got their handbags open. But the laws weren't taken very seriously. Still, I don't think there were as many on the streets as there had used to be, certainly not anywhere near so many as in the great days of opportunity of the war, when the lie was given to the old liberal sociological studies of prostitution which said that women took it up only because they couldn't get any other kind of work. What you saw more of now was women beckoning from doorways and windows and suddenly darting out from the darkness and saying: Want a quickie, darling? I made a very thorough job of my search around Soho—Frith Street, Greek Street, Wardour Street, Old Compton Street, Dean Street, everywhere—but I didn't find Brigitte. In the advertisement-cases of shady tobacconists and bookshops I saw ambiguous announcements: Fifi for Correction

(Leather a Speciality); Yvonne, Artist's and Photographer's Model—40 24 38; Colonic Irrigation administered by Spanish Specialist. Never once did I find anything (like Fräulein with German Novelties) which would lead me to Brigitte. In a pub I found a man who had a brochure—all photographs and telephone numbers—called The Ladies' Directory, but Brigitte wasn't in it. I even went into a police station and said I was looking for my wife, a German girl who, through her innocence, had perhaps let herself be drugged and whiteslaved, but they were very suspicious about that.*

As always happens, I found Brigitte by accident. I went one night to a cinema on Baker Street (nothing I particularly wanted to see; I was just tired and fed up) and afterwards had a couple of small whiskies in a pub just by Blandford Street. A woman entered, well dressed, well made-up, well spoken, bringing in with her a synthetic smell of rose gardens† and a husky Dietrich kind of voice. She said to the landlord: Bottle of Booth's, Fred, and forty Senior. Certainly mavourneen, he said. She crackled a lot of five-pound notes in her bag. I wondered about the mavourneen and then caught on: Bridget sounds Irish to the English. I gave her a long look but it was a fair time before she recognised me, or else she *did* recognise me and pretended that she hadn't. Anyway, she couldn't get away with that. She went out quickly and I followed. Leave me alone, she said, or I'll call the police. That was a good one, that was. I said: The police are the last people you'll call. Besides, there's no law that I know of that prevents a husband speaking to his wife. She said: You'd bet-

---

* They should have been most willing to help, shouldn't they?
† Cut out the frills, Roper. Not your line at all.

ter forget all about that. Divorce me and finish with it. I could now, I said, now that I know where you are and what you're doing; otherwise I'd have to wait three years for desertion (she'd reconciled herself to my following her to where she lived), but once you're divorced you'll be deported as an undesirable alien. I saw that undesirable was the wrong word there. All she said was: I won't be deported.

Her flat was evidently a very expensive one, central heating, corner bar with bar-stools, cushions, erotic pictures on the walls (German ones from the Nazi time; I saw that). There was a kitchenette with a refrigerator humming, an open bathroom-door with bath-smells coming from it, an open bedroom-door showing a big bed with a silk coverlet, dim wall-lights on. Will you have a drink? she said. This is my night off and I was going to get to bed early, but have a drink and say what you want and then go. Perhaps she thought I wanted to know where she'd left the spare front-door key of the house. Thinking of the house made me want to cry. What I said was: I want you. She said: You can have my number; ring me sometime. No no no, I said, I want you. I want you to come back. She laughed at that and said: *Warum?* Her suddenly asking why in German, when her English seemed to have improved so much, brought back the whole past to me, and I really started to cry this time. Don't do that, she said. What has to be has to be. I want to be as I am. I don't want shopping and hausfrauing any more. I meet some very important people now. I'm a lady. You're a whore, I said, the English and German words being very nearly the same. That's what you are, a prostitute. She said: the two words are not quite the same. Oh, why don't you grow up and learn about the great world?

Apart from anything else, I said, I have certain rights. Conjugal

rights. I demand their restoration. You filthy pig, she shouted; I've
never had such filth spoken to me before. Get out of here at once.
And then she gave me a very foul mouthful of German. And then
she said: If you want a woman there are thousands in London willing to do it for the money. Some of them even walk the streets with
little dogs, which is against the law. But do not come to me, no, not
to me, do not come to me. I felt very bitter and ill used then, but I
could not really turn against her. Also I felt triumphant, because I
would have her that night and she would not know it. But I boiled
also within to think that this was my wife and other men could possess her and I could not. I became very cold and cunning outside,
despite the boiling inside, and, when I saw her handbag lying open
on the settee, I said: Give me a drink and then I'll go. A cold drink.
Perhaps you have beer in the fridge. We always used to have it in
the old days. All right, she said, go and help yourself. Then get out.
But I said: For old time's sake, Brigitte, get me a drink with your
own hands. Please. I ask no more. She shrugged and said: Oh all
right, then went to get it. I knew that her key was in that bag. It was
no trouble to get it out and put it in my pocket. When she brought
the beer I drank it off in one draught. She said: You drink like a pig,
just as you ate like a pig. I only smiled and said: A goodnight kiss?
For old time's sake? But she wouldn't give me even that, my right.
I left then and said: Goodbye, dear Brigitte. Look after yourself.
She seemed a little puzzled to see me go without further trouble.
Out in the street I looked up at her sitting-room window till the
lights went out. Then I went home. Lucy was waiting for me with
some nice hot supper.

    I now had something to do every night. What I did mostly at
first was to walk that street, seeing who went into her flat. Her
trade was a high-class one, to judge by the cars that parked there.

Once a policeman looked at me suspiciously but I got in right
away with: Never mind, constable. This is a job. Private detective
agency. He didn't ask to see my card or anything. The pleasure I
got from watching was what, I suppose, is called a masochistic
one. I never thought such pleasure was possible, but it is. It is not
just what Shakespeare calls wearing the horns; it is making a kind
of crown of horns.* I delayed my entering for as long as possible,
letting weeks go by. I felt especially virtuous about submitting to
all this delicious pain, since I'd told Lucy that I was after evidence
for a divorce. When I got back at night she said: You poor dear.
Let's have a nice hot drink before we go to bed.

I watched and watched till one night a very unpretentious car
came to her door and a man got out of the car looking furtive. He
darted up the stairs to the open doorway of the little block of flats
and, in the light from the hall, I saw his profile fairly clearly. I
knew I'd seen that face somewhere, but I couldn't think where. It
seemed to me to be a fairly important face, but whether political
or artistic or even in the ecclesiastical field I knew not. A
Television Personality perhaps? That got closer to it. I felt I'd
seen that face earnestly talking one night on television when
Lucy and I were taking hot soup from our knees, I mean from
bowls on our knees, with crackling slices of Ryvita. The face, I
thought, was both political and televisual—something to do with
a party political broadcast? I had to wait about an hour and a half
before he came out, stuffing his wallet into his inside pocket, still
looking furtive but more *smugly* furtive. It was about the time
when the theatres were finishing, and there were one or two taxis
coming down the street to turn on to Baker Street. This man

* Oh no, Roper. No no NO.

hadn't yet got into his car, but I stopped a taxi and the driver said: Where to, guv? (or it may have been: Where to, mate?) I felt like giggling as I said: Follow that car once it starts. The driver said: I can't very well bleeding follow it while it's stationary, can I? Then he said: You mean it, guv (or mate)? Cor, this comes from seeing too much telly. But he did what I said.

It was a bit difficult, because other cars and taxis got in the way, but eventually we came to the area round about Marble Arch, and this car stopped outside what looked like a block of flats. The taxi-driver drew up very discreetly on the opposite side of the road. Now, he said, go in and get your man. Not too much rough stuff, mind. I paid him and he went off. I waited a little while then I went to the entrance where I'd seen the man go in. There was, as I'd expected, a sort of porter on duty in the entrance-hall. I said: Excuse me, but wasn't that Mr Barnaby who went in just then? He looked at me most suspiciously and said: What's it to you who went in, mate? (Too much of this *mate*, everywhere—the parody of friendliness of an uneasily egalitar-ian state.*) I said: Don't call me mate. My name is Doctor Roper. Sorry, he said, doctor. No, that wasn't no Barny, or whatever you said. That was none other than Mr Cornpit-Ferrers.† And a very nice gentleman too. This porter went on then about his eloquence on television and (though how did he know, obviously no man for the Strangers' Gallery?) in the House. Also his generosity, always ready with the odd half-bar for small services rendered. Like now, going to put his wife's car away for the night, that being it as he'd just come in, him perhaps not wanting to use the

---

* From what pretentious TV play did you pick that up?
† Sir Arnold Cornpit-Ferrers, as he now is? The dawn breaks, Roper.

regular Bentley this evening. I donated 10s or half-a-bar and said: Married then, is he? He said: Thank you, sir, doctor. Yes, a lovely wife and three kids, lovely kids.

Adulterous whoring swine. But at last I saw a way of getting Brigitte back. Next time I would Confront Them both, as that time with that ghastly Wurzel. But no, I'd played no man's role then; I'd had to leave it to Hillier. I watched and waited another week and he didn't come, the House perhaps sitting late. But one evening a man for all the world like that filthy West German Devil came, dropped by somebody in a car. He shouted something like *Guter Kerl*, very foolishly, to the driver, who shouted back something like *Sei gut* before going off. This time I decided to go up, after a decent, wrong word there, interval. I was blazing, that bad time, the first speck of rot in the apple, coming back to me. Outside her door I had to pause and take deep though silent breaths. Then I heard them talking very serious German inside. This made me wonder. Surely there should be none of that going on, the seriousness reserved to a different kind of communication. I listened and I kept hearing the name Eberswalde. Eberswalde? That was in East Germany. Brigitte had spoken a couple of times about some filthy relative she hated who lived in Eberswalde. I listened hard but could take in little. I could not take in very fast German, despite my marriage to one who spoke it when in passion or anger. At one point Brigitte seemed to start to cry very gently. Was this relative in Eberswalde really so filthy? Had other relatives turned up there, not filthy at all? The only other word that came clearly through the door was another name—Maria. I heard it often. Surely Brigitte had spoken of a niece of that name, someone who was, apparently, far from filthy. And then, quite loud, Brigitte cried: But I know nothing, not yet. Softer, the man seemed to say: But you will know. You will know much if you try harder. And then: *Ich gehe.* I got away quickly before he left and walked right down the street, as far from the flat as possible.

What did all this mean? I couldn't tell. It might mean nothing. But, like everybody else, I'd had this security thing hammered into me, and I couldn't help thinking that a German prostitute (terrible thing to call Brigitte) who had relatives in East Germany would, in free and easy London, be all too much a subject for proposals or target for threats from the Other Side. Not that I could take it very seriously. We scientists who were socialists were working out a highminded blueprint about International Co-operation in Research, and we saw, rightly, all research as one—all answers to all questions free to all. War was to be out-lawed, and we were in the vanguard of the outlawing process, the scientist having great responsibilities and terrible powers.

I looked up Mr Cornpit-Ferrers in *Who's Who* and saw that he was a Minister without Portfolio. That was three governments ago. What he is now I neither know nor care. He was, and proba-bly still is, a man highly thought of, not only by his hall-porter, a member of Commissions and Committees, including one that had something to do with Television Teenage Religious Program-mes. The hypocrite. Anyway, the time for Confrontation must come very soon now, so I thought. But I still had to wait three weeks, in which period Brigitte, poor corrupted girl, had many visitors, all of them well-dressed. The night it happened was a rainy night, and I nearly decided to give up. But that remembered car drew up and the remembered face, now with a name pinned on it, looked through the rain with the old furtiveness. Cornpit-Ferrers went in, and I was five minutes after him. My heart went like mad, I could hardly breathe, and I wondered if I would be able to speak. I turned the key boldly in the lock and entered. There was nobody in the sitting-room, but from the bedroom I could hear writhings between sheets and sickening yumyumyum noises. I found I could speak, even cry aloud. I called: Come on out of there, both of you, you sinful bastards. And at the same time I felt the things in my inside pocket that I'd brought with me, just to make sure they were still there. There was a surprised silence, then whispering, then I called again: Come out, hypocritical politician. Come out, you who I'm ashamed to call my wife. Then they came out, she pulling a négligée around her, he in shirt and trousers, smoothing his hair. She said: I thought that's where that other key must have got to. Go on, quickly, what do you want? But Cornpit-Ferrers said: He wants a good firm kick on the arse, straight down those steps. Who is he anyway? Your ponce? Of course, that was something I'd never thought of, that Brigitte might have such a man or half-man in the background. I now felt sick as well as angry and bitter and I said: I, Mr Cornpit-Ferrers, am this woman's husband. He said: Know my name, do you? Hm, that's a pity. To Brigitte: Get him for trespass. Ring up the police. Ah, that's fixed you, hasn't it? (to me). Don't like the sound of that, do you? I said: This woman is my wife. Brigitte Roper. Here (and I took it out of my pocket) is our marriage licence. And here (taking that out too) is our joint passport; the photographs aren't bad likenesses.

He didn't ask for a close look. He sat down on the settee and took a cigarette from Brigitte's cloisonné box. Then he said: What is this? What are you after? Money? Divorce? I shook my head and said: No. All I want is my wife back again. Brigitte cried: I'm not going back to you. Whatever you do, dirty filth. Never never never. Cornpit-Ferrers said: You hear the lady. I don't see how I can do anything about getting her to return to you. Incidentally, I didn't know, obviously. I'm sorry. Just one of those things. I said: And if it were discovered that she receives visits from East German agents?

Brigitte turned pale; it was true then. What I mean, I said, is this: she ought really to be deported. I take it you're reasonably friendly with the Home Secretary? Cornpit-Ferrers said: What the hell's that got to do with anything? (He was blustering badly.) I said: It's up to Brigitte now. I could easily bring pressure on you to see about her deportation. If she comes back with me—not necessarily tonight, as there's somebody else staying with me at the moment, but, say, in the next day or so, we'll take it that none of this ever happened. That I never saw you. I have a responsible position and am not likely to want to discredit anyone in a position of authority. Too dangerous. Nor would I stoop to blackmail. Unless, of course, I have to.

What is this position of yours? asked Cornpit-Ferrers. I told him. He was not unimpressed. He said to Brigitte: Well, what he says seems reasonable enough. How about it? Brigitte said: Never. If you try to have me thrown out then I will say about you coming here. I will say to your wife and to the Prime Minister. He said: Difficult. No witnesses. She said: Here is a witness, my husband. I grinned at that, the silly little fool. She said: I have another. He has seen you come here often. Both Cornpit-Ferrers and I felt that might be true. He said: Well, no need to be hasty about anything. I think it's time you and I (to me) got out of here. A drink or something. Leave little Bridget to sort things out. I must say (he said) you're a forgiving sort of man. I admire you rather. I suppose that's love. I said: No drink, thank you. I'd sick it up at once. If either of you wants to get in touch with me, you know where I am. Then I left. But, before going down the steps, I decided to turn back, open up again, and say, in a twisted disgusted tone, God God God, what a bloody mess you're both in. Then I really left. I was very cheerful with Lucy that night, and she was overjoyed to think that it wouldn't be long now, poor girl.

The things that happened after that I didn't expect. One morning I received a rather grubby envelope through the post. My name and address were typed on it quite neatly, which made the grubbiness of the envelope seem all the stranger. Inside were ten one-pound notes. A typewritten slip said: Sorry to be so long repaying the loan. And then there came the typed initial C. I thought back, frowning, to any time I could remember lending ten pounds to anyone, but I couldn't catch at a memory. Lucy, bringing in breakfast, asked me what the matter was, and I told and showed her. She said: Never frown over buckshee money (her father had been a soldier). You *are* forgetful, you know. Then we ate our cornflakes. I threw the slip and envelope away and put the pound notes in my wallet. That evening two men in raincoats came to the door. Can we have a word with you, sir? they said. I took them to be police officers. Seeing Lucy, they said: Mrs Roper? I said: A friend. Miss Butler. Ah, the older one said, as they came in, of course. Mrs Roper doesn't live here any more, does she? No, she doesn't, does she, sir? And then, to Lucy: We'd like a word with Mr Roper *alone*, if you don't mind, miss. Lucy looked worried. Please, miss, they said. She went upstairs; she had no authority to question or argue or complain.

Now then, said the senior officer. Could we please examine whatever money you have on you, sir? Notes, I mean. I said: Oh, if it's something to do with that ten pounds—Ten pounds is the sum, sir. Could we see the ten pounds, please? I showed them all my money. The junior officer took out a list with numbers on it. They checked the numbers of my notes with those numbers. Hm, they nodded, hm hm. The senior said: You understand, sir, it is a very serious crime to live off a woman's immoral earnings. I couldn't speak. Then I said: Nonsense. Utter bloody nonsense. I got this money in the post this morning. Really, sir? said the junior in a sleepy way. I take it you won't deny that Mrs Roper, who is not living with you but is in fact engaged in prostitution, has received certain visits from you recently? I didn't deny it. But, I said, this money—Yes, this money, sir. Mrs Roper drew out from her bank three days ago these identical notes. I said:

A frame-up. A put-up job. The senior officer said: We'll keep these, if you don't mind, sir. You'll be hearing more about this. Then they got up to go. I said: You mean you're not charging me? The junior said: We have no authority, sir. But you'll be hearing about this in a day or two. I spluttered at them. I even got Lucy to come down and shout at them, but they only smiled and touched their hats (which they'd not taken off in the house) as they left.

It was hard for me to work in the days that followed. Then came the summons, and it was a kind of relief. It was a summons to a small house not far from Goldhawk Road. Cornpit-Ferrers opened the door. With him was a man who looked foreign and, when he spoke, spoke with what seemed to be a Slavonic accent. It seemed to be this man's house we were in, dirty and ill-furnished. But the man himself was clean and rather well-dressed. Cornpit-Ferrers was very urbane. He said: I gather that you and some of your colleagues have been doing a little polemical work on the need for International Co-operation in Scientific Research. I said nothing. He said: It seems there's a chance for you to do more than merely discuss it or draft pamphlets about it. I said: What are you getting at? He said: Oh, by the way, this is Mr—(I didn't catch the name; I never learned it). I don't think I need tell you which embassy he is in. He's making all arrangements. This is a wonderful opportunity, Dr Roper. We politicians talk and talk but we do little. (You do enough, I nearly said, with venom.) You, he went on, represent a sort of spearhead of action. I understand that this is rather a good time for you to leave the country. Am I right? I swore at him; I said: Your filthy bloody trick. But you won't get away with it. He said: Not just *my* trick. She was very ready to help. The Slav man now laughed. Cornpit-Ferrers also laughed, saying: He knows her too. Quite as well as I. And, as for *getting away with it,* to use your term, the two men who called on you are waiting for the word to lodge some sort of information with the police. The law deals harshly, for some reason, with that kind of crime. I don't see (he continued) why you should grieve overmuch at going away. You don't like England all that much, do you? You don't feel all that loyal to England either. I know. You don't want England nearly as much as you want you-know-who. Cheer up, Dr Roper. She's going with you.

I gasped. She's agreed to it? He said: I'm afraid it's all got to be done rather quickly. There's a boat leaving Tilbury tomorrow morning at eleven. Eleven? (looking for confirmation to the Slav man. The man nodded.) The *Petrov-Vodkin,* carrying cargo to Rostock. Some men from Warnemünde will pick you up at the Warnow Hotel. Everything's going to be all right, believe me. A new lease of life. Your career's done for here, you must realise that. What's that in Shakespeare about the man almost damned in a fair wife? Never mind. You'll like your new ambience—hard work and hard drinking, so I understand. Any questions?

I'm not going, I said. He said: That's not a question. As for the disposal of your goods and chattels (you have a house, I believe), that can be done by remote control. The Curtain may be Iron, but it has letter-boxes cut in it. From now on our friend here will be looking after you. Give him your house-key and he'll arrange for bags to be packed. You'll sleep here tonight.

I said: And you call yourself a Minister of the Crown. I knew England was corrupt, but I never dreamed— And then: Will she be coming here too? Will we be going together? He said: You'll meet at the Warnow Hotel. You don't believe me? You think this is all a trick? Well, here's something for you. He took from his top pocket, from behind a handkerchief arranged in seven points, an envelope. He gave it to me. I recognised the handwriting of the note within. *I was a fool. We will make a new beginning.* Cornpit-Ferrers said: No forgery. The genuine article. She *has* been a fool too. In fact, we've all been fools. Live and learn. But you've been the biggest fool of the lot. Of the lot. Of the.*

I said: This is going to be bloody merry England's last betrayal of a Roper. Oh yes. What you did in 1558 you're doing again now. Faith then, still faith. England's damned herself. Warmongering cynical bloody England. His light went out at 15-58. Continental time.† Up all your pipes. Martyr's blood runs through them. He said: No regrets, then. Good. He put on a bowler hat and picked up an umbrella. He was wearing a grey raglan overcoat. He was Trumper-shaved-and-barbered. Eucris. Eucharist.‡ He had a

---

* Watch it, watch it.
† And again.
‡ Do try.

hard handsome look that would soon go soft. I said: On your own head be it. In *my* head I carry things England thought valuable. Good, he said again. International share-out, eh? Plans across the sea. I said: Traitor. He said: To whom or to what? Then: I must be going now. I'm giving lunch to a couple of rather important constituents. He did a sort of mock-salute against his bowler-brim, then ordered arms with his umbrella, lip-farting a bugle-call, grinned goodbye at the Slav man, left. I spat in his wake. The Slav man reproved me for that in thick English. His house, he said. Rented by him, anyway.

The story can end here. Except that, at the Warnow Hotel in Rostock, there was no Brigitte waiting for me. I was not surprised. In a way I was pleased. My sense of betrayal was absolute. I fetched the barnaby out of the cheese-slice, fallowed the whereupon with ingrown versicles, then cranked with endless hornblows of white, gamboge, wortdrew, hammon and prayrichard the most marvellous and unseen-as-yet fallupons that old Motion ever hatched in all his greenock nights.* The men from Warnemünde were very jolly and plied me with gallons of the stuff. I think we sang songs. We hardhit bedfriends in twiceknit garnishes. Oh, the† welter of all that moontalk, such as it was, whistles and all.‡ Whenever an empty trestlestack is given§ more than half of its prerequisite of mutton fibres, you may expectorate high as a HOUSE FULL placard. Implacable.**

---

* ?

† Knocknoise, distant.

‡ Wherewhatwhowhy?

§ Oh, please, please, please. He's dead, I tell you. It's all over. Alan won't wake up.

** Eh? Clara in dressing-gown, weeping. *She* came in to tell me, triumphant almost. He's dead. Oh, what do we do now?

EIGHT

'WHAT DO WE do now?' repeated Hillier, awake again but dog-tired. He stood up, letting the manuscript fall in loose sheets to the floor. She sought his chest, bare under the dressing-gown, and, arms about him, wept and wept. 'My poor darling,' he murmured into her hair. 'But we knew this was going to happen. You have me to look after you now.' The figure of Cornpit-Ferrers danced through his brain, waving its rolled umbrella, another of the bloody neutrals. That was where evil lay: in the neutrals. Clara wept, her face still hidden; he could feel tears rilling down the sternum. She drew in breath for a sob and coughed on an inhaled chest hair. His arms held her tight. He stroked, soothing. But the body of a woman was the body of a woman, even when she was a girl, even when she was a daughter. 'Come,' he said gently. 'You'll feel better soon.' And he led her over to the narrow bunk. She sat there, wiping her eyes with her knuckles, and he sat beside her, still trying to soothe. She said, her voice denasalised by tears:

'She walked right in. To my cabin and. Shook me. It was as if she was. Glad.'

'She's one of the neutrals,' said Hillier. 'And now you'll be rid of her.' He kissed her forehead.

'And then. When she'd told me. She went. Back to bed.'

'There there there there.' But, of course, what was there to do except go back to bed? And tomorrow she would have a blinding headache and expect pity, the widow. Had she already equipped herself with smart black? There would be men all too ready to give comfort. Hillier saw them knocking gently at her cabin door;

they wore bowler hats and carried umbrellas. He saw himself, tomorrow, making all arrangements. I insist on a rebate, he would tell the purser. And, for that matter, it wasn't Mr Innes's fault that he didn't embark at Yarylyuk. I'll bet he didn't nudge out other possible bookings. I want a sizeable chunk of money back. A question of a coffin. Thrown in free, one of the ship's amenities?

'There'll be a lot to do tomorrow,' said Hillier. 'She'll see out the cruise, all the way back to Southampton. A distraught and desirable widow. Leave everything to me. As for now, we both need rest.'

She was tired with the whole evening; it had been a very tiring evening for the three of them: no wonder Alan couldn't wake up. When he woke he would have a memory of a dream of killing a man, then he would hear of the death of his father. It was no way to start a sunny cruising morning. But there was still this merciful night, a whole black sea of it. 'Come,' said Hillier, and he raised her gently from the bunk so that he could draw down the coverlet and blanket and top sheet. Dead-beat, she nodded, sniffing. Hillier helped her off with her silk dragon-patterned dressing-gown; the nightdress underneath was black, bare-armed and shoulder-strapped, opaque but maddening. This was no time for being maddened, though; this was his daughter. She flopped into the bunk, her hair everywhere. Hillier brought his chair closer, sat, and held her hand. Soon the hand tried to drop from his, finger by finger. She slept quite soundly, the power of the sedative Hillier had given her earlier re-asserting itself blessedly. Totally without desire, he stripped himself naked and eased himself into the bunk beside her. Her body, unconsciously accommodating, rolled itself to the bulkhead. He lay with his back to her, almost on a knife-edge of bed space.

A ghost of sobbing possessed her sleep. He could not lie so, averted. He turned to hold her, and his hands strove to avoid those areas of her body where she would cease to be a daughter. Again that sleeping body helped, turning to face him, the head at length cradled in his oxter, tiny gales of her breathing heating his bare chest. It was possible then to sleep, but he slept lightly, awakening to a rougher sea than any they had known yet, outside the half-open light. Sleepless, a man was parading the deck, coughing over a two-in-the-morning cigarette. Wriste looked in, switched on the bunkside lamp, and, dangling from a bloodless socket an eye on a rubbery stalk, said: 'I admire you, sir, I do really. What time your early-morning death, sir?' Hillier shook him out, along with the lamp, but Cornpit-Ferrers, much diminished in size, jumped on to the other bunk and, gripping his lapels in elder-statesman style, addressed the House: 'My right honourable friend has spoken eloquently of duty to the country as a whole, but duty as seen by a government consists primarily not in governing so much as in existing (*Hear hear*), and this applies not merely collectively but (*man thrown out of Strangers' Gallery for crying:* Adulterer!) componentially. Divided we stand even though united we may fall.' Hillier found himself in the House of Commons, waiting to meet his own member to protest about being awarded death instead of a bonus. On the floor he disentangled *Virtue Prevails* and *Love and Fidelity to Our Country* and *Faithful* out of the florid byzantine cryptograms. Then the letters all snaked up again and the meanings were lost. Instead of his member there came along his chief and colleagues—RF, VT,

JBW, LJ. Hue and cry. Guns going off while the Speaker toddled in, preceded by his mace-bearer, followed by his doddering chaplain. 'I appeal,' called Hillier, 'in the name of the Mother of Parliaments.' A policeman with the portcullis symbol on his flat cap said: 'Court of Appeal's not here, mate.' Hillier was told to take it like a man, not to interrupt the grave processes of legislation, question-time just coming up. Foreign tourists disobeying orders, snapped with their cameras the leaping and twisting body of Hillier as bullet after bullet got home.

He awoke to find Clara comforting him. 'A nightmare,' she said, wiping the sweat off his forehead with her bare hand, which she then rubbed dry against the over-sheet. The sea was quiet again; it was grey very early morning. His member; what had that been about his member? Her hands were smoothing his body, girl's curiosity as well as motherly tenderness in them. His body's dream-leaping must have shaken her awake. As one hand went down he arrested it, thinking: Never would I have thought possible, never could I have ever possibly conceived that I would now resist what of all things. But her hand, that had turned the pages of so many cold sex-books, was interested. What she touched was warm, smooth, a bauble rather than a rocketing monster. 'No,' he said. 'Not that. But there are other things.' This was no time, this was no girl, for the big sweating engine of phallic sex. And so, very gently, he showed her. He gave without taking. He imagined shocked faces on the ceiling whispering: 'Necrophily', but he rubbed them out with his own acts of tenderness. To ease her in gently to that world of release and elation which lay all before her, all too easily spoilt for ever by the boor, cynic, self-seeker, was surely a valid part of the office of almost-father he had assumed. This was an act of love.

But had she already perhaps half-corrupted herself with curiosity? It was more avidity for knowledge than acceptance of pleasure that, after the first epiphany, led her to ask for more things, her greed squeaking faintly like the pencil of an inventory-taker. And what is this, that? How is the other thing done? She wanted to turn atlas names into the photographable stuff of foreign travel. Hillier bade her sleep again, they must be up early, there were many things to be seen to before their disembarkation at Istanbul. He fed her one pleasure that brought her to the sword-point of a cry that might wake the whole corridor, and after that she slept, her firm young body mottled with heat-rash and her hair all dark strings. Hillier wearily looked at his watch: 6.20. At seven she wakened him roughly and demanded what he had been loath to give her. He still demurred but soon, the morning advancing and his own lust angry at its bits and snaffles, he led her to the phallic experience. It was then that she ceased to be Clara. His head was too clear now, tenderness bundled out like a passenger who had not paid his fare, and he was able to say to himself: There are no virgins any more; ponies and gym-mistresses are the distracted deflowerers, jolly liquidators of a once high and solemn ritual spiced with pain. Tea-trays began to rattle in the corridor. He muffled the shriek of her climax with a hand over her mouth and then took his own, humbler, orgasm outside her. At once he was able to plunge into the prose-world of the morning—to lock the door against a tea-bringing steward, light a cigar, tell her to cover herself and, when the corridor was clear, seek her own cabin. Love. How about love?

She said: 'Do you think my breasts are too small?'

'No no no, perfect.'

She put on her nightdress and then her dressing-gown with a child's glow of smugness. She said: 'Do you have to smoke those horrible things first thing in the morning?'

'I'm afraid I do. An old habit.'

'An old habit.' She nodded. 'Old. It's a pity one has to wait till one's old to really know anything. You know a lot.'

'What any mature man knows.'

'They'll be jealous at school when I tell them.' She lay on the bunk again, very wide awake, her hands behind her head.

'Oh, no,' murmured Hillier.

'It's all talk with them. And of course what they get out of books. I can hardly wait.'

Hillier was hurt. Early though it was, he gave himself a large Old Mortality and tepid water; the name on the bottle glared at him like his own reflection. She looked indulgently: this was a bad habit, but it didn't smell like a cigar. 'Which,' he asked, 'will you tell them first—that you've lost a father or gained a lover?'

Her face screwed up at once. 'That was a filthy and cruel thing to say.' It was too.

'Sorry,' he said. 'I know a lot but I've forgotten much more. I'd forgotten the coldness of youth till you reminded me of it. It needs to be matched with the coldness of the village initiator. There used to be such men, you know—safe experienced men who showed young girls what it was all about. No love in it, of course. I suppose now you think me a fool for having talked about love.'

She sniffed back the renewed tears of bereavement. 'I shall remember it. It's one of the things I shan't tell the other girls.'

'Oh yes you will.' His mouth tasted sour. He would have liked to be lying in that bed alone, watching the tea brought in. 'It doesn't matter really. I'd forgotten you were a schoolgirl. I've never even asked your age.'

'Sixteen.' She smirked very faintly then looked sad again.

'Not so young. I once had an Italian girl of eleven. I was once offered a Tamil girl of nine.'

'You're pretty horrid really, aren't you?' But she gave him a full gaze of neutral appraisal. *Initiator:* he could see the word being marshalled into position behind her eyes. And on this cruise there was a man who was really what you might call an initiator. A what? Tell us more.

'I don't know what I am,' said Hillier. 'I failed to be a corpse. I dreamed of a regeneration. Perhaps one can't have that without dying first. It was foolish of me to think I could be both a father and a husband. And yet in what capacity do I dread your being thrown to the wolves?'

'I can look after myself. We can both look after ourselves.'

There was a knock at the door. 'Tea at last,' Hillier said. 'You'd better get off that bunk. You'd better look as though you just came in to tell me your sad news.' She got up and went demurely to a chair. Sad news; that was what the Old Mortality tasted like. Have another nip of Sad News. Hillier unlocked and opened up. It was not the strange steward, Wriste's replacement. It was Alan. In his dressing-gown, hair sleek, Black Russian in holder, he looked rested and mature.

'Did she spend the night here?' he asked. Hillier made a mouth and shrugged; no point in denying it. The brother had done murder; the sister had been initiated. 'Well,' said Alan, 'you've certainly shown both of us how the other half lives.' He tasted, like Sad News, the ineptness of that last word. '*She* came,' he said. 'She woke me up to tell me. It seemed rather small stuff really. I hope that doesn't sound callous.'

Very ill at ease, Hillier said: 'He reached Byzantium first.' He could then have bitten out his tongue. Alan looked at him gravely, saying:

'You're what I'd call a romantic. Poetry and games and visions.' To Clara he said: 'She's behaving as I knew she would. Terribly ill after telling everybody the news. Blinding headache. Prostrate with grief. She said it was up to the Captain to see to everything. Get him off the ship. Bundle him out of sight. It upsets the passengers, having a dead body on board. They paid for a good time and by God they're going to have it.'

'You must leave everything to me,' said Hillier. 'You'll want to travel back with him. You can fly BEA from Istanbul. I'll sort it all out for you, the least I can do. I'll get dressed now and go and see the purser. I ought to radio your solicitors, *his* I mean. They can meet you at London Airport.'

'I know what has to be done,' said Alan. 'You're too much of a romantic to be any good at *real* things. I notice you don't say anything about flying to London with us. That's because you daren't, isn't it? Some of your pals will be waiting for you, other romantic games-players in raincoats with guns in their pockets. You talked about looking after us, but you daren't even set foot in England.'

'Things to do in Istanbul,' mumbled Hillier. 'One thing, anyway. Very important. Then I was going to suggest that you both meet me in Dublin. At the Dolphin Hotel, Essex Street. Then we could decide about the future.'

'Our future,' said Alan, 'will be decided by Chancery. Wards

in Chancery, Clara and Alan Walters. A stepmother has no legal
obligation. I suppose you'll start talking about yourself having a
moral obligation. And all that means is our skulking in Ireland
with you. Neutral territory. Opting out of history—that was
your expression. That means the IRA and gun-men and blowing
up post-offices. No, thank you. Back to school for us. We want to
learn *slowly*.'

Hillier looked guiltily and bitterly at the two children. 'You
didn't always think like that,' he said. 'Sex-books and dinner-
jackets and ear-rings and cognac after dinner. You talk about *me*
playing games—'

'We,' said Alan with something like sweetness, 'are only children. It was up to you to recognise that. Games are all right for
children.' Then his larynx throbbed with anger like an adult's.
'Look where *your* bloody games have landed us.'

'You're not being fair—'

'Bloody neutrals. That bitch with the grief-stricken headache
and filthy Theodorescu and grinning Wriste and *you*. But I suppose you feel very self-righteous and very badly done to.'

'There are no real martyrs,' said Hillier carefully. 'One should
always read the small print on the contract.'

'Oh, you even have to make a game out of that,' sneered
Alan. He took out of his dressing-gown pocket a much-mauled
piece of paper. 'Look at it,' he said. 'This is that message you
gave me to de-code.' Hillier took it. The paper was quite blank.
'No come-back there,' said Alan. 'They play the game well.'

'Seven-day vanishing ink,' said Hillier. 'I might have known.'

'It would be lovely if everything could vanish as easily.
Conjuring tricks. Games. Oh, let's get back to the real world.' He
made as to leave. 'You coming, Clara?'

'In a minute. I just want to say goodbye.'

'I'll see you at breakfast.' And, with no farewell to Hillier, he left. His mature smoker's cough travelled down the corridor, perhaps to a boy's tears in his own cabin, the natural self-pity of a newly-made orphan. Hillier and Clara looked at each other. He said:

'A kiss wouldn't be in order, would it? Too much like love.'

Her eyes were bright as from dexedrine. She lowered them bashfully. 'It doesn't look as if you're going to get any morning tea,' she said. 'Why don't you lock the door again?' He stared at her incredulously. 'There's plenty of time,' she said, raising her eyes to him. How often had he seen those eyes before.

'Get out,' he said. 'Go on. Out.'

'But you seemed to like it—'

'Out.'

'You're horrible.' She began to cry. 'You said you loved—'

'Go on.' Blindly he pushed her out on to the corridor.

'Beast. Filthy filthy beast.' And then, as she too made for her cabin, it was just tears. But tears, however public, were in order. Hillier settled in his wretchedness to the bottle of Old Mortality.

NINE

HILLIER HAD three days to wait in Istanbul. His hotel was pretentiously named—the Babi Humayun or Sublime Porte—also misleadingly, since it was nearer the Golden Horn in the north than the Old Seraglio in the south-east of the city. But it suited Hillier well enough. The final act to be performed accorded better with fleas, foul lavatories, stained and carious wallpaper, than with the grand asepsis of the Hilton. His room was shady and smelt shady: the bed had surely known gross and barbaric *gesta*, the paint scratched from its iron by strong and cruel fingers from the hills, fingers unwashed from dipping in rank stews of goat-mutton. Bearded phantoms shuffled the floor in the night in greasy slippers, muttering last words before the striking down for a little bag of coins ill-concealed under the bursting mattress: shadows of murderous thieves danced on the walls in the dim light from the three-in-the-morning street. The room had a balcony long uncleared of Turkish cigarette-ends, old cobwebs thick with white dust; the one chair was rickety. But Hillier liked to sit there and take his early breakfast of yoghurt, figs, unleavened bread and goat-butter, thick syrupy coffee and foul Brazilian cigars, looking into the clear glimmer of the morning Bosporus. He reflected, naked under his dressing-gown, on how wrong he had been about things, believing too much in choice and free will and the logic of men's acts; also the nature of love.

On Cumhuriyet Caddesi he had watched, half-hiding like some native of the city up to no good, the loading of the flour-king's coffin on to the closed BEA van, later the boarding of the flour-king's orphans, two pale and elegant children, with the rest of the passengers on Flight BE 291, and he had waved feebly as the coach ground off to Yesilköy Airport. He had gone to the address given to him by Theodorescu and found it a decent bundle of business offices. At the enquiry-desk he had asked if there were anything for Mr Hillier; a Mongol-looking woman with hair streaked white had given him an envelope. A note inside merely said: FAIL WHOLLY TO UNDERSTAND BUT WILL BE THERE. It was signed T.

And then to wait. Breakfast, the first raki of the day, fried fish or kebab for lunch, raki going all the time. Sleep or a restless wandering of the city, cocktails at the Kemel or the Hilton, a European dinner, then a raki-crawl and early bed. Istanbul disturbed him with its seven hills, as though Rome had tried to build herself on another planet. The names of architects and sultans rang in his mind in dull Byzantine gold—Anthemius, Isidorus, Achmet, Bajazet, Solyman the Magnificent. The emperors shrilled from a far past like desolate birds—Theodosius, Justinian, Constantine himself. His head raged with mosques. The city, in cruel damp heat, smelt of wool and hides and skins. Old filth and rusty iron, proud exports, clattered and thumped aboard under Galata's lighthouse. Ships, gulls, sea-light. Bazaars, beggars, skinny children, teeth, charcoal fires, skewered innards smoking, the heavy tobacco reek, fat men in flannel double-breasteds, fed on fat.

In the early evening of the third day, Hillier arrived back at the Babi Humayun from a trip to Scutari. He was damp and tired and his head ached. His pulse raced when he saw in the entrance-hall a small pile of good leather luggage. Someone had arrived from somewhere. Who? He did not dare ask the squinting bilious-skinned porter. He took the lift (old iron for export) to his floor, went to his room, stripped, and checked the Aiken and silencer before loading. He hid the weapon among his few remaining clean shirts in the top drawer of the dressing-table. He drank raki from the flask by the window. Dressing-gowned, towel round his neck, he went out to the bathroom, feeling slightly sick, eyes focusing badly; he noted the tremor of intent in his fingers as they reached for the bathroom door. He knew what he would see inside.

Miss Devi stood under the shower's cold trickle. He surveyed her nakedness as coldly as she suffered his gaze. Fronds and dissolving islets of water flowered and fell upon the baked skin; the tar-black bush glistened. She had hidden her hair in a plastic cap; her face seemed more naked than her body. The nipples were pert after the shock of the douche; like eyes they met his eyes. 'Well,' he said. 'Is he here?'

'Later. He has things to do. He found your message very mysterious. He will not trick you, of course. No tape recorder. But his memory is very good.'

Mine too, thought Hillier. His flesh crawled as it remembered that night in her cabin. Was it proper now to feel desire? That past desire had been used to betray him; this time it would be different. Shatter that child's body; those scents that lingered in his nostrils and the feel that was stitched into the whorls of his hands could only be exorcised by the ranker contacts of a knowing, mature, corrupt routine. Hillier said: 'Would you now? I take it there is time.'

'Oh, there's time. Time for the *vimanam* and the *akaya-vimanam. Mor* and the *taddinam* and the *Yaman.*'

'*Yaman?* That's the god of death.'

'It's just a name. My room is 47. Wait there.'

'Let's go to mine,' said Hillier.

'No. I have the instruments of the *Yaman.* Wait for me there. I must perform the triple washing of the *vay.*' Hillier noticed that she had a little waterproof bag on the chair by the bath. There would be other engines there than those of the *Yaman.* He went to her room. It was as seedy as his own, but her presence rode it strongly, sneering at the accidents of decay. He washed himself in cold water from her basin and briskly dried himself. Then he got into her bed (the sheets must be her own: crisp black linen) and waited. In five minutes she came to him, plunging into the bed naked from the very door.

'It's no good,' said Hillier, after the simple movements of the *vimanam*. 'I want something too direct and easy and tender for you. I want a simple tune, not a full orchestra. It's just the way I am.'

She went cold and stiff beneath him. 'A little English girl,' she said. 'Blonde and trembling and talking about love.'

'She never talked about love,' said Hillier. 'She left that to me.'

With a swift muscular convulsion she rejected him. He was not sorry to be rejected. 'I'm sorry,' he said.

'You'd better go.' The voice was glacial. 'Mr Theodorescu said something about business first, dinner after. He'll see you in your room as you requested. He asked me to see that you have drinks sent up. *Not* raki. It can go on his bill, he told me to tell you. And now get out of here.'

Hillier sat in his room waiting. The marine sky insinuated itself, through phases of pink and madder, into a velvet transformation. Stars over the Golden Horn, its gold in darkness now like the gold of Byzantium. On the table by the balcony were whisky, gin, cognac, mineral water, ice, and a box of cigarettes whose paper was like silk and whose tobacco tasted like burnt cream. Hillier checked his gun once more and placed it in the right-hand pocket of his moygashel jacket. He waited.

Theodorescu entered without knocking. He was in a lounge suit and silk shirt; he smelled of an ideal Orient, not the gamy real Asia that started here east of the Bosporus. He was huge; his baldness was massive smoothed stone; he was urbane, genial, saying: 'I'm sorry you've had to wait, my dear Hillier. There

were things in Athens that had to be seen to. Miss Devi enter-
tained you, I take it? No? You seem very serious, glum almost.
This is not the naked Hillier I knew and respected on shipboard.'
There were chairs on either side of the drink-table. Theodorescu
took a whole gill of whisky; ice clinked in with the tones of a tiny
celeste.

'You respect me no longer?' said Hillier. 'Now that I'm going
to give you something for nothing? Now that I'm going to give
you *everything* for nothing?'

'My trade is a crude one. I'm used to buying and selling only.
I doubt if anybody's ever genuinely given me something for
nothing. Presents, bribes—those are different. There's a tag,
isn't there, about *dona ferentes*? You say you have things to give
me. What do you want in return?'

'Release,' said Hillier. 'I've a burden to jettison. A general
confession that justifies my staying alive. Do you understand
me?'

Theodorescu shone both eyes full on him. 'I think I do.
You're turning me into a priest. I'm honoured, I suppose. And
now I have to take the burden over. I see. I see. I see why you
wanted no mechanical recorders. Well, go slowly—that's all I
ask.'

'A confession,' said Hillier. 'But also a gift horse. I'll take my
own time.'

'Begin, then. *Bless me, father, for I have sinned*—' Hillier did
not answer his smile; Theodorescu ceased smiling.

'That's not for you. But this is, these are.' And he started.
'The identity of Avenel is H. Glendinning of Seyton House,
Strand-on-the-Green, London. Abu Ibn Sina, known to the
Baghdad police, runs the radio station known as Radio Avicenna.

The three international saboteurs who call themselves the Adullamites are Horsman, Lowe, and Grosvenor; you will know the names, I think.'

'Indeed. Hypocrites.' He took another gill of whisky. 'Pray continue.'

'Operation Aegir is to be mounted near Gellivare six months from now. H. J. Prince, at Charlinch near Bridgwater, Somerset, England, is in charge of a training school for subversion called Agapemone. A pocket television transmitter called, for some reason, Nur-al-Nihar, is in process of development at a station near El Maghra, south-west of Alexandria. Twin missiles named Aholah and Aholibah are near completion on the Jordan border, east of Beersheba. The assassin of Sergei Timofeyevich Aksakov is in retirement at Fribourg; he goes under the name of Chichikov—a pretty touch. T. B. Aldrich, an importer, runs our station at Christinestad; he is in radio contact with GRT, as it's called, which is in the Valdai Hills, south of Staraya Russa. The scheme known as Almagest is already being mounted at Kinloch on Rhum Island. Escape route Gotha starts three miles north-west of Cöpenick. Barlow, Trumbull, Humphreys and Hopkins, a so-called pop-group named the Anarchists, have plans of the San Antonio installations in a villa outside Hartford.'

'Are you sure of that?'

'One can never be totally sure. They may have other things too. That's why there's been no pounce as yet.'

'I doubt if I shall remember more than a fraction of all this. You're a hard man, Mr Hillier.'

'C. Babbage is in charge of the Cambridge team which is developing the Zenith PRT calculator. A very corruptible man.

John Balfour of Burley leads the Cameronian sect with its head-quarters in Groningen—mad but potentially dangerous. The Nero Caesar cryptogram has been broken by Richard Swete in Taranto. The sea-trials of the Bergomask have been indefinitely postponed. Watch very carefully the activities of the Bismarck Group in Friedrichsruh. The Black Book of the Admiralty has disappeared: don't try and sell that to the press. Rolf Boldrewood is forging roubles in Bolt Court off Fleet Street, London. The air-exercise known as Britomart will be photographing the base at Varazdin. An atomiser-gun provisionally named Cacodemon is being tested at Gonville Hall. The French nuclear scheme is phased according to the revolutionary months. Completion stage is designated Fructidor. At present the Thermidorian tumbrils are coming—that was the message received.'

'Good God.' Theodorescu had finished three-quarters of the whisky.

'Watch Portugal. Leodogrance has, we gather, seen plans of an ICBM called Lusus. But Leodogrance was raving from the cellars at Santarem. Watch Spain. There are rumours of what is known as a Pan-Iberian doctrine being drafted underground at Leganes. There are some very strange installations at Badajoz, Brozas, and in camps in Southern Pontevedra.'

'That I knew.'

'That you knew. But you didn't know that Colvin was in Leningrad as a fur-buyer. Nor that a certain Edmund Curll is fab-ricating indecent photographs to compromise Kosygin. His shop is on Canonbury Avenue, London, N.1. Our agents in Yugoslavia are at Prijepolje, Mitrovica, Krusevac, Novi Sad, Osijek, Ivanic and Mostar. They all give English lessons. The password till September 1 is *Zoonomia*.'

'Please spell that.'

'The UAR call their long-term anti-Israelite attrititive scheme by the Koranic name of Alexander the Great—Dhul'karnain. Hence arms-dumps are indicated by the sign of the two horns. Johann Döllinger has recently been expelled from the under-ground neo-Nazi *Welteroberungs*-bund. He drinks all day in a rooming-house on Schaumkammstrasse, Munich. The Druidical movement in Anglesey is not to be laughed off: it is financed by Böltger and Kandler, late of Dresden. Laurence Eusden was seen with a Moorish boy in Tangier.'

'I have photographs.' Having finished the whisky, Theodorescu started on the cognac.

'Give me some of that,' said Hillier. His brain was becoming a jumble of names. He drank. He must push on. He said: 'Miniature nuclear submarines called Fomors are to be launched secretly off Rossan Point, Donegal. *Gabriel Lajeunesse* is the code-name for the graminicidal experiments to be carried on south of Carson City, Nevada. Joel Harris is the official executioner of J24, at present residing in Lübeck. Godolphin still seems to be at large: Hodgson reports having seen a man answering to his description in Zacatecas.'

'Very small stuff.'

'Perhaps. Remember that this is a team of gift horses.'

'Jades. Nags. Rocinantes. But I see I'm presenting myself as ungrateful and discourteous. My apologies.' He looked at his watch, a flat gleaming Velichestvo. 'Do continue. Or, if you can, conclude.'

'Watch Plauen, watch Regensburg, watch Passau. America looks east with new-mark 405 installations. Ingelow has been sent to Plovdiv in time for the Dzerzhinski visit. There's an American military mission, disguised as travelling evangelists, visiting Kalatak and Shireza. The Kashmir business is being forced into blowing up again soon: those packing-cases in Srinagar contain flameguns.'

'Yes yes yes. But you know what I really want.'

Hillier sighed. 'What you really want. But you're not entitled to anything. You bloody pederastic neutral.'

Theodorescu laughed. 'Would you address your priest so? I suppose you could. We shrink to our offices, or expand.'

'Evil,' said Hillier between his teeth, 'resides in the neutrals, in the uncovenanted powers. Here it all comes, then—what you really want.' Theodorescu leaned forward. 'Number One Caribbean Territories is F. J. Layard,' said Hillier, all his instincts telling him to be sick, faint, gag. 'Savanna la Mar, Jamaica. The office is at the rear of a bicycle-store called Leatherwood's. Layard goes under the name of Thomas North.'

'Come nearer home.'

'Number Two (Operations) is F. Norris, on six months' leave, living with his aunt at Number 23, Horne Road, Southsea.'

'Never mind about the Caribbean. It's London I want.'

Hillier retched, then swigged some cognac. 'Headquarters in Pennant Street—Shenstone Buildings, tenth floor, Thaumast Enterprises Limited. The Chief—'

'Yes yes?'

'Sir Ralph Whewell. Albany and a house called Trimurti, Battle, Sussex.'

'Old India man, eh? Good. Never mind about other names. Just give me the frequencies you work on.'

'On the Murton scale, 33, 41, 45.'

'Book codes?'

'Very seldom.'

'Thank you, my dear Hillier. You said I was evil a minute ago. I quite probably am. But I'm *honest*, you know. I couldn't stay in this business if I cheated. When I place that envelope on the table in Lausanne, when I say: "Gentlemen, this contains the name of the Chief of the BES" or "Here is the exact location of Intercep", my potential bidders never doubt that I'm telling the truth. And they know I never sell the same information twice. I'm honest, and I'm fair. You insisted, out of your generous heart, on giving me all those titbits, dry and succulent alike, for nothing, so I would never insult you by offering a token gift in return. But I took something of yours—or rather Miss Devi did—and I insist on giving a fair price. Shall we say two thousand pounds?' From his inner pocket he extracted the blue-scrawled Roper manuscript and waved it. 'She stole this, my dear Hillier, while you waited in her bed just now for the ecstasies some block of guilt prevented your consummating. You'll probably regard me as greedy and ungrateful, but I always take what I can when I can how I can.'

'You knew I had it?'

'Not at all. Routine rummaging, you know. I was rather pleased. I first heard of the libidinous Sir Arnold Cornpit-Ferrers from a young lady in Güstrow. She had some little secrets to sell and was put in touch with me—pathetic rags and tatters of information they were, picked up while she worked as a prostitute in London.'

'Brigitte.' A letter to Roper. One of these days.

'Was that her name? You're remarkable, Hillier. Is there anything you don't know? Evidently you too have been interested in the Roper case. But why not? Our world is small. I always take a very special interest in defectors—they're endlessly corruptible. Well now, will you take a cheque on my Swiss bank?'

'I'll be fair too,' said Hillier, drawing out his silent Aiken. 'I may give without taking but—I can't say I'm sorry about what I'm going to do now. You're the enemy, Theodorescu; you straddle the Curtain jingling the joy-bells in your pocket. Unlike Midas, I didn't even blab to a hole in the ground. I blabbed to nothing.' And he fired.

Theodorescu laughed through the harmless smoke. Hillier fired again, and again. Nothing happened. He could almost hear the sudden bursting of sweat all over his body.

'Blanks,' grinned Theodorescu. 'We knew we'd see that delightful little Aiken again. Miss Devi effected the exchange in your brief interim of sad lecherous waiting. A very useful girl. And handsome. I wish sometimes I could be attracted to her sex. But we remain what greater powers make us. Ultimately we're impotent. Life is, I suppose, terrible.'

Hillier hurled himself but was hurled back by a single gesture of the arm. Theodorescu marched towards the door, laughing. Hillier clawed at him, but his nails turned to plastic. 'If you're going to be a nuisance,' said Theodorescu, 'I shall have to call on my friends down-town. I have some work to do in Istanbul and I don't like *little* people getting in the way. Be a good fellow and sit over a nice drink looking out at the Golden Horn. You've done your work. Rest, relax. Go and see Miss Devi again—her nature is forgiving. For my part, I'm going out to dinner.' And he went out laughing.

Hillier dashed to the dressing-table. His syringe and ampoules were still in their resting-place under handkerchiefs, apparently untouched. He cracked open two ampoules and filled the syringe; he had to be quick. When he got out on the corridor he found the lift already creaking ferrously down, a slow song of rust, and fancied he heard Theodorescu laughing in it. Hillier tore down the stairs, all worn hazardous carpet, past huge Byzantine pots of dead plants, a stately Turkish couple coming up to their room, a tooth-sucking waiter in filthy white. He stumbled on one of the treads, cursing. He saw, down the lift-well, the cage approaching ground-level, its top laden with fruit-skins and cigarette-packets, even rare condoms. He would, he thought, just make it.

A man in a cloth cap, perhaps Theodorescu's driver, read with gloom a Turkish newspaper near the lift-gates. Hillier pushed him aside, saying *'Pardon'*. Theodorescu was opening the flimsy lattice-work of the cage, the only passenger. 'Allow me,' said Hillier, taking hold of the knob of the outer gate. He pulled, allowing only a narrow chink between gate and slotted gatepost. Impatiently, Theodorescu tried to push, fine strong ringed white hand in the opening. Hillier pushed the other way with all his strength, jamming the hand so that its owner cursed. To have that hand at his mercy for just five seconds— The cloth-capped Turk was not happy; he was going to get away from here. The force which Theodorescu exerted was formidable; it was time for Hillier to swing round, change his hand-position, and pull. He did this athletically, finding a good foothold in the worn tiles of the floor; he gripped a wrought-iron rod of the outer gate and heaved. The hand itself seemed to curse, flashing all its rings like death-rays. Hillier took the syringe from his breast-pocket, uncapped the needle with his teeth, then jabbed hard into the veins of the thick wrist. Theodorescu yelled. Two old men coming down the stairs looked frightened and turned back. There were noises as of hotel staff clattering down coffee-cups off-stage, preparing to consider whether to see what was happening. 'This won't hurt,' promised Hillier, and he pressed the plunger. The vein swelled as the viscous fluid went in, its overflow mingling with the needled gush of black blood. 'That will do,' said Hillier. He left the syringe sticking in, like a lance in a white bull's flank, then let go of the outer gate and fled.

He cowered in the shadows by the ill-lighted entrance of the hotel. Soon he heard singing. Theodorescu, whom nothing could make drunk, had been made drunk. The song sung was the anthem of a minor British public school: 'Porson was founded in days of old, When learning was in flower, And mighty warriors strong and bold Brought England peace and power.' The organ-tones of the voice had been somehow diluted to the reediness of a harmonica, though there was still much strength there. Theo-dorescu, trying to remember the second verse, then saying 'Dash it', then merely humming, appeared at the hotel entrance, smirk-ing sillily in the globe-light above against which moths beat, his left arm around a decay-mottled barley-sugar pillar, his right hand dripping blood. 'A jolly nice night for a bit of fun,' he told the street. 'Hey, you fellows there,' he called to a knot of Turks in old brown suits, 'let's go and write dirty words on Form Five's blackboard.' He began to stagger off now to the right, towards the maze of dirty streets which at length led to uncaulked craft bobbing on the water, thieves, little food-stalls. He sang a maturer song of school, naughty: 'We're good at games like rug-ger And snooker and lacrosse, And once aboard the lugger We are never at a loss. Look at the silly sod, pissed on half-a-pint of four-half.' He roared with boyish laughter, zigzagging on the greasy cobbles. Hillier followed well behind.

From a ramshackle raki-stall came thin Turkish radio-noise, skirling reeds in microtonal melismata with, as for the benefit of Mozart, gongs, cymbals, jangles. Theodorescu cried loud his contempt of foreign art: 'Nigger-stuff. Bongabongabonga. Chinks and niggers.' And, like a true Britisher, he rolled seawards, Istanbul possessing three walls of sea and one wall of stone. Lowly people of various inferior races stared at him, but with neither fear nor malice: this big man was lordly drunk, Allah or the shade of Atatürk forgive him. The time, thought Hillier, had come to steer him whither it was proper for him to be steered. As he lessened his following distance, he was suddenly turned upon by Theodorescu, though jovially. Theodorescu called: 'Ah, Biggs, you little squirt, if you try and pin that insulting filthy card to my back I will have you. I know your nasty tricks, you boily son of a cut-price haberdasher.'

'It's not Briggs,' said Hillier.

'Oh, isn't it?' said Theodorescu. Three filthy children, Turko-Graeco-Syrian or something, were capering round him for baksheesh. Theodorescu tried to cuff them off, but his co-ordination was bad. Still, they ran to an alley of foul dark, jeering. 'No, it's not Briggs,' agreed Theodorescu. 'It's Forster. Well, Forster, is it to be war or peace?'

'Oh, peace,' said Hillier.

'Jolly good,' said Theodorescu. 'We'll fare forward together. In peace peace peace. Arm in arm, Forster. Come along, then.' Hillier was up to his side, but he resisted the fierce and podgy embrace that was offered. 'You say peace,' said Theodorescu, tottering downhill along a sinuous mock-street, 'but you told Witherspoon that I was a dirty foreigner.' The street seemed full of torn posters advertising long-done Turkish entertainments, though one showed two American film-stars embracing grimly among words umlaut-spiked. A gas-lamp flickered like a dying moth. A fat woman with creamy Greek skin suddenly peered out from a derelict shop, calling hoarsely. 'I am a true-born Englishman,' said Theodorescu, 'despite the name. I will make the second eleven next year, so Shaw said. The eye and the hand.' He began to demonstrate batting strokes but nearly fell.

'Let's go down,' said Hillier, 'for a breath of the old briny.' A ghastly odour of decaying water-rack came up to them on the warm breeze. With a finger-tip prod he impelled Theodorescu to descend a wider street with food-and-drink shops open to the night. Here radio music of various kinds contended; a plummy, somehow Churchillian, voice read through farts of static the news in Turkish. There was the hissing of nameless fish and meat being dropped into hot fat. Theodorescu sniffed hungrily. 'Old Ma Shenstone's fish and chips,' he slavered. 'The best in town.' There were knots of merchant seamen about, some quarrelling over money. Hillier could swear that he saw, for an instant only, a woman thrust a fat white belly over the window-ledge of an upper room; she was dressed only in a yashmak. Hadn't Kemal Atatürk forbidden yashmaks? Then her light went out.

'Theo,' said Hillier, 'you're a dirty young squirt. What have you been doing with the younger boys?'

'It was Bellamy,' cried Theodorescu in distress. 'Bellamy did it to me. They all stood around in the prefects' room. The door was locked. I yelled and nobody came. They only laughed.'

'You have the habits of a dirty foreigner,' said Hillier. 'I know what you did with that little boy in the choir.'

'I didn't do anything with anybody. Honest.' Theodorescu started to cry. An unshaven sailor, streaked with hold-dirt, stood outside a food-hell called *Gastronom*. He belched on a long and wavering note. Theodorescu decided to run. He did this clumsily, crying. 'They're always on to me,' he yelled. 'I only want to be left alone.' He Charlie-Chaplin-turned the corner. Two linked seamen swerved out of the way of his impending bulk, calling strange words.

'Easy, easy, Theo,' soothed Hillier, catching up with him. 'You'll feel tons better after a lovely sniff of sea.' They were on a minor wharf, its stones broken or slimy. The Bosporus lapped orts of shipping. Two youths, hairy and dark under a faint working-light, one of them unshod, were trying to open a packing-case with an old iron bar. Seeing Hillier and Theodorescu, they ran off with unsure Turkish guffaws. There were crates lined up against dismal sheds, rat-scufflings behind. A gull somewhere seemed to cry out at a bad dream. 'I say,' said Hillier, 'we could have a jolly good bit of fun here. Let's go aboard one of these boats.' Father out, small merchantmen did a dance of dim lights; there was a party going on somewhere— cries of joy that sounded Scandinavian, desperate under the euphoria. Hillier led Theodorescu to the quay's edge. It was green and slippery. 'Careful, careful,' said Hillier. 'Don't want to fall in, do we?' Theodorescu's eyelids were drooping; Hillier peered at the sagging mass of the face, all fat nobility dripped off. 'You're a bloody foreigner,' he said, 'not British at all. I dare you to jump on that barge with me.' It was a coal-barge emptied of coal; only its residue of dark dust, film everywhere, mole-mounds of it here and there, glistened under the thin rising slip of a Turkish moon. The empty vessel rocked over a subdued glug of water, its lip not more than three feet from the quay.

'Can't,' said Theodorescu, looking seaward with filming eyes. 'Not like warrer. Ole Holtballs no blurry good. Took us to the baths, not teach swim proper. Wanner go ome.'

'Coward,' jeered Hillier. 'Dirty dago coward.'

'Fishin ships. Ole Ma Shenshtin.' Hillier reached up and slapped him on the left jowl. He tried not to think. Ah God God God. Was he so much the ultimate villain? He could have taken all that information that time without asking, without paying out dollars. Even the identity of, the location of. Free will, choice: he had spoken of those things. 'Choose now, Theodorescu,' he said into the sea-breeze. 'Go in now. A narrow bed, it will just hold you.'

'Murrer send big cake for dorm. Bellamy buggers eat the lot.'

'Five shillings, Theodorescu. I bet you five whole bob you daren't jump after me.'

'Five?' It had shaken him awake. 'Not supposed to gamble. Old Jimballs will be in a hell of a wax.'

'Watch this.' Hillier gauged keenly. There was a wooden ledge a foot or so down from the gunwale. That would be all right. 'Now then, Theodorescu.' It was an easy leap. Panting only slightly, Hillier looked up the brief distance to the quay's edge, where Theodorescu swayed doubtfully. 'Come on, coward. Come on, foreign dirty dago coward. Come on, you flaming neutral.'

'British,' said Theodorescu. He stood erect, as to the National Anthem. 'Not neutral.' He too leaped. The water was so shocked by the impact of his weight that it launched to the air curious ciphers of protest: ghostly caricatures of female forms, Islamic letters big enough for posters, samples of lace curtaining, lightning-struck towers, a wan foam-face of dumb and evanescent horror. Its chorus of hissing after the splash was for an outraged audience. Theodorescu was between quay wall and unpainted barge-side, gasping: 'Rotter. Beastly rotter. No right. Know I can't.'

'You forgot to give me the absolution,' said Hillier. And, he remembered, the Roper manuscript. That tale of betrayal was being fast soaked down there, along with wads of money. A fortune was going down in the Bosporus. Theodorescu's rings gleamed dimly as he tried to scratch his way up the weedy stonework. Howling, he tried to keep himself afloat by, in a crucified posture, pressing both walls of his gulped and glupping prison. The barge moved its skirts away from his grope, tut-tutting. He cried out again and a fistful of dirty water stopped his mouth. 'Bellamy,' he choked, 'bou fwine.' The prefects were tee-heeing all about him. Oh God, thought Hillier: finish it off. He clambered into the barge well, searching. He found only a heavy shovel. He climbed up with it, hearing before he saw Theodorescu fighting the wet, the solids of stone and wood. He foresaw himself, in a cannibal breakfast, tapping that skull-egg, seeing the red yolk float on the water. It wouldn't do. But there was the drug, the drug was still working. Theodorescu seemed to fold his arms, like a stoic placed in the Iron Maiden. He said something in a language Hillier didn't understand, then he visibly willed himself—eyes tight shut, lips set firm—to go under. He went under. Odd burps and glups, as of marine digestion, rose after him. Then the water settled. After a short while, Hillier flawed the air with a Brazilian cigar. Then, puffing, he minced along towards the prow of the barge. At that point, on the quay wall, a worn lifebelt had been fixed as a sort of buffer. By means of this he was able to climb with ease on to the wharf. Now, with his work finished (though suddenly, briskly, Cornpit-Ferrers danced in, thumbing his nose, going Yah like a schoolboy), he could go home. But, as he walked through the odorous Turkish evening, he wondered again where the hell home was.

PART IV

ONE

'NOW THEN, EVERYBODY,' CRIED THE TELEVISION PRODUCER, 'drink, but not too self-consciously. Talk, but not too loudly. No singing, please. You're just background, remember. And let me say now, in case I forget, how much I appreciate your co-operation. And,' he added, 'the BBC too. Ready for rehearsal, everybody? You ready, John?'

The man addressed was grey with hangover. He was sitting at the bar with a camera looking at him, a microphone impending, waiting for his words. On the bar-counter stood a large Irish whiskey, untouched, un- (shudder) -touchable. 'Make it a take,' he said. 'Let's get it over.'

'Boom shadow,' said the cameraman. There was some adjusting.

'A take, then,' said the producer. 'Quietish, please.'

'Will we be seen?' asked one of the drinkers, in sudden agitation. 'Will we all be on the film?'

'I can't guarantee it,' said the producer crossly. 'You're just part of the background, you know.'

'But we *may* be seen? *I* may be seen?' He finished his draught stout in one shaky throw. 'I don't think I can risk it.' He got up. 'Sorry. I suppose I should have thought of this before. But,' he said, with a touch of aggressiveness, 'this is where I normally drink. I've as much right here as anyone.'

'Stay where you are,' commanded the producer. 'I don't want an empty seat there. What's the matter? You got enemies in England or something?' Then he soothed: 'Never mind. Read this newspaper. That'll cover your face. A nice touch, too.' He took from his overcoat pocket a folded copy of *The Times*— yesterday's or the day before's. He had not read it; he had not had much time for keeping up with the news.

The drinker said: 'That'll be all right. Thanks.' And he unfolded *The Times,* raising its front page to eye-level. A grizzled man, an electrician, brought a chalk-dusty clapperboard to the camera.

'Turn over,' said the producer.

'Scene ten, take one,' said the clapperman.

'Mark it,' cried the sound-recordist. The board clapped.

'Action.'

'It was in pubs like these,' said the hungover man called John, earnest dead-beat eyes on the camera, 'that he spent much of his spare time. He would come in with his little bits of yellow paper and his stub of pencil and scrawl down what he heard—an obscene rhyme, a salty anecdote, a seedily graceful turn of phrase. In a sense, he never had any spare time—he was always working. His art was Autolycan, snapping-up, catching the mean minnows of the commonplace when they were off their guard.

Perhaps his devotion to the speech-scraps and decayed eloquence of this city derived from the fact that he was not of this city, nor of any city of this mean and vindictive fairyland. He was a foreigner, a wanderer, a late settler, a man who had lived secretly in Europe—anywhere between Gibraltar and the Black Sea. This ambience was new to him. He came with a sharpened ear—'

'Is it some sort of a bloody queer ear you'll be wanting yourself?' said a bearded young man, a drunken country singer. 'Mean and vindictive, is it? And he's a fine one, sure, to be talking about fairylands.'

'Cut,' said the producer.

'Smash him,' said the young man, whom restraining hands now clutched. 'Smash the bloody camera and the whole bloody bag of tricks. Foreigners coming over here with their dirty libels.'

Indifferent, the technicians readjusted—light, shadow, angle, level—seeking perfection with cold passion. The bearded singer was carried off cursing still. The producer said to the man called John: 'Leave out that mean and vindictive bit. We may want to sell this to Telefís Eireann.'

'I rather liked it. And it's true.'

'We're not concerned with the truth. We're concerned with making a bloody cultural film.' He then shouted: 'Ready, everybody?' And, after, having absorbed something of the country in his three or four days here: 'Don't interrupt till he's finished, please.'

A Trinity College man spoiled the second take by suddenly saying: 'Well, isn't it mean and vindictive? Isn't it just what the man said it was?'

'Cut.'

The third take was ruined by the drinker with *The Times* suddenly shaking so violently that the sound-recordist said: 'It's coming through loud and clear. Rustle of that paper. Like an army on the march.'

'Cut.' The producer came over to the man and said: 'I think you'd better leave. If you don't mind. No hard feelings, eh? When you come back there'll be a pint of Guinness paid for.'

And so he went out. Autumn sun gilded Duke Street. He turned into Dawson Street and then walked south to Stephen's Green. They knew then, or somebody knew. The shadow of a gunman, the regular dream of the two courteous strangers in raincoats. He still had *The Times* gripped in his left hand. He glanced again at the box-number. And, had it not been for this chance today, he would never have known. The fear could have remained a dream. The only thing to do was to answer, no longer to remain in hiding. But, before he wrote, there was something important to be done. He had parked his small car just off Baggot Street. He strode nervously to get it. Then he drove through the shining traffic north, across the river—Capel Street, Dorset Street, Gardiner Street.

The big room was cool, a sanctuary. When the tall man came, he said: 'I've made up my mind. I've been thinking about it a lot.'

'It's a very momentous decision.'

'I've done what you suggested, thought of other roads. But this is the only one I can take.'

'If you're quite sure.'

'Sure as I'll ever be. I can be useful.'

'You can that. Well, I'll do what I said. The wheels can be put in motion. I don't think you'll have to wait long.'

'Thank you.'

His drive to what he called home was a long one, along the

coast road, the sea on his left. When he saw Blackrock Park on one side, Blackrock College on the other, he felt calmer. The sun was brilliant on Kingstown Harbour, what they now called Dun Laoghaire. Monkstown Road. Larry, one of his dig-mates, a man who had no second name, worked in a pub just off there. A curate. Holy name, holy office. George's Street, Lower, Upper. Summerhill Road. Glasthule. Sandycove Road. Scotsman's Bay down there, Sandycove Harbour. And one of the towers that Pitt had had built for the protection of British soil. The French are on the say, they'll be here without delay, and the Orange will decay. It always seemed a very small consequence of a very big invasion. A decaying orange. Things shrunk here to sweetness. It was time to engage the bitter world again. He turned right into Albert Road.

It was a decent little house, newly painted, painted often: the sea salt tended to get at it. A gull wheeled and mewled above the sugar-candy roof. He opened up with his Yale. Mr Sullivan, who had once worked in the Castle, could be heard coughing loudly from his room. The hall had a damp comfortable smell, vaguely bready. There was a barometer, also a coat-rack. On the walls were crude pictures of the Sacred Heart, the BVM, St Anthony, the Little Flower. These were the work of a man who sat all evening in the cellars of the Ormond Hotel, making his hagiographs among hot pipes like pythons, a bottle of beer occasionally brought down by an art-admiring waiter. 'I'm home, Mrs Madden,' he called. The word no longer seemed forced or conventional. Soon he would be deeper home. Mrs Madden came out from the kitchen, huge-bosomed, crazy-eyed, wiping her hands on her apron.

'Will you be wanting it now?'

'I have a letter to write. Then I'll be down.'

'Don't be too long now. I'll start it right away.' And she went to get down her frying-pan. He mounted the stairs. There were other holy pictures on the wall of the stairwell, but these were Italian—olive-skinned Christ, swooning Madonna. There was a photograph of the late Pope John. He entered his bed-sitting-room. It looked out on to Dundelea Park with its little hand-shaped lake. Beyond was Breffni Road, then the sea. He had no pictures on the walls, only maps of cities. The scales were tiny; to read the names of the streets he had to use a magnifying-glass. All the cities were beyond what was known as the Iron Curtain.

Well, he had worked, he had kept himself, but it had all been so much marking time. After his weeks at the Dolphin, he saw that his money would not last for ever. He had taught foreign languages in a little private commercial school in, of all places, Booterstown. He had eaten sparely, had kept to draught stout with the odd ball of malt, as they called it. He had not been with a woman at all. Marking time. He sat down now at his little table, took out his writing-pad and ballpoint and set down his few lines of reply to the advertisement in *The Times*. He put down the date, but not his address. He said: 'I am alive. I am not very much afraid. Put that same enquiry in *The Times* one year from now to the day and I will not be afraid at all. I will then say where I am and you can come for me.' He signed his name: they would find the signature genuine. After lunch he would go down to Dun Laoghaire and see that the letter went aboard the packet, to be posted in England. It was a return to the old way of cunning. Soon that cunning would be in the service of a more interesting end.

TWO

IT WAS RAINING heavily when he took his car to meet them at
Dublin Airport. Five, not four, seasons had gone by, and for him
they had been crammed with a renewal of work, discipline, obe-
dience. They had been punctual with their message and he had
been punctual in replying, but, they had said, they would have to
delay coming, they could not get away so easily. He smiled to
remember his relief and yet annoyance. He had been discharged
dead, after all. Only after death, he had once said, was regeneration possible. He pulled up his raincoat collar and tightened the
muffler round his neck: a little throat trouble lately, and that
would not do. The flight, it was announced, would be ten minutes
late. He had a large JJ in the bar. It had been strange to meet
Father Byrne again, that very old man, up from Cork for a visit
to his great-nephew, still with a healthy thirst for JJ, less anti-
semitic than in the old days, not too sure about the way these ecu-
menical things were going, but we have to change with the times,
my boy. And how is that friend of yours, the clever one, God forgive him, Hoper or Raper or something? He'd heard from
Roper, said Hillier, in East Germany. Once apart from his wife
but now reunited. Working for the Bolsheviks, did you say? A
terrible world, sure. A Godless boy, that was all his science. Wait,
Hillier had said.

The aircraft descended from heaven. Umbrellas on the tar-
mac. And then. The shyness was to be expected.

'To think,' said Hillier, 'I'd been frightened. I suppose I'm a
little frightened now. I need a lot of forgiveness.'

'I suppose we do too,' said Alan. 'You don't look all that much

older. Thinner, though.' Alan had grown into young man's grav-
ity. He refused a cigarette. Clara was still beautiful.

'Where are you staying?'

'At the Gresham. That's a good place, isn't it?'

'Oh, yes. A film-star place. Jet-set stuff. I can't afford even to
drink there.'

The luggage came sailing through on the endless belt. 'Only
one bag each,' said Alan. 'We can't stay more than a couple of
days. Clara's going to be married.'

Hillier tested his nerves for jealousy then grinned at himself.
'Felicitations, if that's the right word. Who is he?'

She blushed. 'He's a sculptor. But doing very well, really. The
GLC commissioned him to do a symbolic group, representing
Comprehensive Education. There's plenty of work coming in,
honestly.'

'Honestly,' echoed Hillier, as he took one of the two suitcases,
fine new pigskin, 'I didn't think for one moment that he was mar-
rying you for your money. Does Alan approve of him?'

'There've been too many smelling around after the money,'
said Alan. 'This chap seems all right to me.'

'And who gives the bride away?'

'You may think it funny,' said Alan, 'but at one time we actually thought of you.'

'Oh no.'

'But Hardwicke insisted it was his job. I suppose I should say
George—that's what we're supposed to call him. We live there
during the vacations. In Surrey. He's all right, but he laughs too
much. Of course, he's got plenty to laugh about. He became
Chairman, you know.'

'Really? This is my car.'

'I always pictured you,' said Alan, 'with one of these real spy jobs. But that's all over, isn't it? You're respectable now.'

'Not really all over. Not really respectable.'

Atha-Cliath, said the signpost. The road to Dublin was all wet greens. The windscreen-wiper didn't work very well. Hillier asked after their stepmother.

'That bitch? She didn't do too badly, but the lawyers said some nasty things about her. She's married somebody quite different, not her regular boy-friend at all. She was a desirable widow, you see, even though she didn't get as much as she expected. I think they're in Canada or somewhere. He's a Canadian, something to do with typewriters.'

'Not an impostor?'

'I was very young then,' said Alan. 'I knew too much, and it was all quiz-rubbish. Now I start learning, something deep and narrow. I want to specialise in Mediaeval.'

'Interesting. But will it equip you for the running of flour-mills?'

'We both eat bread now,' said Alan, 'but we don't care for it very much. No, somebody else can get on with Walters' Flour, the Flower of Flours. I rather fancy useless scholarship.'

'That's Findlater's Church,' said Hillier. 'Can you see it? This is a terrible place for rain.'

'Why did you come here to live?' asked Clara.

'It's the only place for a Catholic Englishman forced into exile. A Western capital, not too big. The sea. It produced great men. Tomorrow you must come with me to St Patrick's. Swift and Stella, you know. And with the Irish, this is another attraction, history is timeless. Friend and enemy are caught in a stone clinch. It looks very much like the embrace of lovers.'

'Neutral,' sneered Alan. 'It opted out of the modern age. Good God, look at that laundry van. It has a swastika on it, look. Can you imagine that anywhere else in the world?'

'We have to be careful about that word "neutral",' said Hillier. 'You don't need bomb-ruins to remind you of wars. The big war can be planned here as well as anywhere—I mean the war of which the temporal wars are a mere copy.'

'Good and Evil you mean,' said Alan.

'Not quite. We need new terms. God and Notgod. Salvation and damnation of equal dignity, the two sides of the coin of ultimate reality. As for the evil, they have to be liquidated.'

'The neutrals,' said Alan. 'If we could get down to the real struggle we wouldn't need spies and cold wars and spheres of influence and the rest of the horrible nonsense. But the people who are engaged in these mock things are better than the filthy neutrals.'

'Theodorescu died,' said Hillier. 'In Istanbul.'

'Ah. Did you kill him?' It was a cool assassin's question, professional.

'In a way, yes. I made sure he died.'

'I seem to remember there was an Indian woman with him,' said Clara. 'Rather lovely. In his power, I should have thought.'

'I never saw her again. She had great gifts. She was a door into the other world. Does that sound stupid? It wasn't the world of God and Notgod. It was a model of ultimate reality, shorn of the big duality however. Castrated ultimate reality. In one way she purveyed good, that other neutral. But good is a neutral inanimate—music, the taste of an apple, sex.'

'Not an image of God, then?' said Alan.

'Knowing God means also knowing His opposite. You can't get away from the great opposition.'

'That's Manichee stuff, isn't it? I'm quite looking forward to doing Mediaeval.'

They had arrived at the Gresham Hotel. Some little girls were waiting in the rain with autograph-books. They weren't sure whether to accost Clara or not. 'This place,' said Hillier, 'is a terrible place for film-stars.' A porter with a big umbrella saw to the luggage. Alan and Clara went to the reception-desk. 'I'll see you in that lounge there,' Hillier said. 'Among the film-stars. We'll have a drink.'

'On me,' said Alan.

When they came down from their rooms they gaped. Hillier had had his raincoat and muffler taken to the cloak-room. He sat there smiling in a clerical collar. But, a gentleman, he rose for Clara. Clara said the right thing:

'So I can call you Father after all.'

'I don't get it,' frowned Alan. 'You spouting that Manichee stuff. *Most* unorthodox.'

'If we're going to save the world,' said Hillier, 'we shall have to use unorthodox doctrines as well as unorthodox methods. Don't you think we'd all rather see devil-worship than bland neutrality? What are we going to have to drink?' A waiter was hovering, as though for a priestly blessing. Alan gave the order and, when the gins came, signed the chit with the flourish of a flour prince. He said:

'My real bewilderment is in seeing you got up like that. I'm sure it's just another of your impostures.'

'What they call a late vocation,' said Hillier. 'I had to go to

Rome for a kind of crash-course. But one of these days we'll meet again on a voyage, and I'll be a real impostor. Another typewriter technician or perhaps a condom manufacturer or a computer salesman. I think, though, I'll be travelling tourist. Otherwise, it'll just be like old times—sneaking into the Iron Curtain countries, spying, being subversive. But the war won't be cold any more. And it won't be just between East and West. It just happens that I have the languages of cold-war espionage.'

'Like the Jesuits in Elizabeth's time,' said Alan. 'Equivocation and all that.'

'But will you kill?' asked Clara too loudly. Some neighbour drinkers, solid Dubliners, looked shocked.

'There's a commandment about killing.' Hillier winked.

'Champagne cocktails,' said Alan with excitement. 'Let's have champagne cocktails now.'

'You a priest,' wondered Clara. Hillier knew what she was remembering. He said:

'The appointment isn't a retrospective one.'

'That's where you're wrong,' said Alan. 'I wasn't such a fool that time, after all. On the ship, I mean. I knew you were an impostor.'

'*Samozvanyets*,' translated Hillier. 'You remember the man on the tram that night in Yarylyuk?'

'The night I—' It was quiet assassin's pride.

'Yes. He knew as well. And yet everything's an imposture. The real war goes on in heaven.' He fell without warning into a sudden deep pit of depression. His bed would be cold and lonely that night. The times ahead would be even harder than the times achieved. He was ageing. Perhaps the neutrals were right. Perhaps there was nothing behind the cosmic imposture. But the very ferocity of the attack of doubt now began to convince him: doubt was frightened; doubt was bringing up its guns. Accidie. He was hungry. Alan, who could see through impostures, could also read his thoughts.

'We'll have a *good* dinner,' said Alan. 'On me. With champagne. And we can drink toasts.'

'Lovely,' said Clara.

'Amen,' said Father Hillier.